Enrollment Form

☐ *Yes!* I WANT TO BE A *Privileged Woman.*
Enclosed is one *PAGES & PRIVILEGES*™ Proof of
Purchase from any Harlequin or Silhouette book currently for
sale in stores (Proofs of Purchase are found on the back pages
of books) and the store cash register receipt. Please enroll me
in *PAGES & PRIVILEGES*™. Send my Welcome Kit and FREE
Gifts -- and activate my FREE benefits -- immediately.
More great gifts and benefits to come.

_____
NAME (please print)

_____
ADDRESS   **APT. NO**

_____
CITY   **STATE**   **ZIP/POSTAL CODE**

PROOF OF PURCHASE
ONLY

**NO CLUB!
NO COMMITMENT!**
*Just one purchase brings
you great Free Gifts and
Benefits!*

Please allow 6-8 weeks for delivery. Quantities are limited. We reserve the right to
substitute items. Enroll before October 31, 1995 and receive one full year of benefits.

Name of store where this book was purchased_____

Date of purchase_____

Type of store:
    ☐ Bookstore   ☐ Supermarket   ☐ Drugstore
    ☐ Dept. or discount store (e.g. K-Mart or Walmart)
    ☐ Other (specify)_____

Which Harlequin or Silhouette series do you usually read?

_____

Complete and mail with one Proof of Purchase and store receipt to:
U.S.: *PAGES & PRIVILEGES*™, P.O. Box 1960, Danbury, CT 06813-1960
Canada: *PAGES & PRIVILEGES*™, 49-6A The Donway West, P.O. 813,
       North York, ON M3C 2E8

SIM-PP6B

▶ DETACH HERE AND MAIL TODAY! ▶

"I'm not going to sleep with you, David,"

Paige announced. "Not until I know who you are."

"You know who I am."

"No, I don't! Until a few hours ago, I thought you were an engineer."

"I am an engineer. I've never lied to you, Paige. Except by omission."

"Well, you omitted a few rather significant details. A whole secret identity, in fact. How could you do that?" She searched his face. "Didn't you trust me?"

"It's not a matter of trust."

"Then what?"

He raked a hand through his hair. "I wanted to keep you separate from this side of my life. It's too dark. Too dangerous."

"I see," Paige responded. "Look at me, David."

A faint half smile curved his lips. "I'm looking."

She smiled. "What do you see?" Then her smile faded. "Because...maybe I'm not quite the woman you thought you knew, either."

Dear Reader,

This is another spectacular month here at Silhouette Intimate Moments. You'll realize that the moment you pick up our Intimate Moments Extra title. *Her Secret, His Child,* by Paula Detmer Riggs, is exactly the sort of tour de force you've come to expect from this award-winning writer. It's far more than the story of a child whose father has never known of her existence. It's the story of a night long ago that changed the courses of three lives, leading to hard lessons about responsibility and blame, and—ultimately—to the sort of love that knows no bounds, no limitations, and will last a lifetime.

Three miniseries are on tap this month, as well. Alicia Scott's *Hiding Jessica* is the latest entrant in "The Guiness Gang," as well as a Romantic Traditions title featuring the popular story line in which the hero and heroine have to go into hiding together—where of course they find love! Merline Lovelace continues "Code Name: Danger" with *Undercover Man,* a sizzling tale proving that appearances can indeed be deceiving. Beverly Barton begins "The Protectors" with *Defending His Own,* in which the deeds of the past come back to haunt the present in unpredictable—and irresistibly romantic—ways.

In addition, Sally Tyler Hayes returns with *Our Child?* Next year look for this book's exciting sequel. Finally, welcome our Premiere author, Suzanne Sanders, with *One Forgotten Night.*

Sincerely,

Leslie Wainger
Senior Editor and Editorial Coordinator

Please address questions and book requests to:
Silhouette Reader Service
U.S.: 3010 Walden Ave., P.O. Box 1325, Buffalo, NY 14269
Canadian: P.O. Box 609, Fort Erie, Ont. L2A 5X3

MERLINE LOVELACE

UNDERCOVER MAN

Silhouette®

INTIMATE™MOMENTS®

Published by Silhouette Books

America's Publisher of Contemporary Romance

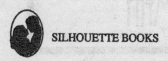

SILHOUETTE BOOKS

ISBN 0-373-07669-X

UNDERCOVER MAN

Books by Merline Lovelace

Silhouette Intimate Moments

Somewhere in Time #593
*Night of the Jaguar #637
*The Cowboy and the Cossack #657
*Undercover Man #669

*Code Name: Danger

Silhouette Desire
Dreams and Schemes #872

MERLINE LOVELACE

As a career air force officer, Merline Lovelace served tours of duty in Vietnam, at the Pentagon and at bases all over the world. During her years in uniform she met and married her own handsome hero and stored up enough adventures to keep her fingers flying over the keyboard for years to come. When not glued to the word processor, Merline goes antiquing with her husband, Al, or chases little white balls around the golf courses of Oklahoma.

Undercover Man is the third book in Merline's "Code Name: Danger" series for Silhouette Intimate Moments. Look for Maggie and Adam's story coming in February 1996.

Merline also writes sweeping historical romances for Harlequin Historicals. She enjoys hearing from readers and can be reached at P.O. Box 892717, Oklahoma City, OK 73189-2717.

To Al, who's given me a life filled with wonderful adventures. Who would've thought that bowl of raspberries would someday show up in a romance!

Prologue

Her heart thumped painfully against her rib cage as she approached the security station. Only one more checkpoint to pass through. One more screening.

Despite the chill March air pervading Washington's Dulles International Airport, sweat trickled down between her breasts. But she allowed no sign of her inner trepidation to show as she strolled toward the conveyor with a long-legged grace that made men crane their necks to watch her and women sniff disparagingly.

Smiling at the wide-eyed girl on the stool behind the X-ray screen, she dropped her white chinchilla coat and her little leather purse, with its discreet designer logo, onto the conveyor, then moved toward the metal detector with an air of assurance. When she caught the hefty, red-faced guard's openmouthed stare, her smile deepened into the sensual, teasing pout she'd perfected for hicks like these.

Without seeming to, she rolled her shoulders. The

narrow, slithery front panels of her gold mesh halter shifted, baring most of her generous breasts. The guard's mouth sagged, and she sailed through the detector. No alarms sounded. No beeps distracted the security specialist from his gawking.

Almost choking with relief, she retrieved her purse and her coat and joined the stream of elegantly dressed passengers heading for the Concorde's gate. With each step, her terror lessened by imperceptible degrees.

Still, she wished she hadn't let herself get talked into this. It was too nerve-racking. And too damned dangerous. The last woman who followed this route hadn't ever returned. Sure, the money was fabulous, but she made enough from her regulars to live well, very well, in L.A. She didn't need this kind of—

"Miss Ames?"

Her stomach heaved. Swallowing the sudden, acrid taste of bile, she turned to face the broad-shouldered man who stood behind her.

Under any other circumstance, she might have appreciated his square, cleanly shaven jaw and severely cut brown hair, with its subtle mahogany tints. She liked a man who dressed in his conservative style. They usually paid most generously for the decidedly unconservative services she provided.

But the expression in his gray blue eyes killed her flicker of professional interest instantly. There was no trace of the admiration she was used to. No masculine appreciation of her well cultivated beauty. Instead, those steely eyes sliced through her with an intensity that made her tremble in pure, unadulterated fear.

"Are you Meredith Ames?" His deep, even voice sent danger signals screaming along her nerves.

"Y-yes."

"Come with me, please."

She threw a frantic glance around the waiting room, seeking an escape route.

"Don't even think it," he growled, taking her arm in an iron grip.

Chapter 1

Cold March winds swirled along the uneven brick sidewalks of a quiet side street just off Massachusetts Avenue, in the heart of D.C.'s embassy district. Late-afternoon shadows marched down the facades of the elegant Federal-style town houses on either side of the street, casting many of them into preevening darkness.

The shadows dulled the sheen on the discreet bronze plaque mounted beside the door to a brick-fronted three-story structure midway down the block. Anyone who glanced at the plaque would learn that this particular town house was home to the offices of the president's special envoy—a nebulous position created a decade ago to give a wealthy campaign contributor a fancy, if meaningless, title and a chance to rub elbows with the Washington elite.

Only a handful of the most senior government officials were aware that the president's special envoy also served as director of OMEGA, a secret agency whose initials comprised the last letter of the Greek alphabet.

An agency that, as its name suggested, served as the president's last resort in certain situations with international implications.

Not ten hours ago, an urgent call from the president to the current director had activated an OMEGA response. Now, a small team of dedicated professionals was gathered in the control center on the third-floor of the agency's headquarters, preparing to send two of their own into harm's way.

"Now *this* is more like it!"

Maggie Sinclair twirled slowly in front of the crew room's full-length mirror. A wide, sequined gold band circled her throat like a shimmering dog collar. From the collar, narrow folds of gold mesh draped sensuously over her breasts to be caught at her waist with another band of sequins. Everything else above her waist was skin.

She faced the mirror once more and grinned at the men hovering just behind her.

"You guys should take notes. This is just what every well-dressed secret agent should wear into the field."

The pudgy, frizzy-haired genius who headed OMEGA's field dress unit snorted. "I'm just glad the suspect was carrying a purse. Even I couldn't figure out how to conceal a weapon in that outfit."

Her grin widening, Maggie smoothed her palms down over hips encased in sleek, cream-colored spandex leggings.

"This outfit *is* a weapon," she purred.

Splaying a hand across her chest to keep the narrow ribbons of mesh in place, she leaned toward the mirror and squinted at the glittery collar through green-tinted contacts.

"Which one is the microdot?"

Maggie still found it hard to believe that one of the tiny disks sewn to the collar contained over a million lines of computer code. Code that translated into the latest secret technology in fiber optics. Code that was worth hundreds of millions of dollars on the black market.

She'd known, of course, that both the FBI and CIA had been watching the cadre of very beautiful and very expensive call girls jetting between L.A. and the pleasure centers of Europe for some time, suspecting them of acting as couriers in the dangerous and often deadly game of industrial espionage. But until the president called the director with the shocking news that highly classified fiber-optic technology was at that moment being smuggled out of the country, Maggie hadn't realized just how high the game stakes were.

This technology had been developed by the military and now formed the backbone of their command-and-control networks. Using the new optical fibers, electrical impulses could be transmitted at many times the speed and a hundred times the capacity of the old cables.

The same technology would soon be available for civilian use, with certain modifications. To say it would revolutionize the global transfer of visual or digital information was a gross understatement. Huge broadcast news and entertainment conglomerates, particularly, were clamoring for its release.

The sequin-and-fur-clad woman who'd been eased off a plane at Dulles International Airport a few hours ago and whisked away to a secret holding center in Virginia hadn't known what information she carried. Nor had Meredith Ames known who she was delivering it to, only that someone would contact her after she arrived in Cannes.

Now Maggie would make contact for her.

The chief of the field dress unit squinted at the collar, then pointed to one of the small gold circles. "That's the microdot. I think. You need a hand-held infrared scanner to tell for sure."

Maggie squinted at the tiny dot, no different to the naked eye than any of the other glittery sequins. "You could have fooled me," she murmured.

Rolling her shoulders to settle the slithery gold halter into more graceful folds, she picked up a leather purse and a cream silk jacket that matched her leggings.

"If you guys will pack the rest of this stuff for me, I'll go downstairs. Doc's waiting with the director for our final mission clearance."

"Will do, Chameleon."

The chief clucked disapprovingly as one of his subordinates started to transfer the rest of Meredith Ames's wardrobe, hastily altered where necessary to fit Maggie, into her suitcases. "Careful! Those Guccis aren't knockoffs, you know."

Maggie snapped open the flap of the white-and-gold Paloma Picasso purse to make sure it held her lipstick, her newly doctored passport, the diamond-studded compact the Special Devices Unit had given her an hour ago, and her Smith & Wesson .22. Satisfied that all items rested securely in their special nest that would shield them from airport metal detectors, she hooked the bag's chain over her shoulder and strolled out into the control center.

A long, low wolf whistle rolled across the banks of communications equipment. Grinning, Maggie did a slow pirouette for Joe Samuels, the senior comm technician, with whom she'd shared many tense hours and cold cups of coffee.

"Not bad for a small-town Oklahoma girl, huh?"

"You look like a million dollars."

"Well, a couple thousand, maybe," she countered with a laugh. "Which is about what this little ensemble cost, and about half what the woman I'm impersonating earns a night."

The other occupant of the control center, a serene, dark-haired woman with dove gray eyes and a luminous ivory complexion, smiled. "You look stunning, Maggie."

"Thanks, Claire. Do I fit the profile you compiled on Meredith Ames?"

"Perfectly."

A psychologist with a string of degrees, Claire Huffacker had quietly become one of the world's foremost experts on hostage negotiations after the death of her husband some years ago at the hands of terrorists. Not content just to passively provide information to those combating terrorism's deadly effects, Claire had recently joined OMEGA as an agent. Her code name, Cyrene, was drawn from Greek mythology, and alluded to her hard-won serenity.

Maggie couldn't think of anyone she'd rather have acting as headquarters controller for this mission than this remarkable woman. Her tranquil expression hid a mind as keen as any in the organization, and an astounding ability to anticipate the reactions of the sort of dangerous characters that Maggie and Doc, her partner for this mission, might have to tangle with in the field.

"Generally, the more expensive call girls dress rather conservatively," Claire commented, surveying Maggie's dramatic appearance. "They tend toward neat suits, pearls and leather pumps, particularly when meeting their clients in public. The businessmen they service don't want it known that the deal being negotiated over drinks and dinner is for sex, instead of stocks and bonds. But Meredith is in a different class."

"*Was* in a different class," Maggie interjected. The tall, sultry blonde in the Virginia interrogation center would be out of business for some time.

"Was in a different class," Claire agreed calmly. "The women who work the international scene, as Meredith did, are at the absolute peak of the prostitution hierarchy. Their clients are usually so wealthy, they're beyond the reach of the law. These men want their escorts to dress with style, and a sensual allure." She hesitated, then tacked on a quiet warning. "Because they're so powerful, however, they can be absolutely ruthless. Be careful, Maggie."

"I will," she promised, heading for the door to the control center.

"Good luck on this one," Joe called out. "Soak up some of those Riviera rays for me."

"Will do. You just keep Terence away from the twins' homework. You know how he likes to eat paper."

"Yeah. He's a ready-made excuse when the boys 'forget' to get their assignments done."

Joe shook his head, mumbling something about not quite knowing how he'd ever gotten talked into baby-sitting for Maggie's pet in the first place. Wisely, she kept silent. There were few enough people willing to watch the German shepherd-size blue-and-orange striped iguana while she was on assignment. The creature had been a gift from a certain debonair Central American colonel who wanted to establish much more than a working relationship with her. Joe's twins had unofficially adopted Terence, and Maggie secretly hoped to make that arrangement official one of these days.

With Joe mumbling behind her, she flattened a hand against the hidden sensor beside the control center's door, spoke her code name and waited for security's computers to process the positive palm, voice and video identification. In a few seconds, the heavy titanium-shielded oak door hummed open. She swept down the stairs that led to the second floor, the heels of her cream-colored ostrichskin boots beating a tattoo on the oak treads. After a quick scan of the monitors to make sure the second-floor offices were clear, she stepped into the reception area. The gray-haired, matronly receptionist glanced up at her entrance.

"You look like one of those angels on top of a Christmas tree," Elizabeth Wells exclaimed, beaming. "All spun gold and cream."

"Good grief, I hope not! I was aiming for the other end of the spectrum! You don't think Field Dress overdid it a bit on the hair?"

"That particular shade of ash blond is very attractive on you," Elizabeth declared staunchly.

"Think so?" Maggie wrapped a finger around one of the wispy tendrils that escaped her smooth French twist. "Well, at least this is a commercial color, right out of the box. I'm not trusting those guys upstairs with dyes anymore, not after that so-called temporary blemish they tattooed on my chin for the last mission. It took two months for that thing to fade completely."

When she dipped a shoulder to examine the pale white-gold strand of hair, the halter slid to one side.

So did Elizabeth's smile. "Er, won't you be a bit cool in that top, dear?"

"Not in the least. Honestly, Elizabeth, there's a white chinchilla coat waiting with my bags that you have to see to believe. Apparently high-class hookers don't worry about being politically correct. They're still into real fur!"

"If you say so." The grandmotherly woman cast another doubtful glance at the skimpy halter and picked up the intercom.

When Maggie walked down the short corridor that led to the spacious office of the president's special envoy a few moments later, excitement bubbled in her veins, as it always did at the start of a mission. But this time the bubbles were two parts professional and at least one part

personal. With an unabashedly feminine sense of anticipation, she couldn't wait for Adam Ridgeway to see her
in this particular field uniform.

During her three-plus years as an OMEGA agent,
Maggie's unique ability to alter not only her physical appearance, but also her very personality, to fit whatever
role she was playing had earned her the code name Chameleon. She had gone underground as everything from
a nun to a streetwalker. Had slathered every substance on
her skin, from camouflage soot to bone-white makeup.
Had traveled in every conveyance from a mule cart to an
air force jet.

For the first time, she was going first class. In slinky,
sinfully expensive clothes. Bathed in the subtle scent of
Bal de Versailles, at three hundred dollars an ounce.
Flying via the Concorde to Paris, and then by chartered
jet to a sun-soaked playground for billionaires on the
Mediterranean. She was definitely going to enjoy this
mission.

She stopped just outside the director's office and drew
in a deep breath. Feeling the effects of that breath on the
slippery halter, she hastily let it out. If this little number
didn't get a reaction from the iron-spined Adam Ridgeway, she thought with an inner grin, nothing would.

It did.

With a dart of sheer feline satisfaction, Maggie saw his
blue eyes narrow sharply as they swept her from the tip
of her silver-blond head to the toe of her thousand-dollar-
a-pair ostrich boots, lingering for long, heart-stopping
moments on parts in between. When his gaze worked its
way back to her face, it held a combination of blatant
masculine appreciation and an almost reluctant approval.

Feeling unaccountably pleased with herself, Maggie
sauntered into his spacious office and took her favorite
perch, on the corner of the huge conference table.

The two men who waited while she made herself comfortable couldn't have been more different. Tall, dark, and leanly handsome, Adam exuded an aura of unshakable authority and sophistication that only a moneyed background and a Harvard education could produce. Most Washington insiders thought he'd been appointed to the juicy sinecure of special envoy because of his hefty campaign contributions and first-name familiarity with the man who now occupied the Oval Office. Few knew that, in addition to his largely ceremonial duties as special envoy, Adam Ridgeway also directed a dozen or so highly trained OMEGA agents.

The operative who stood beside him was one of the most skilled in the agency, although few would have guessed it to look at him. If Maggie had been forced to come up with one word to describe David Jensen, it would have been *solid.* Brown-haired, broad-shouldered and square-jawed, he had honed his muscular body to tempered steel through rigorous self-discipline and regular exercise. He moved, spoke and thought with the precision of an engineer, which he was. His code name, Einstein, referred to his reputation in his civilian life as a world-renowned expert in electronics, although the OMEGA agents had shortened that to Doc.

Doc had been recruited into OMEGA from the navy, where he'd been their foremost demolition expert. He'd pulled a number of combat tours, and could detonate explosives underwater, on land or in the air. Maggie sincerely hoped he wouldn't have to use his expertise on this particular mission.

His smoky gray blue eyes now looked her up and down with careful precision. Maggie hid a smile, knowing that Doc was cataloging her appearance in minute detail and filing it away for future reference. When they met again in Cannes tomorrow afternoon, he would know if she'd altered so much as ...

Well, there wasn't much she could alter about the two pieces of clothing she wore.

"Nice," he told her with an approving smile.

"How nice?"

Doc's brows rose at the husky, sensual purr. "Very nice. Did you pick that accent up from Meredith Ames?"

Maggie nodded. With her extensive training in linguistics, duplicating Meredith's distinctive southern-California accent had been a piece of cake.

"Miss Ames was *very* cooperative," she confirmed. "In fact, she was so frightened, she spilled her guts—literally and figuratively—as soon as I got her alone. You must have scared her half to death at the airport."

"I had her under surveillance from the time she left L.A.," Doc said with a small frown. "She was scared before I approached her."

"With good reason," Adam put in dryly. "She faces espionage charges for trying to smuggle technology that's still highly classified. What's more, the last courier suspected of carrying information like this was found dead in a Cannes hotel room, of a supposedly accidental drug overdose."

Maggie tucked a strand of hair behind her ear, taking in Adam's cool air. Although he rarely displayed any emotion, she knew that even the unshakable Adam Ridgeway had to have his breaking point. One of these days, she sincerely hoped, she'd find it.

"Supposedly?" she asked, watching his face as he tapped a gold fountain pen against his desk blotter.

"Supposedly. There's no proof her death wasn't accidental, but she was transporting a prototype of the same technology you're now carrying." Adam's blue eyes skimmed her face, their expression unreadable. "A lot of people would go to any lengths to get their hands on that microdot. Be careful."

"I will, Chief."

"Have you memorized the list of potential buyers I put together?" Doc asked quietly.

Maggie smothered a grin. Doc's lists were famous around OMEGA. In his quicksilver but methodical way, he could pull together seemingly random facts and scraps of information, analyze them, and draw parallels others had missed. He also made lists of his lists, and occasionally cross-indexed them. People like Maggie, who tended to operate more on instinct, could only watch him in awe.

"I've memorized the list of buyers," she assured him. "And the list of possible middlemen. And the long list of ramifications to international command-and-control systems if this technology is compromised. I've got so many lists floating around in my head, it's a wonder there's any room for anything else under this fluff of—" She brushed a hand through the wispy tendrils. "This fluff of white."

"Silver," Adam said.

"Platinum," David amended in his precise way, then his handsome face softened into a crooked smile. "It happens to be one of my favorite shades. It's very similar to my fiancée's, although perhaps hers has a few more gold tints."

"Really?" Maggie tilted her head in surprise.

Although David had been engaged for almost a year now, he kept his civilian life and his undercover activities so separate, so compartmentalized, that none of the close-knit OMEGA cadre had ever met him outside the environment of a mission. And no one had even glimpsed so much as a photo of his longtime fiancée.

"Really," Doc replied.

Maggie tapped an ostrich boot impatiently. When no more details were forthcoming, she shook her head in exasperation.

"Just when are we going to meet this elusive fiancée of yours, Doc? You could introduce us without blowing

your ties to OMEGA. A few of us have socially acceptable covers in our civilian lives, you know."

The tanned skin at the corners of his eyes creased.
"You wouldn't think so, to look at you now. But I was
hoping I could convince you to stay an extra day or two
in Cannes after this mission," he added, reaching for his
trench coat. "To act as a witness. I've already cleared it
with Adam."

"Witness?"

"At the marriage ceremony."

"Wait a minute!" Maggie yelped. "You're getting
married? In Cannes?"

"If we complete this mission within acceptable time
parameters. If not, I'll have to reschedule the ceremony
for after our return." He picked up his briefcase and
turned to Adam. "I'll leave this list of contacts with
Elizabeth and—"

"Doc!" Maggie jumped off the edge of the conference table, remembering just in time to keep her shoulders back and the halter snug against her chest. "For
Pete's sake! You can't just announce you're getting married and leave me hanging like that."

"Like what?"

"How on earth can you plan a wedding when you're
about to leave for a mission?"

He stared at her in genuine puzzlement. "The two are
hardly incompatible. I've built enough flexibility into the
agenda to allow for unforeseen circumstances. My fiancée understands that the 'symposium' I'm attending may
extend indefinitely. Assuming I don't pack it in on this
mission," he added with a small shrug, "she'll fly to
France when I call her."

"I should have known," Maggie groaned. "I'll bet she
has a detailed timetable sitting on the kitchen table."

His lips curved. "On the nightstand, actually. I've laid out her agenda from the hour she leaves L.A. to the minute she arrives in Cannes."

Maggie couldn't help wondering what kind of woman would live her life to one of Doc's precise schedules. "I'm looking forward to meeting her," she said honestly.

"You'll like her. She doesn't have your confidence and exuberance, perhaps, and she's a little timid at times, but she's...she's..."

Maggie waited in surprised anticipation. If the articulate, precise Doc had to fumble for an adjective to describe this woman, he must have it bad. A tiny pang of envy curled through her. Carefully she avoided looking at Adam.

"She's sweet," Doc finished.

With a final nod to Adam, he picked up his trench coat and folded it over his arm. His eyes held a gleam that only two people who have shared dangerous, desperate hours could understand.

"See you on the Riviera, Chameleon."

"See you, Doc."

Maggie's soft sigh floated on the air for a moment after Doc left to catch his plane. She turned to find Adam's inquiring gaze on her.

"I wish I could manage my life as well as Doc does," she said with a small shrug. "I have enough trouble just working in the care and feeding of one small house pet, let alone a fiancé or even a significant other."

"Perhaps if you got rid of that repulsive reptile you call a pet," Adam suggested dryly, "you might find it easier to acquire a fiancé or a significant other."

Maggie refused to rise to the bait. She and Adam had agreed to disagree about the relative merits of a large iguana as a companion.

"Something tells me I won't have too much trouble 'acquiring' male companionship in this little outfit," she responded, with a seductive toss of her shining white gold hair.

To her absolute delight, Adam's jaw squared a fraction. Maggie couldn't have pinpointed exactly when ruffling his formidable equilibrium had become such a personal challenge to her. In the three years they'd worked together, he'd never given any indication of anything other than a professional interest in her well-being. And she would've died before admitting how much the media shots of the dashing special envoy out for an evening on the town with any one of his several elegant and very eligible companions disturbed her.

Yet there was no denying the intensity of the awareness that arced between them. Or the way her heart seemed to flip-flop in her chest whenever they were alone together. Or how much it secretly delighted her when Adam raked her face with those steel blue eyes, as he did now.

"I have no doubt any number of men will try to purchase your services during this mission," he said after a moment.

Flashing him a mischievous grin over one shoulder, Maggie headed for the door. "I just hope they can afford my price."

For long moments after she left, Adam stood still and silent, one hand in the pocket of his tailored gray suit. Without realizing he was doing so, he fingered a gold money clip that held a fold of hundred-dollar bills.

Chapter 2

Paige could sense the Mediterranean before she saw it. As her tiny rental car putt-putted up steep hills, then coasted down winding inclines, the air took on a softer, balmier feel. Even the scent from thousands of acres of roses and jasmine and mimosa and wild lavender around the mountain town of Grasse, the perfume capital of France, couldn't disguise the tang of the sea only a few more miles ahead.

Double-clutching to downshift around a hairpin curve, Paige winced when the gears growled a protest. After three days of driving through the French Alps, she still hadn't quite mastered either the winding roads or the art of changing gears on an incline. Sending the gearshift an apologetic glance, she wrapped both palms around the steering wheel and aimed the little car forward.

When she crested another steep hill, she gave a sudden gasp. Tires crunched on loose shale and brakes screeched as she pulled off onto a narrow overlook. While the engine shuddered and died, Paige gazed, awestruck, at the dazzling vista before her.

Laid out below in a hazy, shifting pattern of azure and ultramarine and indigo was the Mediterranean. Far out to sea, huge tankers plowed through the waters, while closer in, smaller ships weaved through the waves and left sparkling white wakes. They were cruise ships, Paige mused, or those fabulous yachts she'd read about, with their own helicopter ports and twenty-six staterooms. In the distance, a gray green island rose out of the blue. Corsica, she thought. Or Sardinia.

But it was the spectacular shoreline that drew her awed gaze. The famous, sun-drenched Riviera.

Almost directly below her, the city of Cannes clung to the curve of the bay. A narrow strip of sand and a wide boulevard lined with palms and flowering shrubs separated the city from the sea. Tall luxury hotels faced the Mediterranean on the inland side of the boulevard, like a row of white-fronted sentinels guarding Europe's most unselfconscious pleasure port.

Crossing her wrists on the steering wheel, Paige propped her chin on top of them. She couldn't believe she was here. She couldn't believe she'd actually torn up David's careful, typed instructions, called the airline and booked her own flight. She wasn't supposed to arrive in France for another week, at least. She certainly wasn't supposed to have rented a car in Paris and driven the long, tortuous route through the Alps to reach the sea. By herself, yet!

The first few days on the road, she'd been terrified of losing her way, of unintentionally offending someone with her execrable French, of ordering the wrong things from the menu. Even now, her stomach gave a funny little lurch every time she remembered the calf brains in a rich brown sherry sauce she'd been served her first night on the road. She hadn't realized what they were until the second or third bite.

She'd almost turned around right then. Almost scurried back to Paris and called home to leave a message for David on her recorder that she'd wait for him there. But the same desperate need that had driven her to leave L.A. early had kept her on the road. She'd needed this time by herself, away from the bustle of the city. She'd needed quiet to think. Privacy to sort through her jumbled feelings. She'd needed to find a way to tell David she wasn't going to marry him.

Painfully, Paige swallowed to ease the lump that seemed to have taken up permanent residence in her throat since the day David had calmly suggested they combine his business trip to the south of France with their honeymoon. Blinking back a sting of tears, she shook her head. She wouldn't cry again! She wouldn't! She'd cried all she was going to.

Still, her throat was raw as she lifted her left hand and stared at the square-cut emerald on the plain white-gold band. The ring was simple. Unadorned. Filled with a quiet, soothing beauty, David had said, like Paige herself.

So quiet, she could only nod when he'd slid the ring onto her finger.

So simple, she'd believed that his deliberate restraint when he made love to her was a mark of respect.

So soothing, that even now, after almost a yearlong engagement, he still kissed her with that same combination of fond affection and control. He could ignite every one of her senses with his skilled hands and mouth, yet he always kept a small part of his inner self distant from her.

Only a woman who loved a man as desperately as Paige loved David Jensen would ache with longing at the memory of his kisses. And be so devastated by the knowledge that she wasn't woman enough to engage his whole heart.

He deserved better, Paige told herself in a now-familiar litany. He deserved a woman who would make him lose himself in her arms. One who would throw him into a tailspin once in a while. Would make him forget his careful schedules. Toss out his endless lists. One whose wedding he wouldn't work in neatly with an international symposium on digital electronics, she thought with a little spurt of resentment.

That tiny spark of indignation gave her the courage to tug the emerald over her knuckle and off her finger. She fumbled in her purse for a tissue, then wrapped it around the ring. Still, she had to blink furiously to hold back her tears as she tucked the wad of tissue into the zipper pocket of her purse.

Drawing in a deep breath, Paige reached down to shove the little car into gear. An agonized screech made her jump, then hastily tromp down on the clutch. This time the gears engaged, and the mini edged back onto the road.

As perspiration gathered between her breasts, Paige pressed the heavy knit of her sweater with one hand to blot the dampness and tried to ignore a small niggle of guilt. David had left specific instructions about what clothing to bring. He'd even given her the range of temperatures to expect, and the average number of sunny days—three hundred!—that the Riviera enjoyed each year. But the weather in L.A. had been gray and overcast and decidedly chilly when she impulsively tossed her things in a suitcase and dashed to the bank to transform her entire savings account into travelers' checks. It had been just as cool in Paris when she landed, and downright cold driving through the Alps.

Now that she'd left the snowcapped peaks behind, however, Paige was forced to admit that David had been

right. As usual. The Riviera was not the place for heavy
sweaters and plaid wool jumpers.

Feeling utterly depressed, she realized that the first
thing she'd have to do after checking into her hotel was
buy some clothes. She sighed, thinking of the neat list of
shops David had left for her. Boutiques suitable for her
own quiet style, he'd told her, in the deep voice that always sent shivers of delight down her spine. Shops where
she could pick out her trousseau.

As she inched around the hairpin turns, Paige sighed
again. She'd left the careful list of shops in L.A., knowing that she wouldn't be shopping for her trousseau.
She'd just have to find something suitable on her own
before the shops closed for the afternoon.

Two hours later she pushed open the door of yet another boutique. The store window displayed only one
item, a sequined ball cap in lavender on a black marble
stand, so Paige wasn't quite sure exactly what she'd find
inside.

As soon as she saw the single rack that ran the length
of the small shop, she almost turned around and walked
back out. A quick glance told her the beaded and jew-
eled garments weren't the kind of clothing she wore.
What was more, she knew they would be well out of her
price range.

Paige paused with her hand on the door latch. She was
tired and hungry and absolutely appalled at the prices
she'd encountered. Unfortunately, she was also smoth-
eringly hot and not in the mood to search for the kind of
shops David had indicated carried items more to her
taste. Gritting her teeth, she closed the door and walked
over to the rack. Maybe they'd have something on sale.

The shop attendant called out a musical greeting, ad-
vising Paige that she'd be right with her. A moment later,
the dark-haired woman glided into the back room in

search of some item for the only other customer in the boutique, a tall, leggy blonde in a short tomato-red jacket worn over a gold mesh halter.

Paige flipped through the few padded hangers on the rack, without much hope. She suspected that the prices for these sequined, Madonna-ish corsets and lacy see-through tank tops would be in direct inverse proportion to the amount of material that went into them. The skimpier the article of clothing, she'd discovered in the past hour, the more outrageous the price.

She lifted a hanger from the rack and gazed at a narrow band of gold lamé. The stretchy loop couldn't be more than a couple inches wide. Steeling herself, she glanced at the tag.

"Good Lord!"

The sound of a soft chuckle brought her stunned gaze from the handwritten tag to the shop's other customer.

"Kind of hits you right in the solar plexus, doesn't it?"

Surprised and unaccountably pleased to hear another American accent after so many days on her own in France, Paige sent the stunning blonde a weak smile.

"Is this the price or an inventory number or something?"

The American's vivacious laughter added a gemlike sparkle to her green eyes. She strolled out from behind the rack, and Paige blinked at her short—*extremely short*—shorts, which were in the same eye-catching shade of red as her jacket.

"It's the price. The starting price. One doesn't pay that, of course."

"One doesn't?"

"No. Don't you know that Cannes is the world's most opulent bazaar? You don't quite haggle like a street merchant, but you certainly don't pay the asking price. For anything!" She nodded toward the tag still clutched in Paige's hand. "Besides, that figure includes the TVA."

"The TVA?"

"*Taxe à la valeur ajoutée.* A luxury tax. About forty percent on that little piece, I'd guess. You have to deduct the TVA when you calculate the cost, since you'll get reimbursed for it when you leave the country."

"Oh." Paige stared down at the tag dubiously. She'd never been good with numbers, and the simple mathematical exercise required to estimate the price of this strip of gold daunted her.

"It's not that difficult," the other woman assured her with a grin. "Really. Just divide that figure in half to incorporate the TVA and a ten percent-discount, then convert to dollars, and you have the approximate cost."

Scrunching her forehead, Paige struggled with the mental calculation. "So this . . . this . . ."

"I call it a boob tube, but I think a more polite term is bandeau."

"So this bandeau only costs the equivalent of my monthly car payment, and not what we're planning to put down on our house in—"

Paige broke off, biting her lip against a wash of pain. The realization that she'd never live in the hillside home she and David had made an offer on just two weeks ago closed her throat.

The other woman cocked her head. She didn't say anything, but she couldn't have missed the sudden, bleak expression on Paige's face.

Shy and somewhat withdrawn, Paige rarely confided in her few friends. To her shame, she couldn't even fully express herself to David. He was so self-contained, so confident, that she'd always felt a little intimidated by him. Yet she found herself responding to the unspoken question in the other woman's eyes. Drawing in a slow breath, she articulated the decision she'd come to so painfully over the past few days.

"I was engaged . . . until very recently. We were planning on buying a house together."

"And now?"

Paige swallowed the constriction in her throat. She wouldn't cry. She wouldn't!

"Now?" She lifted her chin. "Now maybe I'll buy this bandeau instead."

A smile curved the blonde's generous mouth. "Good for you. I can't think of any better cure for a broken engagement than a new wardrobe. And Cannes is just the place to acquire one."

Paige eyed the woman's flamboyant red jacket and minuscule shorts. They would look just as stunning when worn with the gold lamé breastband she clutched in her hand as with that glittery mesh halter.

"Did you get that outfit here?" she asked.

"The shorts and top? Yes, earlier this morning. This is my second foray into the shops."

"I wonder if they have another one, in a size eight. My name's Paige, by the way. Paige Lawrence."

"I'm Meredith," the other woman replied. "And if they don't have this in your size, they'll have something just as sinful."

The saleswoman produced the red hot pants and jacket in a perfect size eight. Clutching the bandeau, Paige followed her to a small curtained fitting room that smelled of lavender potpourri and money.

For the next half hour, Maggie pushed her simmering tension to one corner of her mind and indulged in the serious pleasure of shopping.

When Paige Lawrence first walked into this shop, she'd wondered if the younger woman could possibly be the contact she'd been waiting for since she'd arrived in Cannes early this morning. A few moments of idle conversation with the younger woman had killed that idea.

If Paige had any connection with the ring of high-class hookers that Meredith Ames was a member of, Maggie would eat the pink satin bustier she'd purchased just two shops ago.

Still, she had to give the slender young woman credit. She'd gulped once or twice, but she'd soon got into the spirit of things. One by one, she'd shed her layers of worsted wool and cable knit. What had emerged was a delicate beauty, less dramatic than Maggie herself, in her carefully orchestrated role, but similar enough to make Maggie feel like a mother hen with a newly hatched chick.

When they'd finished outfitting her in the jaunty red two-piece outfit and matching three-inch-high platform shoes, Paige struggled with the effort to convert the bill from francs to dollars.

"Can I help?" Maggie asked.

"Would you? I don't do well with numbers," she confessed.

Maggie did a quick conversion, skillfully negotiated the saleslady down to a less outrageous commission, and computed the amount of the TVA so that Paige could complete the necessary forms.

The younger woman managed not to flinch at the total, although she did turn a little pale and her fingers fumbled with the pen as she signed the traveler's checks.

"Shall I have your packages sent to your hotels, ladies?" the attendant asked.

"Yes," Maggie replied. "I have more shopping to do yet."

The real Meredith Ames had indicated that she'd been instructed to stroll the shops that lined Cannes's world-famous boulevard, the Croisette, until the nameless, faceless individual who'd arranged shipment of the stolen technology made contact. Maggie had followed the same routine, secretly delighting in the fact that she'd been *forced* to purchase an item or two to keep up her cover. Still, she'd be glad when she finally made contact and got this mission under way.

"Send my things to the Carlton, suite 16," she told the attendant.

"I'll take mine with me," Paige murmured as she stuffed her traveler's checks into her purse. Gathering up her various bundles, she tugged self-consciously at the back hem of her shorts to make sure the red material covered both cheeks. It did. Barely.

"I haven't found a hotel room yet," she said with a hesitant smile. "When I do, can I give you a call? Maybe I could buy you lunch sometime, to thank you for all your help."

"Maybe," Maggie returned easily, although she had no intention of responding if Paige called. She wasn't about to draw anyone else into the games she'd be playing once the operation swung into high gear.

The tension she'd kept at bay during the interlude in the boutique flickered along her nerves. She should've met her target by now. She'd been in Cannes for six hours, and she'd been strolling the shops off and on for three. The sixth sense that had served her so well during her years with OMEGA told her the contact had to come soon.

"Well, thanks again," Paige said shyly. "I'd...I'd better go find a hotel." She flicked an uncertain glance at the front door and tugged once again at the back hem of the shorts.

Maggie hid her amusement at the younger woman's obvious reluctance to step outside in her new, abbreviated look. Slipping a pair of star-shaped sequined sunglasses off the top of her head, she held them out.

"Here. You need a finishing touch. Try these."

Paige slid on the bright red shades with barely concealed relief.

"Perfect," Maggie told her, grinning.

An answering smile tugged at the other woman's lips as she glanced at herself in the wall of mirrors behind the rococo desk that served as a sales counter.

"Perfect," she agreed.

With a rustle of tissue paper and a final farewell, she gathered her bags in one hand, opened the shop door and stepped out into the late-afternoon sunshine.

She was still smiling when she turned left to walk along the palm-lined boulevard.

And when the long, sleek Rolls-Royce slid to a halt beside her.

Her smile slipped a bit when a dark-haired chauffeur stepped out of the car and took her arm.

It disappeared completely when he hustled her toward the rear passenger door.

Watching through the shop's tinted window, Maggie gave a sudden gasp. "Oh, my God!"

She raced for the boutique's door and dashed into the street just as the Rolls merged into the traffic flowing along the Croisette. Before Maggie could catch more than a few numbers on its license tag, it disappeared into the streaming flow.

"Dammit!"

She stood on the sun-washed pavement, her mind racing with a dozen different possibilities. Unfortunately, only one of them made any sense.

Unless she missed her guess, Paige Lawrence had just made the contact Maggie had been waiting for all afternoon!

Chapter 3

Great! Just great!

Grinding her teeth in frustration, Maggie searched the lanes of traffic for a likely pursuit vehicle. Just as she stepped off the sidewalk, intending to flag down a sleek German sports model, the flow of cars slowed. To her intense disgust, traffic quickly ground to a halt.

She'd seen some horrible traffic snarls in her lifetime, but few to match those of the Croisette. In the short time she'd been in Cannes, she'd discovered that these hopeless backups occurred frequently, usually when carloads of tourists slowed to gawk at the sun-bronzed, topless and often bottomless bathers on the beach.

While she waited with mounting impatience for the tangled, honking vehicles to sort themselves out, half a dozen possible courses of action flitted through her mind, only to be immediately discarded.

Given the sensitivity of her mission, she couldn't involve the local authorities and ask them to track the Rolls for her. Only two French officials at the highest government levels knew OMEGA operatives were in place on the Riviera. One was the French president himself. The other was the chief of security, who would supply any assistance Maggie might need in-country.

She'd have to work through OMEGA control to extract Paige Lawrence from this situation without compromising her own or Doc's cover. And she had to do it immediately, before the shy, innocent tourist was harmed!

To her intense relief, the traffic began to flow again. Hailing a cruising cab, she flung herself into the backseat and instructed the driver to take her to the Carlton, fast! While the swarthy Mediterranean weaved back and forth across three lanes, gesturing obscenely but good-naturedly at every angry honk, Maggie dug in her purse for her diamond-studded compact. Flipping open the lid, she pressed the square stone in the center of the lid with one finger.

"Doc, do you read me?" she murmured. She doubted the driver would hear her or notice her talking to her own reflection, seeing as he was engaged in a shouting match with a trio of youngsters on motor scooters who seemed to think they had some right to use the road, as well. Just to be authentic, however, she stabbed at her nose with the powdered sponge.

Pressing the stone once again to shift the communications device in the compact's lid into the receive mode, Maggie waited impatiently for Doc to respond. His own device, an elegant gold cigarette case, would hum with an ultralow-frequency resonance only he could hear until he acknowledged her transmission. While she waited, she searched her mind, trying to remember just where he would be at this moment. He'd given her a detailed schedule to memorize, then destroy. She hoped he hadn't yet left for the international symposium that was providing his cover.

"Doc here," he replied calmly a few moments later. "Go ahead, Chameleon."

Maggie threw a quick glance at the cab's rearview mirror. The driver was still too engrossed in his vociferous argument with the teens on the scooters to notice her prolonged preoccupation with powdering her nose.

"Doc, get hold of control, quick. Have Cyrene run a check through the IIN on a silver Rolls, 1991 or '92 make, French tags, the first two digits of which are 74."

"Will do."

That was Doc, Maggie thought with a surge of sheer relief. No questions, no panic. By the time she got back to the Carlton, he'd have all the information immediately available on the owner of the Rolls through the IIN, the International Intelligence Network. And probably have it synthesized into a list of possible connections with all known fiber optics firms in Europe and North America. What was more, Claire would have started a psychological profile on the possible target.

"I'll be back at home base in five minutes. Make that three," Maggie gasped as the driver swung recklessly across two lanes of traffic, cutting ahead of the motorbikes and a rather large truck in the process. "Meet me in my suite."

"Roger."

"Oh, and ask Cyrene to check out an American by the name of Lawrence. Paige Lawrence. I think our friends have just picked her up by mistake."

Maggie grabbed at the handgrip as the cab swerved around a corner. Righting herself with some effort, she pressed the stone again.

"Doc?"

There was no response. She pressed the transmit button again.

"Doc, did you copy that last transmission?"

"I copied it."

Frowning, Maggie stared down at the compact. She'd never heard quite that element of savage intensity in Doc's voice before. It was clearly audible, even after being bounced off a communications satellite orbiting some two hundred miles overhead.

"Where are you?" he growled. "Right now."

Maggie glanced through the windshield. Just ahead, the distinctive twin cupolas of the Carlton rose above a wavy line of palm fronds. Supposedly modeled after the breasts of a gay French mistress of the Prince of Wales—before he became King Edward VII—the conical domes crowned either end of the hotel's fanciful facade.

"I'm about a half mile from the hotel," Maggie responded.

"Get the hell up here. Fast! Out."

She blinked at the abrupt termination, then shrugged and tucked the compact in her bag again. She wasn't any more pleased than Doc at this complication in their mission before it even got started. She only hoped she could extract Paige from this damnable mix-up before the players in this deadly game of industrial espionage discovered they had the wrong woman.

Clenching both hands around her purse, she scooted to the edge of her seat and waited for the driver to sweep to a halt in front of her hotel.

A preposterous, thoroughly marvelous wedding-cake structure, the Carlton had been built just prior to World War I. White-painted bricks set in intricate patterns decorated its caramel-colored facade, and gleaming marble columns rose in majestic splendor at the colonnaded entrance. A stately, liveried doorman marched forward to open her door, but before he reached it, Maggie was already out of the cab and rushing for the entrance.

She thrust a wad of francs into his gloved hand, asked him to take care of the fare and add a substantial tip, and hurried inside. Wrought-iron elevator doors clanged shut behind her as she waited, foot-tapping in impatience, for the old-fashioned cage to take her to the fifth floor. She had barely thrust her room key into the lock when her door flew open and a hard hand yanked her inside.

Years of intense training kicked in immediately. Without thought, without hesitation, Maggie swung at her attacker.

Luckily, Doc had undergone the same training she had. He threw up an arm to deflect her blow just in time, then hauled her inside and slammed the door.

"What in the world—?" she exclaimed in astonishment.

Frustration, and an emotion Maggie couldn't quite identify, blazed in his gray blue eyes as he swept the sitting room. She knew he was searching for a place where they could talk undisturbed. A place where he could be sure they wouldn't be "overheard" by the anonymous individual who'd reserved this opulent, high-ceilinged suite for Meredith Ames in the first place.

"It's clean," she told him, still stunned by his uncharacteristic behavior. "I cleared it this morning."

Using the electronic "sweep" Special Devices had designed to fit into the handle of her hairbrush, Maggie had surreptitiously checked for bugs and hidden cameras when she first arrived.

She'd found one, a sophisticated listening device that she'd foiled with a simple countermeasure. The small gadget looked like a travel clock, and would filter a conversation just enough to make the words indistinguishable. It would also drive any listener batty with the effort to make them out, the chief of Special Devices had informed her smugly.

Doc, however, didn't appear particularly gratified by the knowledge that they could talk in the open.

Although dressed in a conservative business suit of fine gray worsted, his powerful body radiated a fierce, controlled tension as he swung Maggie around to face him. His dark brown hair, gleaming with subtle mahogany tints, lacked its usual neat style. In fact, it looked as though he'd thrust his hand through it. Several times.

"Control is checking the license tag. Claire should get back to us in five minutes or less," he informed her in a low, ominous voice. "Which means you have exactly four minutes and fifty-nine seconds to tell me just how Paige Lawrence got into the picture. And what do you mean, she got picked up by mistake? By whom? When? Dammit, Maggie, how in the hell did you get her involved in this?"

Maggie took an involuntary step backward as Doc leaned over her. She'd never seen him like this. And she'd never realized just how intimidating he could be when all one hundred and ninety pounds of him emanated a cold, hard fury.

"I didn't get her involved," she protested. "Well, I did, I suppose, by encouraging her to buy an outfit similar to mine. That must have been what caused the mix-up. That, and our coloring. But..." She craned her neck back and stared up at David in utter perplexity. "But..."

"But what?" he snarled.

Enough was enough. This was her partner, for heaven's sake. She would trust David Jensen with her life. She'd done just that, in fact, one hot, muggy night in Malaysia, two years ago.

"But what's with this 'Paige' business?" she retorted. "You say her name as if you know her."

His smoky eyes narrowing to dangerous slits. "Of course I know her. She's my fiancée."

"Your fiancée!"

Ignoring Maggie's surprised gasp, he pinned her with a hard look. "What I *don't* know is why she came to Cannes before I called her, and why you involved her in this operation."

She debated which issue to address first—the fact that David apparently no longer had a fiancée, at least according to Paige Lawrence, or the fact that Maggie hadn't involved the younger woman in this operation. After another quick glance at Doc's tight jaw, she decided to take the easy one first.

"I don't know why she's here a week early, and I didn't involve her in the mission. It was a mistake. A mix-up. My contact evidently mistook her for me."

Doc ran an eye down her bright gold-and-red-clad form. "Unless your contact is completely blind, there's no way he could mistake Paige for you. She wears dresses, not spangles. And sensible shoes, not elevators."

"Platforms," Maggie said, trying to find a way to break the news that the last time she'd seen Paige Lawrence, she was wearing spangles and three-inch platforms and not much else.

"Look, Doc, I don't understand this any more than you do. It's incredible that she's here and we just happened to bump into each other. Just a crazy coincidence." She paused, her brows drawing together. "Or is it?"

"What the hell is that supposed to mean? What else could it be?"

Still frowning, Maggie folded her arms across her chest. "Just what do you know about Paige Lawrence? Who is she, Doc?"

He stared at her for a long, incredulous moment. "I know all there is to know about her," he stated with savage intensity. "I've been engaged to her for over a year, and we dated for almost that long before deciding to marry."

"You don't know what she's doing in Cannes," Maggie pointed out.

He drew in a sharp breath, obviously struggling to contain himself.

"No doubt she got the dates confused. She does that occasionally. Well, regularly. Last month, she took me to her parents' home for their fortieth anniversary party. She got that date right. Even the day of the week. Just the wrong month."

The tenderness Maggie had glimpsed in his eyes when he told her of his wedding plans a few days ago flickered in their depths once again.

"Paige has a mild form of dyslexia. One that causes her to transpose numbers. It's what drew me to her in the first place," he added wryly. "That, and the two-hundred-dollar fee she mistakenly charged my department for a two-dollar technical publication. She's smart and generous, and far too trusting for her own good, but she gets a bit muddled at times. She needs someone to look after her."

The tenderness vanished, to be replaced by a fierce, flaring protectiveness. "Which is why I intend to find her, and quickly. However she got involved in this operation, she's out of her depth here. Way out of her depth. Tell me exactly what happened," he ordered.

Maggie did, although she found herself glossing over Paige's hesitant confession that she and Doc wouldn't be making a down payment on a house together. When they located the young woman and extracted her from the situation she'd inadvertently been drawn into, Paige could tell Doc about that herself, Maggie decided.

He listened to her brief account without interruption, absorbing every detail. When she finished, he began to pace the spacious suite.

"All right. We know the problem. This driver appears to have mistaken Paige for you. Now let's break it down into small pieces and find the solution."

Maggie felt a surge of admiration at the way Doc deliberately, ruthlessly controlled his emotions and engaged his mind. She tended to operate more on instinct, yet she knew firsthand how many potentially dangerous situations Doc had neutralized with just this kind of swift, brilliant analysis.

"The driver will have instructions to take her someplace private. Someplace where your contact can remove and examine the chip. Someplace with access to a computer sophisticated enough to read the lines of code and verify that they contain the fiber-optic technology."

His face set with intense concentration, Doc paced the blue-and-green Savonnerie carpet that covered the sitting room's parquet floor.

"I'd guess we have a half hour, an hour at most. When this contact discovers that Paige doesn't have the microdot, he'll either let her go or..." His jaw worked. "Or he'll make sure she doesn't tell anyone about her visit to wherever he's taken her."

"We'll find her, Doc."

"Yes, we will. All right, here's how I think we should—"

He broke off and dug in his pocket. Maggie's pulse leapt in anticipation as he pulled out his gold cigarette case. With the information control would provide, they could kick into action.

"Doc, here. Go ahead, Cyrene."

For a second or two, the only sounds disturbing the sunny stillness of the sitting room were the wash of the waves on the beach across the street and the hum of traffic that drifted in through the open balcony doors. Then Claire Huffacker's calm voice filled the air.

"There are more Rolls-Royces per capita in Cannes than in any other city on earth..." she began.

"Why doesn't that surprise me?" Maggie murmured, glancing at the priceless antiques scattered about the sitting room.

"But I found two that fit your description. One belongs to a reclusive film star, Victor Swanset. He's an English expatriate who owns a villa on avenue Fiesole, in La Californie."

From her intelligence briefings prior to this mission, Maggie knew La Californie was an exclusive residential area that clung to the rugged hills above Cannes. According to the intel briefer, its grandiose Edwardian villas had once been home to a sparkling mix of European royalty and distinguished diplomats and their bevies of mistresses. They sat tucked away among fragrant stands of pine and eucalyptus trees, and the only access to them was via a steep, winding mountain road.

"No one has seen Victor Swanset in public for over a decade," Claire continued. "My sources indicate he's an anonymous, driving force behind the Cannes Film Festival. Supposedly he's donated millions to preserve his art. I don't have anything else on him right now, except..."

"What?"

"The computer cross-referenced a missing-persons report with Swanset's name listed as a contact. The report was filed about a year ago, on a cook who disappeared from his villa. I'm following up on that now."

"What about the owner of the other Rolls?" Maggie asked.

"It checks to a French banker. Gabriel Ardenne. He was in Tokyo at an International Monetary Fund conference until two days ago. He supposedly stopped over in Cannes for a few days' rest before flying back to Paris."

Claire paused, then added softly, "I've verified that he was also in Cannes last month, when the prototype fiber optics technology was smuggled out of the States."

Maggie and Doc exchanged swift looks.

"Do you have a fix on his location here?" Doc growled.

"Nothing firm. He keeps a condominium in one of the beachfront palaces, but isn't using it on this trip. His staff doesn't have a clue why. From what I've been able to gather on him so far, he's a Donald Trump type. Early forties. Wildly extravagant. Overextended financially. Enjoys the finer things in life, including a string of very expensive ex-wives and mistresses, but is having trouble paying for them. I'll have more for you when I get his health and social history over IIN."

"Thanks, Cyrene," Doc replied, then quickly signed off. "Get changed," he told Maggie, his eyes a flat steel blue. "We're going hunting."

She nodded, already on her way into the bedroom. Slamming the door behind her, she peeled off the halter and stuffed it into her purse. That little dot was going with her wherever she went.

Working frantically at the zipper of her red shorts, she hurried toward the ornate wardrobe that held Meredith's clothes. She had the shorts halfway down her hips when she heard a sharp pounding on the door to her suite.

Kicking off the clingy shorts, Maggie grabbed a pale lavender silk kimono from the wardrobe door and flung it on. She dug in her purse for her .22 and dashed out of the bedroom as another staccato rap sounded on the oak panel.

His weapon in his hand, David melted back into the shadows beside the huge nineteenth-century armoire that housed the suite's entertainment center.

"It's probably the boutique, delivering my purchases," she told him softly.

"Could be," he replied. "Or it could be one of Meredith Ames's customers, sent up by the accommodating concierge. Whoever it is, get rid of him. Fast!"

"Right."

Tucking the .22 into a pocket of her kimono, Maggie pulled open the door.

If the individual standing in the corridor was a delivery boy, he'd forgotten his packages. If he was one of Meredith's customers, he was a precocious one. Small and wiry, with a shock of red hair and a splash of freckles across his thin nose, he couldn't have been more than ten or twelve years old.

To Maggie's considerable amusement, he gave her a cheeky grin and ran his eyes over her bare legs with a blatant masculine approval that was all French.

"Mademoiselle Ames?"

"Oui?"

"Bon." He turned and called out, to no one in particular that Maggie could see, "Your friend is at home, *mademoiselle.* You can come out now."

Keeping a firm grip on the weapon in her pocket, Maggie leaned out the door and peered down the corridor. When a pile of laundry in a wheeled hamper a few yards away began to heave, her eyes narrowed. Sheets and towels tumbled over its sides, and then a disheveled blond head poked its way out of the mound.

While Maggie gaped in astonishment, the street urchin went to help Paige Lawrence climb out of the laundry cart.

The woman looked as though she'd run a marathon—and finished dead last. Her hair straggled down her back in wet, tangled snarls. Her bright red jacket had disappeared, along with one of her shoes. The narrow gold bandeau covered only the center of her breasts, leaving

the full curves above and below bare. Her shorts rode
down in front and up in back as she clambered awkwardly over the side of the cart and clumped down the
hall on one high-soled platform shoe.

"I'm sorry to bother you like this," she murmured
distractedly, "but I'm in something of a predicament."

"So I see."

Paige shoved her wet, tangled hair out of her eyes with
one hand. "I fell into the bay and lost my purse, along
with my passport and all my money."

She'd lost a lot more than that, Maggie thought wildly.
She couldn't even begin to anticipate Doc's reaction when
he saw his sweet, demure former fiancée.

"Why don't you tell me about it inside?" she suggested faintly.

Paige flashed her a relieved smile. "Thank you. I was
hoping I could count on you. This is all so embarrass-
ing."

When she limped awkwardly into the foyer, the cocky
boy strolled in right behind her. Hooking both thumbs in
the waistband of his rather scruffy-looking shorts, he
gave the ornate sitting room a quick once-over and whistled softly.

"A palace, *mademoiselle*," he commented in swift,
idiomatic French. "You must do very well of a night."

"I do all right," Maggie returned dryly.

It didn't surprise her that this young tough had guessed
Meredith's occupation with one sweeping glance. In fact,
it wouldn't have surprised her to learn that he occasionally acted as a middleman in negotiations for just the type
of services Meredith offered. His thin, pinched face and
shrewd, too-knowing eyes hinted at a life on the streets.

"May I borrow fifty francs?" Paige asked, wrapping
her arms around her chest to ward off the cool, breezy air
in the suite. "Just until I arrange to have my traveler's
checks replaced? I promised to pay—"

She broke off, her mouth dropping, as a tall, broad-shouldered figure stepped out from beside the armoire.

Glancing from her to Doc and back again, Maggie couldn't tell who was the more thunderstruck.

"Paige?" he growled.

"David?" she squeaked

A cheerful young voice broke the stark silence that followed. "Me, I am Henri. Someone will pay me fifty francs, yes?"

Chapter 4

Stunned, Paige stood unmoving.

Some distant corner of her mind registered the whisper of cool air that raised goose bumps on her damp skin. She heard the muted roar of the sea across the street. She tasted the tang of salt as she ran the tip of her tongue along suddenly dry lips.

"David?" she repeated weakly.

He didn't answer, except to stride forward and sweep her into his arms.

With a tiny sob, Paige lost herself in his solid, comforting warmth. Her fingers clutched at the scratchy wool of his jacket, and she strained against him for endless, wonderful moments. Then his hand tangled in her hair. He brought her head back and crushed her mouth with his. For once, he didn't control his emotions.

His rough kiss was all that she'd dreamed of. Hard. Searing. Scorching in its intensity.

And over too soon.

Far too soon.

Paige gasped an indistinct protest as he dragged his mouth from hers and held her head steady in both hands, scrutinizing her face with narrowed eyes.

"Are you all right?"

Still dazed by the raw power of that kiss, she could only stare back at him. It took her a moment to realize that whatever he'd experienced in that brief, shattering moment, he'd already managed to bring it under control.

While her heart was thudding erratically in her chest, David showed only an icy calm.

While her lips ached for his touch, his were drawn into a thin, tight line.

"Are you all right?" he repeated, his eyes searching hers.

Still unable to speak, she pushed herself a little way out of his arms. Or tried to.

As she stumbled back, the narrow lamé band caught on David's tie clip. To her horror, the fabric dragged downward. She splayed one hand across her breasts and tugged frantically at the soggy band with the other.

David unsnared her and shrugged out of his jacket. "Here, take this."

Her face flaming, Paige stood rigid as he dropped the worsted around her shoulders. She heard a stir behind her and remembered that there were others present. The heat in her face intensified even more.

She glanced behind her and caught the other woman's eyes. Friendliness shone in their green depths, and a carefully banked curiosity. Paige started to respond to the unspoken question there, and then noticed for the first time Meredith's short dressing gown. The pale lavender silk brushed the tops of her legs. Her very long and very bare legs.

The soaring combination of relief and joy that had swept through her when she saw David faltered.

Meredith moved forward, the silk swishing against her bare skin. "Why don't you bring her into the sitting room, Doc? So we can find out what happened?"

Doc?

The easy familiarity with which this woman addressed David plummeted through Paige like a stone dropping into a well. Numbly she felt him take her elbow and steer her toward the huge, vaulted room.

Glancing down at the woman beside him, Doc struggled to bring his soaring relief and astonishment under control. His senses were still reeling from the vivid image of Paige standing before him, her green eyes huge in her pale face, wearing only a narrow strip of gold, a pair of red shorts that displayed a good portion of her firm, rounded rear cheeks, and one ridiculously high shoe. He gripped her arm in a tight hold, as if to reassure himself that this wet, unfamiliar creature was actually Paige.

They hadn't taken two steps when a high, piping voice stopped them.

"But first my fifty francs, no? Me, I have business I must attend to."

Doc turned back, wrenching his attention away from his bedraggled, nearly naked fiancée to survey the boy. The youngster cocked his head and waited expectantly, his thumbs hooked in the waistband of his grubby shorts and a confident expression on his freckled face.

Malnourished, Doc noted in a swift mental list. Undersized for his age, which was about eleven or twelve. A faint scar on his chin that probably hadn't come from falling off a bike. Tough as shoe leather, if the cocky expression on his face was any indication.

"Fifty francs?" Doc asked. "For what?"

"For fishing *mademoiselle* out of the sea."

At Doc's quick frown, the boy gave a little wave of one hand. "She wades ashore some distance from here, you understand, and I bring her to the hotel. Fifty francs is a small fee, no? For such a service?''

Reaching into his pocket, David withdrew his wallet and pulled out a hundred-franc note. *"Merci."*

To his surprise, a white-faced, trembling Paige pushed his hand away before he could pass the bill to the youth. ''No.''

Her voice wavered and almost broke on the single syllable. His protective instincts soaring, David moved to take her into his arms again.

''No!'' she repeated, backing away.

Sudden, swift fear curled in Doc's belly. Although she appeared unhurt and had walked into the suite unassisted, something must have happened to make her shy away from him like that. Exerting immense control, he remained still.

''What is it? What's the matter?''

''Before I let you pay my debts for me, I think you'd better explain—'' She swallowed and darted a quick look at Maggie's bare legs and scantily clad body. ''I think you'd better explain what you're doing here, in this woman's suite.''

Cursing to himself, Doc realized that he'd made a tactical error. He, the precise, flawless engineer, who always thought problems through step by step before acting, who never made mistakes, had screwed up. Royally. He'd let his concern for Paige drive clear out of his mind the fact that she had no idea why he was here, in ''Meredith Ames's'' suite.

And he couldn't tell her.

He met Maggie's eyes in swift, silent communication and gave an almost imperceptible shake of his head, determined not to involve Paige in this any more than she already was. Still, the agent in him had to draw whatever she knew out of her.

"We'll talk about what I'm doing here later," he said. "Right now, you need to tell me what happened."

"No, I think we'd better talk about it now," she insisted, squaring her shoulders under the gray wool suit coat.

Despite himself, Doc felt heat spear through his belly as her small movement threatened to dislodge the thin strip of gold once more.

Rigidly he controlled the urge to reach out and tuck the folds of his jacket across her front. He'd seen Paige in less than she now wore, he reminded himself. He'd caressed and kissed her soft flesh a number of times in the past year. Not as often as he'd wanted to, but he'd deliberately held himself back. He hadn't wanted to overwhelm her, to frighten her with the passion he kept ruthlessly in check. She was so shy with him, so delicate in her responses.

Yet seeing her there, with that barbaric band around her breasts and her eyes flashing a challenge he'd never seen in them before, he had difficulty remembering that this was Paige. Sweet, shy Paige.

"I can't explain it," he replied in an even tone. "Not now."

Henri gave a small, derisive snort and lifted one red brow. "Me, I can."

"Keep out of this, half-pint," Maggie murmured, jerking at the back of his ragged, less-than-pristine navy sweater.

Doc ignored the two of them. "You'll just have to trust me," he said quietly.

When she hesitated, her eyes searching his with desperate need, he smiled reassuringly.

"Come on, sweetheart, we'll sort this out later. Right now we need to talk about what happened."

Ever afterward, Paige would wonder what might have happened if he hadn't used just that tone with her, as though he were speaking to a recalcitrant child.

If he hadn't assumed she would meekly comply with his soft but unmistakable order.

If she hadn't seen the swift, silent communication between David, *her* David, and this sophisticated, elegant... female.

It galled Paige no end that she'd actually liked Meredith! That she'd come to her for help after losing her passport and her money. That she hadn't wanted to contact David, because she hadn't been ready to face him yet.

She was ready now. Jerking her arm out of his hold, she lifted her chin defiantly.

"I'd like an explanation, David. Now."

He blinked, looking as surprised as if a pet kitten had suddenly arched its back and dug its claws into his hand. Over her head, he sent Meredith a quick, puzzled look.

When she saw the exchange, hot, fierce jealousy seared through Paige. It was emotion she hadn't ever felt before where David was concerned. In its wake came another, even more shattering emotion. Pain. Pure, unadulterated pain.

She'd been right.

In those moments perched high above Cannes, in that little turnout, when she slipped her engagement ring from her finger, she'd been right.

She wasn't woman enough for this man.

In her heart, she believed David, *her* David, had some logical explanation for being in this suite. In her soul, she knew he wasn't the kind of man to dally with one woman while he was engaged to another.

But that quick glance, that unspoken communication between the two of them, told Paige that David shared a special bond with Meredith Ames. She was a part of his life Paige hadn't known about, for some reason. A part of himself she'd often sensed that he held back. A part that, despite the fierce, searing kiss of a few moments ago, he still kept separate from her.

"Paige..." he began, once more in that placating tone she suddenly despised.

"Never mind! It doesn't matter anymore." Blinking furiously to dispel a sudden sheen of tears, she lifted her chin. "I'm sorry I arrived in Cannes early and disrupted your...your business conference. I'll let you get back to it."

Spinning around on her one platform heel, she limped toward the door. "Come on, Henri. I'll get the francs to pay you from the American Express office."

"Dammit, Paige! Wait!"

She flashed him a furious glance as he planted one big hand against the painted door and prevented her exit.

"Get rid of the kid," he instructed Meredith tersely, then took Paige's arm in a hold that wasn't quite as gentle as before.

She started to resist, but one look at his face quelled her brief spurt of rebellion. She'd never seen David look so hard. Or so determined. Biting her lip, she allowed him to lead her a little way into the suite.

"Here, Henri." Meredith shoved a bill into the boy's hand and gave him a little push toward the door.

His birdlike black eyes darted from one adult to the other, then fastened on Paige. "I am often at the telephone kiosk at the corner of the Croisette and the Allées de la Liberté. The kiosk is my headquarters, you understand. You will find me there, yes? If you need me."

Paige swallowed. "Yes. Thank you."

He lifted his hand and rubbed the bill between his fingers. "I thank you, *mademoiselle*."

With a wide grin and another quick glance at Meredith's legs, he was gone.

For a long moment after the door closed behind the boy, no one moved. It was as though they were all measuring each other, mentally adjusting to the unfamiliar personalities that had just emerged.

David, as Paige might have expected, recovered first. His hand gentled on her arm, and his gray blue eyes shaded with concern as they swept over her.

"Sit down, sweetheart, and tell us what happened."

Mutely Paige sank down on a damask-rose satin settee swirling with ornate curves and exquisite detailing.

David sat beside her. Reaching out, he took her cold hand in both of his and began to rub some warmth into it.

Meredith curled a leg under her and occupied a rose-and-green patterned armchair.

Confused, hurting, and close to the tears she'd held at bay until this moment, Paige stared down at David's large, square hands. Those blunt-tipped fingers had worked such magic on her body. Those palms had shaped her breasts and her waist and her future. Now she had no future. Not the one she'd envisioned with David, anyway.

With a fresh wave of pain, she tried to tug her hand free. David's fingers suddenly tightened on hers.

"Where's your ring?" he asked. His face subtly altered, taking on stark planes and rigid angles. "Did those bastards take it?"

She blinked, startled by the savage fury in his voice.

"Did they hurt you?"

"Did who hurt me?"

His jaw worked. "You can tell me, sweetheart. What did they do to you?"

"They?"

"Let her tell us what happened, Doc," Meredith interjected.

The quiet words tore at Paige's soul. If she'd needed any proof that the man she loved and the woman she'd admired during their brief encounter in the boutique shared a special bond, that casual nickname was it. She couldn't imagine any of David's associates at the engineering firm where they both worked calling him "Doc." His impressive credentials and professional stature were such that everyone, from suppliers to the president of the firm, regarded him with a respect bordering on awe.

As chief of the technical library, Paige had been more than a little intimidated the first time she'd been summoned to David's office. Especially since she'd overcharged his department by several hundred dollars for a publication he'd requested.

She'd been equally overwhelmed when he followed up that first meeting with several visits to her crowded little work center. So overwhelmed, she hadn't even realized he was asking her to dinner one drizzly Saturday morning, until he tilted her chin and smiled down at her in a way that made her stutter in confusion.

Correctly interpreting that stammering reply as an affirmative, he'd picked her up that night. And the next. Shortly afterward, he'd begun a slow, measured courtship that left Paige simmering with anticipation for each new plateau in their relationship and aching with loneliness during his frequent business trips abroad.

With a slow sinking sensation, she wondered how many of those business trips David had taken with Meredith Ames. And just what their relationship was.

She glanced at the other woman now, cataloging her vitality, her glowing beauty. Paige's hurt became a dull, throbbing ache.

"What happened?" Meredith asked. "After you left the boutique?"

"A limousine pulled up," Paige replied, with a small, defeated sigh. "No, not a limo. A Rolls-Royce. It was sent for you, you know. The chauffeur called me Mademoiselle Ames several times.''

''That's what I was afraid of.''

''I tried to explain, but I was so surprised that my little bit of French deserted me.'' She made a little grimace of distaste. ''Besides, the driver was rather rude about it all.''

David's hand tightened on hers. ''Rude?''

''Yes. He practically pushed me into the back seat. Then there was a glass partition between us, and I couldn't even talk to him until we pulled up at the marina.''

''What marina?''

''I don't know. One of the ones along the Croisette.''

''And then?''

''And then he gestured toward the boat. Since he didn't seem to understand me and I couldn't get through to him, I decided to explain the situation to whoever was on the boat. But when I tried to walk up the ramp in these shoes, I fell off.''

''What?''

''You did what?''

The simultaneous questions jumped at her from opposite directions.

The swift, startled look that passed between David and Meredith set Paige's teeth on edge. These two might not be lovers, but they certainly could communicate with an economy of words. A tiny, healthy anger began to nibble at the edges of her hurt.

She pulled her hand free of David's tight hold and wove her fingers together in her lap.

''I fell off the ramp,'' she repeated through stiff lips. ''The gangplank. When I was walking up it, onto the yacht.''

''What yacht?''

''I don't know. A big one. With white sides.''

"Did you see the name?" David asked.

"Or the registration number?" Meredith added.

"There were some numbers painted on the side of the boat. Three-six-one something." Her forehead scrunched. "Maybe it was six-one-three. Or three—" Embarrassed by the disability that had dogged her all her life, Paige clamped her lips shut.

"Never mind," David replied. "We'll check all possible combinations. What happened after you fell off the gangplank? It's important. Tell us everything, exactly as it happened."

Gripping her hands together in her lap, she recounted the details of her unexpected swim in the Mediterranean.

"The tide swept me under the dock. There were so many boats berthed at the marina that when I finally surfaced, I didn't know where I was. I could hear shouting some distance away. I thought I heard a splash or two, like oars hitting the water. But by that time, I'd started swimming for shore. I had to shrug out of my jacket, and I lost my purse, but I made it."

David's brows drew into a dark slash, but he didn't interrupt.

"That's when Henri came along," Paige finished. "On his scooter. He saw me wading through the water and helped me to shore. I...I remembered that Meredith had told the saleslady to send her packages to the Carlton, so I asked Henri to bring me here."

With a challenging tilt to her chin, she met Meredith's eyes. "Other than David, you were the only person I knew in Cannes."

David shifted beside her, drawing her attention back to him as he stared at her in some puzzlement. "Why didn't you just come to me? You knew I was staying in this hotel, as well."

It was here, the moment Paige had dreaded and worried about and cried over for weeks. She wet suddenly dry lips, unable to speak.

"Why didn't you come to me, Paige?" A small frown etched across his forehead. "And you still haven't told me what happened to your ring."

In the small silence that followed, Meredith uncurled her long legs and rose. "Why don't I go get dressed?"

Neither of the two people facing each other on the settee paid any attention to her as she moved across the wide, luxuriously furnished sitting room. The tall double bedroom doors closed behind her.

Paige ran her tongue along her lower lip, her whole being focused on the man beside her. She let her eyes drift over the strong planes of his face, storing up memories of the lines at the corners of his eyes, the slight bump in the bridge of his nose, the square chin.

"My emerald ring is in my purse, David," she said slowly. "Which is resting somewhere at the bottom of the bay right now. I took it off before I arrived in Cannes."

"Why?"

"Because I was going to give it back to you."

He went completely still.

Her heart hammering, Paige searched his face. She thought she saw confusion, and hurt, and a sudden fierce denial, flicker in his intent eyes, but in typical David fashion, he didn't express any of that. Instead, he sought to understand the root cause of the problem.

"Why?" he asked again.

Paige groped for some way to explain the feelings that had haunted her for weeks. "Because we have different ideas of marriage. To me, it's a communion between two beings, an equal partnership, with nothing held back." Her gaze flickered to the closed bedroom door. "To you, it's obviously something else."

"I see. You think that I—"

He broke off as the door flew open and Meredith burst into the sitting room.

"I just went to draw the curtains and saw Paige's little friend, Henri, on the sidewalk below. He's talking to someone who looks very much like the chauffeur of the Rolls."

"Hell!" David surged to his feet. "Stay with Paige. And lock the door behind me."

In a few swift strides, he was out the door and into the corridor.

Meredith turned the dead bolt behind him and hooked the old-fashioned chain into the guard for good measure. Without speaking, she crossed the wide expanse of carpeted floor and flattened her back against the wall beside the open balcony doors. She peered out for long, tense moments, while Paige watched in growing confusion.

After a few seconds, Meredith shook her head in disgust. "I can't see anything from here. The palm trees block the sidewalk."

She came back to the grouping of graceful carved rosewood furniture and dropped into the chair she'd vacated just moments before.

"What's going on?" Paige asked. "Why did David rush out like that?"

"We'd like to know who the chauffeur's working for."

"You don't know? I thought... I thought the driver came to the boutique for you."

"He did."

"But you don't know who he's working for?"

Struggling to make sense of the confusing situation, Paige tucked a strand of limp white gold hair behind her ears. "Who are you?"

The tall, self-assured woman hesitated, then gave a small shrug. "I told you. I'm Meredith Ames."

"How do you know David?"

"That's something he'll explain to you."

Frowning, Paige stared at Meredith, then did a slow survey of the opulent suite.

"What do you do? For a living?"

Maggie stifled a groan. She hated having to perpetuate this deception on a woman she was coming to like, for herself as much as for the fact that she was Doc's fiancée. Had been Doc's fiancée. Whatever. But she had no choice, not if there was any chance at all that she could maintain her cover and salvage what was left of her mission.

She drew in a slow breath, suspecting that Paige wasn't going to appreciate the answer to her question.

Chapter 5

"A call girl?" Paige looked Meredith up and down, then shook her head emphatically. "I don't believe it."

"You believed it, or something close to it, when you first walked in the door."

"That was then," she stated with irrefutable logic. "This is now."

Meredith hesitated, then made a small gesture that encompassed the elegant suite. "Do you think your average American tourist can afford to stay at the Carlton or shop on the Croisette?"

Paige glanced around, taking in the opulent furnishings and the huge vases filled with freshly cut flowers that were scattered on every level surface. Her work as a technical librarian involved her more with research in engineering and the applied sciences than with general references, but she'd studied enough sourcebooks in college to recognize a few of the priceless antiques that graced the sitting. A beautiful rosewood secretaire, its roll top inlaid with an intricate mother-of-pearl woodland scene, sat in one corner. The ornate, marble-topped table set against the opposite wall was Italian, she guessed, as was the massive gilt mirror that hung above it.

No, she acknowledged heavily, your average American tourist couldn't afford this suite.

Still, Paige refused to accept that Meredith and David, *her* David, shared an illicit relationship. "You may be a...a call girl, but I don't believe David's one of your customers."

An understanding smile tugged at the other woman's full lips. "No, he's not one of my customers."

Paige stared at her for a long moment, and then her eyes widened in startled disbelief. "Good heavens, you're not trying to tell me he's your...your pimp?"

Half groaning, half laughing, Meredith shook her head. "Women at my level of the profession don't have pimps. Our clients are referred to us by reliable sources, and usually contact us over the phone, which is where the term came from in the first place."

Paige chewed on her lower lip, thinking furiously. She might be naive, and a little timid on occasion, but she wasn't stupid.

"I don't believe it," she said flatly. "There's something else going on here, something you won't tell me. Either of you."

The other woman hesitated, then gave a small sigh. "Look, I'm not cleared to tell you anything. Obviously you realize you've stumbled into the middle of something Doc and I are working on together. All I can say is that it's dangerous. Very dangerous."

Meredith threw a quick glance over her shoulder as a soft knock sounded on the door. She rose, her hand slipping into her pocket. Paige's eyes widened at the faint outline of a gun she saw in the lavender silk. Open-mouthed, she watched Meredith glide to the door on bare feet, not making a sound, then peer through the peep-hole.

Her shoulders lost their coiled tension, and she opened the door for David.

"We're okay," he said quietly. "It cost me another fifty francs, but I verified that our pal Henri didn't disclose anything to the chauffeur other than the fact that he brought an American woman back to this hotel. Apparently the driver still thinks it was Meredith Ames who went into the sea."

"We're close enough in appearance," Meredith said. "Maybe we can still pull this operation off."

"What operation?" Paige asked.

David walked to her side. "You aren't cleared to know. Tell me, did anyone besides this driver get a good look at you before you nose-dived into the bay? Anyone on board the yacht?"

"I don't know. There were some people—crewmen, I think—on the back deck. But I didn't see anyone else."

"We'll just have to chance it," Meredith said quietly to David. "We've taken greater risks before. Or we can take the chauffeur out for a little while."

"Right." He gave Paige's hands a little squeeze. "Come on, let's get you out of here. I'll take you back to your hotel so you can get your things."

"My things?" she asked, startled.

"You're flying out of Cannes in forty-five minutes—sooner, if Meredith can arrange it."

"Leaving? But what about my purse? My passport? I don't have any papers, or money."

"You won't need any," the other woman assured her, moving toward the bedroom with a confident stride. "I'll take care of everything."

"Let's go," David said, tugging her to her feet. "I'll write out your itinerary for you as soon as it's confirmed, and make you a list of contacts at each stop, in case you need them.''

Her forehead creased as she rose, still wrapped in the soft wool of his suit coat. ''How can you get me out of France with no papers?''

His mouth firmed in an effort to control his impatience as he tugged her to her feet. ''I can't explain it to you. Not right now. But you don't have to worry. I'll make sure you're safe. Someone will be covering you every second until you walk in your front door. When I return,'' he added firmly, ''we'll work through this matter of our engagement.''

It was that firm, no-nonsense tone that did it.

At that moment, Paige decided she would not walk out of this hotel room like a chastened child, to be sent home to wait and wonder and worry. If there was any hope for her and David at all, if he was ever going to share this private part of his life with her, it had to be now.

Digging in her one bare and one shod heels, she resisted his efforts to escort her to the suite's door. ''I'm not leaving.''

''I know this is confusing for you,'' he said, in that even voice that made Paige's back teeth grind together. ''I'll explain what I can when I get home.''

''I'm not leaving,'' she repeated, folding her arms across her chest. ''I want to know what's going on.''

His jaw squared a bit at that. ''We don't have time for this.''

''Then we'll just have to make time.''

His blue eyes hardened for an instant, and he gave her slender form a quick, assessing look that suddenly made Paige just a little nervous. How ridiculous, she thought, dismissing the shivery sensation that darted down her spine as the product of overstretched nerves. David would never use his physical strength against her. He was always so careful with her, so solicitous of her comfort.

The thought reassured her, yet somehow depressed her at the same time.

"You weren't listening before," she told him, with a tilt to her chin. "I was trying to say that marriage has to be an equal partnership. All the strength can't be on one side, nor all the sharing."

"What about all the trust?"

"I trust you. I trust you enough to believe you're not one of Meredith's customers."

"Thank you for that much, at least."

Paige's back stiffened at the hint of sarcasm in his voice. She tossed her damp hair over her shoulders in a gesture that held an uncharacteristic rebelliousness.

"Someone has mistaken me for Meredith, correct?"

"Correct. And we're getting you out of here before they discover that mistake."

"What happens if they do discover Meredith isn't me? Or I'm not her?"

"That's not your concern."

There it was again. The closed door. The sealed chamber. The locked part of himself that he refused to allow Paige into. Her mouth settling into mulish lines, she met his look.

"I'm not leaving, David."

"It's not your choice," he told her, his face hardening.

"Is that right? Just what are you going to do? Drug me and carry me unconscious aboard the plane?"

"If I have to."

Paige's jaw dropped. Shock held her immobile for long, silent moments. Then the welter of emotions that had weighted her down for so many weeks exploded. Uncertainty, wrenching unhappiness, insecurity and a debilitating sense of inadequacy all erupted into searing anger.

Planting her hands on her hips, she glared up at David. "Now you just listen to me, Mr. Take-Charge-Stone-Face-Macho-Man! I don't know who you think you are or where you got the impression that I'm some kind of windup doll you can play with when it suits you, then set conveniently out of the way when you've got better things to do. But we're going to correct that impression right here and right now."

"Calm down, Paige."

"Don't 'Paige' me. And do not, *do not ever,* use that patronizing tone of voice with me again. Assuming I allow you to speak to me at all, that is. I want to know what's going on here."

They faced each other like two combatants, arms crossed and bodies tense. Neither one heard Meredith walk back into the room.

Maggie could see at a glance that the course of true love hadn't run smooth during her brief absence. David and Paige stood toe-to-toe, looking for all the world like a sleek, well-muscled California brown bear squared off against a delicate gazelle. He towered over Paige, his face set in hard, unyielding lines. Chin lifted, eyes flashing with a surprising bravado, she glowered up at him. The gazelle wasn't giving an inch, Maggie realized with a start of surprise.

"It's all set," she announced, drawing their reluctant attention. "A helicopter will pick Paige up at the heliport atop the Carlton in thirty minutes. She'll fly to the U.S. air base at Ramstein, in Germany, then take a transport to the States."

"I'm not going."

Her eyes widening in surprise, Maggie glanced from Paige's set face to David's thunderous one, then back again.

"Someone thinks I'm you," the younger woman said belligerently. "Or rather that I'm the person you're obviously pretending to be."

"What makes you think I'm pretending?" Maggie asked sharply.

Paige waved an impatient hand. "I admit I don't know anything about call girls or pimps or this particular line of work. But I do know David. He may be overbearing and obnoxious and entirely too arrogant in his own quiet way," she said acidly, "but he's not the kind of man to become involved with . . . with prostitution."

Doc didn't look particularly pleased with her somewhat backhanded vote of confidence.

"Besides," Paige added, with a cool look in her forest green eyes, "a call girl doesn't just whisk a person out of a foreign country aboard military transports. Who do you work for? Military intelligence? The CIA?"

Maggie and Doc exchanged silent looks.

"If you two do that one more time," Paige stated through clenched teeth, "I'm going to throw something."

Her mind racing, Maggie assessed the situation. Obviously, there was more to Paige Lawrence than the shy, somewhat timid young woman she'd met in the boutique this morning. She was intelligent, too intelligent for her own good. She'd guessed enough to put herself in danger if those on the yacht managed to connect her with this operation. OMEGA would have to send her to a safe haven for the duration of the mission.

Assuming the mission wasn't already hopelessly compromised, Maggie thought with bitter honesty. She and Paige were close enough in appearance to be mistaken for each other at first glance, but not close enough to carry off the deception if the driver, or anyone else, had gotten a clear look at either of them.

Which was why, when Paige suggested a few moments later that she stay in Cannes and meet with whomever had sent the Rolls, Maggie didn't object immediately.

David, however, did.

"Absolutely not."

Paige ignored him, addressing herself to Maggie. "The driver thinks I'm Meredith Ames. I never managed to correct that impression before I fell into the bay. Those people aboard the yacht may have seen me. Whoever was waiting on that boat now expects me, not you."

"True."

"Why were you going there? Other than the obvious reason?" She stared at Maggie, her eyes thoughtful. "You must be delivering something. A message. Or information. Or money."

This woman was definitely too intelligent for her own good.

"That's enough," David interjected. "You've just run out of time to gather your things, Paige. I'll have them sent to you. Come with me."

"No."

"Dammit, you have no idea what's going down here."

"No, I don't. So tell me."

"You don't need to know. I'm not going to allow you to—"

She interrupted him in a soft, dangerous voice. "David, if you harbor even the faintest hope that we might marry someday, which I'll admit appears very unlikely at this moment, you won't finish that sentence."

His jaw tight, Doc refrained from finishing his sentence.

While he scowled down at her, Paige fired her final shot. "I love you, David. I think I've loved you since the moment I walked into your office and you helped me sort out the mix-up on that rather expensive publication I ordered for you. I . . . I know you love me, too." She held up a quick hand when he moved toward her. "Let me finish!"

"You've just said all that matters."

"No. No, I haven't." She drew in a deep breath. "I see now that we don't really know each other. You think I need to be coddled and protected and cherished all my life, and..."

She slid Maggie a quick, sideways glance. "And I think you need a more adventuresome partner, a woman who stirs more than just your protective instincts. I want the chance to prove I'm that woman. I need to do this. For you. For me. For us."

Maggie held her breath, feeling much like a voyeur watching a riveting, compelling personal drama. She probably should've gone back into the bedroom some time ago, she told herself ruefully. But there wasn't any way she was going to miss the ending to this particular scene.

"Whatever you're doing must have some desperate consequences," Paige added softly. "For you, or for our country. I can help. I have a right to help."

When he didn't respond, she drew in a deep breath. "I'm not leaving, David. Not willingly. I'm going to deliver whatever it is that Meredith's supposed to deliver. When this is over, we'll decide who we really are and where we go from here."

Endless seconds ticked by. Outside the open balcony doors, a shrill horn honked on the boulevard below. Inside the suite, a soft breeze stirred air redolent with the scent of white carnations and tall velvet blue irises.

"When this is over—" Doc snapped "—I just hope we *know* who the hell we are."

*   *   *

Sometime later, Maggie studied the two figures on the settee as she waited for control to acknowledge her transmission.

Paige fidgeted a little, hunching shoulders still wrapped in Doc's coat against the cooling breeze. Her eyes were wide with excitement.

David didn't move. Not a muscle. Not an eyelash.

Maggie had worked with him on a number of missions in the past three years. She'd seen him up to his elbows in an Asian swamp and flat on his stomach, inching his way across a thin crust of ice that cracked ominously under his weight with every movement. She'd watched him at the high-speed computer in the control center, his jaw tight and small beads of sweat rolling down the side of his brow as he pulled together a list of possible Irish terrorists just hours before visiting British royalty were scheduled to land in Washington, D.C.

But she'd never seen him as tightly coiled as he was now.

Claire's clear voice cut through the heavy silence at last.

"Cyrene here. I've got Thunder with me. Go ahead, Chameleon."

Maggie smiled as she lifted the transceiver. She'd just won a bet with herself. She'd fully expected Adam Ridgeway to come up to the OMEGA control center once Claire had given him the startling news that Doc's fiancée needed immediate extraction. The director would make it his personal responsibility to ensure his agent's loved one was out of danger.

"The situation I briefed you on a few moments ago has changed a bit," Maggie announced, with slight understatement.

"How so, Chameleon?"

"We won't need the transportation I requested for the subject. Not just yet, anyway."

"Why not?" Adam asked sharply. "Is she all right?"

"She's fine. She's right here, with me and Doc. But she understands that she's been mistaken for me. She wants to make the contact in my place." Flicking an apologetic glance at Doc, Maggie finished her transmission. "I think we should let her."

For several long moments, Adam didn't respond. Maggie held her breath, not quite sure whether or not she wanted the director to approve this highly irregular request. What they were proposing was well outside OMEGA's operating parameters. As far as she knew, Adam had never allowed anyone other than fully cleared, well-trained agents to become involved in the organization's desperate and often deadly operations.

On the other hand, he had two of his best-trained operatives in the field with Paige right now. If anyone could keep her safe, and still pull off this dangerous charade, Maggie and Doc could. She hoped.

"Let me get this straight," Adam said at last. "You want me to authorize a civilian to impersonate a secret agent who's impersonating a call girl?"

"That's it," Maggie confirmed.

"Does Doc concur with this?"

Maggie flicked a quick glance at David's rigid face. Strange she'd never quite appreciated the phrase *carved in granite* before. Without a word, she handed him the compact.

David sent his former and perhaps current fiancée a cold stare.

Paige started to shrink back into the cocoon of his wool jacket, but caught herself just in time. Squaring her shoulders, she returned his look.

His mouth compressed to a thin line, David lifted the compact. The gold case looked tiny and fragile in his big hands, but he operated the transmit button with a sure, competent touch.

"Doc here. I concur. With specific conditions."

Maggie frowned. In the heated discussion that had preceded this transmission, David hadn't mentioned any conditions.

"The subject isn't to be out of our contact, not for a moment," he stated with grim emphasis. "I want to know where she is every second. She'll need a tracking device implanted under her skin. Today."

"I can have someone there in a few hours," Adam replied slowly.

"Wait a minute!" Paige protested. "What tracking device? Implanted where under my skin?"

"Don't worry," Maggie assured her. "It's just a small chip. So tiny, you won't even know it's there."

"I won't know it's *where?*"

Ignoring their exchange, David continued laying out his conditions. "I'm altering my cover to provide her closer surveillance. I haven't worked out all the details yet. I'll get back to you as soon as I do."

"Fine."

The lines bracketing either side of his mouth deepened. "And I reserve the right to extract her without prior consultation. Anytime I deem it necessary."

"Agreed."

"Not by me!" Thoroughly indignant, Paige reached for the compact. "I want to talk to him."

With obvious reluctance, David handed her the communications device. "Press the stone in the center of the lid once to transmit, twice to receive."

She fumbled with the small gold case for a moment or two, then held the mirror up in front of her face.

"What did you call him?" she asked Maggie, peering over the lid. "Thunder?"

"Thunder," Maggie confirmed. "It's his code name."

The satellite transmissions were secure, and so scrambled they couldn't be interpreted even if they were intercepted. Still, none of the OMEGA agents ever took unnecessary chances.

Paige squeezed the small stone. "Mr. Thunder, this is . . . this is Jezebel."

David grimaced in disgust.

After a pregnant pause, Adam replied. "Go ahead, Jezebel."

"I just want to let you know I'm well aware of Dav— of Doc's concerns. I'll do whatever he and—?"

"Chameleon," Maggie supplied.

"Whatever he and Chameleon say. Within reason. I want to check out this implant before anyone pokes it under my skin."

"I can understand your reservations," Thunder replied. "However, Doc has made the tracking device a condition of your involvement in this operation. If you don't agree to it, you'll be out of Cannes within twenty minutes."

Whew! Maggie had felt the whip of Adam's authority a few times herself in the past. It wasn't a particularly pleasant experience, even at a distance of some five thousand miles.

To her credit, Paige didn't wilt under the force of Adam's edict. The prospect of adventure, Maggie decided wryly, must have brought out some inner qualities that she suspected the younger woman hadn't displayed very often in the past.

Paige scowled at the compact, then at Doc, then at the compact again.

"Fine," she said testily into the transmitter. "But the thing had darn well better be removable. I don't want to walk around on an electronic leash for the rest of my life."

Fumbling with the receive button, she didn't catch the hard glint that deepened David's eyes to a gunmetal gray.

Maggie did, however.

Something told her that Paige was going to find it a lot more difficult to shed her leash after her adventure than she imagined.

Chapter 6

For Paige, the next few hours seemed like something right out a spy novel.

David made no effort to hide his anger at her stubbornness, but as soon as Thunder confirmed the decision, he moved into action. Coolly directing Paige to slip into something more suitable for an intense training session, he sat down at the secretaire and pulled a sheet of the hotel's elegant stationery in front of him.

Chameleon, who had confided that her real name was Maggie, took Paige into the bedroom and dug out a pair of tan linen slacks and a sleeveless, backless silk top in a vivid jade.

"Come out as soon as you're changed. We've got a lot to do, and not much time to do it in. Our...your contact could call at any moment."

Maggie paused, her hand on the door latch. "Are you sure about this, Paige? Or I suppose I'd better call you Meredith?"

Paige glanced over her shoulder into the sitting room. David's broad back was to her. She could see the play of his muscles under his starched cotton shirt as he wrote. The afternoon sunlight picked out the deep reddish tints in his brown hair. He seemed so achingly familiar to her, and yet suddenly such a stranger.

Her heart thumped with the knowledge that she was going to discover a side to him she'd never known before.

"Yes, I'm sure."

When she emerged from the bedroom a few moments later, David held several neat handwritten lists.

"All right," he said, "let's get to it."

She'd known he was a skilled engineer and a born leader, of course. The several hundred electronics engineers and technicians who worked for him at the huge firm where they were both employed worshiped him. Personnel turnover in David's division was minimal, and output was well above that of any other department in terms of both quality and quantity. He'd rarely talked about his work when he and Paige were together, preferring instead to explore their similar preferences in old movies and spicy foods and biking through California's glorious national parks. But she'd heard enough cafeteria scuttlebutt and office gossip to know that when David set his mind and his energy to a problem, everyone considered it solved.

He now orchestrated Paige's transformation from technical librarian to high-class hooker with the same skill he brought to his job. And with a merciless, unrelenting thoroughness that almost overwhelmed her.

The first task was to teach her the emergency signals.

Taking into account her difficulty with figures, David and Maggie grilled Paige on each and every signal, over and over. By the time they were done, she was sure she'd be able to verify everything from "Agent in place" to

"Situation desperate, request immediate backup" sixty or seventy years from now.

Then they instructed her in the use of the various implements Maggie laid out on the square, marble-topped coffee table. Paige fumbled a bit with the electronic "sweep" in the hairbrush handle, and gasped when a small but lethal projectile shot out of a tube of mascara and embedded itself in the opposite wall. On her second try with the mascara, she aimed for a thick folded pad David had propped against a chairback and hit a rare Meissen figurine of a young girl on the mantel. While David picked up the shattered porcelain pieces, Maggie quietly tucked away the evil-looking gun she'd laid on the table, saying that Paige would be safer without anything more lethal than the mascara.

When a fussy little waiter knocked at the door to the suite an hour later, Paige, in her new role as Meredith, answered. But it was David who took charge when the waiter set the silver tea tray on a marble-topped table and extracted a set of surgical tools from the snowy linen napkin.

"Is this the chip?" David asked, holding up a clear cellophane package containing a paper-thin sliver of plastic no bigger than a newborn baby's thumbnail.

"Yes, Dr. Jensen," the waiter confirmed in a clipped European accent Paige couldn't place. "It's been tested in labs both here and in the States, and several times in the field. It has not failed us. Not once."

David sent the man a cold look. "It had better not fail now."

"No," he replied, blinking. "No, of course not."

When the little waiter picked up what looked like a scalpel, Paige swallowed nervously. "Is this absolutely necessary? I mean, I'll have the compact with me, and you've said that one of you will be in visual contact at all times."

The look David turned on her was almost as cold as the one he'd given the waiter. "It's not too late to get you out of here."

Paige gulped. "Bring on the knife."

Still, she couldn't help tensing as the waiter wiped the scalpel with an antiseptic gauze, then approached her.

"This won't hurt, *madame*," he assured her. "I will deaden the area a bit. Just sit there, in that chair, and relax."

"Easy for you to say," Paige muttered as she perched on the edge of a side chair.

Her nervousness evidently communicated itself to the little waiter-surgeon. He hovered over her, frowning.

"*Madame*, you must relax. I make only the slightest of incisions, no more than the scratch of a pin. Just here, at the back of your neck, where your hair will cover it."

He indicated the area with a swipe of the anesthetizing pad. Despite herself, Paige flinched.

With a small, savage curse, David strode to her side. Lifting her bodily out of the chair, he resettled her on his lap. Gratefully Paige turned her face into his shoulder. He brushed her hair to one side with a big, warm hand, then cradled the back of her head.

Closing her eyes, Paige buried her nose in his jacket. The distinctive blend of fine wool, woodsy after-shave and the subtle masculine scent that was David's alone filled her senses. She felt the strength of his arms around her, the solid security of the body pressed to hers.

What in the world was she doing? she wondered for a wild, tumultuous moment, burrowing deeper into his hold. How did she think she could play this dangerous game, when she trembled at the thought of a scalpel? Why didn't she just nest here, in David's arms, for the rest of her life?

Because she didn't want to nest, Paige reminded herself. Because she wanted to...to soar with the eagles. Or at least with David. To share whatever danger and excitement and . . .

"So, *madame,* it is done."

"What?" Paige turned her head sideways and opened one eye to peer up at the little man standing beside her.

"It is done."

"It is?"

Cautiously she lifted her nose from David's shoulder. His arms tightened around her for a fraction of a second, as though he were reluctant to let her go.

When he eased his hold, Paige tried to convince herself she didn't miss the security of his arms. She moved her head a few careful degrees in both directions, but didn't feel a thing.

"This is the receiver," the waiter-surgeon said, holding out a small, flat rectangle that looked much like a miniature calculator with a liquid crystal digital display. "Using the signals from the chip, it will pinpoint the subject's exact location, either in global coordinates or in radial meters from a specific center."

"I'll take that." David slipped the small device into his suit pocket.

Paige watched it disappear with an odd sensation. She might have lost her emerald ring, but she was now bound to David by a stronger, far more intimate link. One she couldn't take off if she wanted to.

The thought unsettled her. And reassured her. And confused her.

Once the odd little waiter departed, the pace became frantic. Maggie and David worked through each item on his list to complete Paige's transformation.

A summation of Meredith Ames's leisurely, pampered life-style. Check.

A rundown of the wealthy, elite clients she catered to. Check.

A brief description of the technology she'd carried from L.A. and how she'd carried it. Check.

A precise step-by-step plan for Paige to hand over the microdot, then disappear from the scene. Check.

And in the event the unknown contact didn't surface within the next few hours, a detailed schedule for the rest of Meredith's day and night. Check.

Paige stared at the schedule. "The casino? I'm supposed to go to the casino?"

"It's part of Meredith's normal routine when she's in Cannes," Maggie explained.

"Does she gamble?"

"Occasionally."

"You won't, however," David interjected, his face softening for the first time in what seemed like hours. "You'd probably put down a five-thousand-dollar chip, thinking it was five."

"Probably," Paige agreed, more relieved by that almost-smile than she'd allow herself to admit. "So what do I do at the casino, if I don't gamble?"

Maggie gave her a wry grin. "You advertise. You're a businesswoman, remember? In addition to acting as a mule for smuggled technology, you have a product to sell. One that commands rather incredible prices here in Cannes."

"Oh. Yes."

Ignoring David's sudden frown, Maggie rose to her feet. "Come on, Meredith. It's time we went to work on packaging your product."

David rose also, only to be stopped in his tracks when both women murmured protests.

"We can handle this part," Maggie assured him. "We don't need one of your lists for this."

His gaze rested on Paige's face for a moment. "I have a pretty good feel for what she looks best in."

"Doc," Maggie replied gently, "what you think Paige looks best in and what Meredith Ames looks best in might be two entirely different bests."

Closing the door to the huge, luxuriously appointed bedroom, the two women went to work adapting Maggie/Meredith's working wardrobe for Paige/Meredith's more slender frame.

Digging through the drawers of a high chest-on-chest, Maggie pulled out a stunning silver belt, Italian leather sandals, and a jaunty emerald green rhinestoned ball cap. They would add Meredith's distinctive touch to the linen slacks and green top Paige was now wearing, she explained. Just in case the contact called and she had to go out immediately.

That done, Maggie threw open the doors to a magnificent walnut armoire that must have once belonged to French royalty. Paige's mouth sagged at the array of silks and satins, seductive teddies and whisper-thin negligees, see-through organza blouses and stiff-boned bodices displayed within.

"The Grand Casino is one of the most exclusive men's clubs in the world," Maggie told her as she flipped through the padded hangers. "It's patronized by movie stars and oil sheiks and billionaires who like their play deep, their cigars hand-rolled, and their women elegant. Here, try this little number."

Dubiously Paige eyed the two-piece ball gown she held out. While the full, floor-length black taffeta skirt was demure enough, the bustier that went with it was something else again. An eye-catching, glowing fuchsia in color, the strapless bodice was trimmed with black satin ribbon along its heart-shaped upper edge and the deep V of the lower edge. More ribbon traced the stiff boning that ribbed its front and covered the front closure, which hooked together like an old-fashioned corset.

Paige slipped on the skirt, then struggled with the hooks of the constricting bodice. As she tugged it into place, she discovered that it was fitted with padded lifts that pushed her breasts up to create a dramatic cleavage. Far more cleavage than she'd ever dreamed she possessed.

Maggie handed her a black velvet ribbon with a heart-shaped diamond pendant. "Here, this is perfect with that outfit."

Paige tied the thin ribbon around her throat, then stared at her image in the floor-to-ceiling dressing room mirror.

"Now *that's* what I'd call superior product packaging," Maggie said with a grin.

Paige nodded, ashamed to admit that she wasn't sure she'd have the nerve to go out of the bedroom, much less to a crowded casino, in this decadent, delicious, totally erotic gown.

Yes, she would, she told herself fiercely. It was time a certain broad-shouldered, overprotective engineer learned that there was more to her than long bike rides through the California parks and lazy Sunday mornings sharing the paper. There was excitement. Romance. Mystery. Adventure.

She gave the bustier a last, uncertain look, then changed back into the tan slacks.

Laying the eveningwear on the bed, Maggie smiled as she trailed a fingertip along black satin piping. "This was one assignment I was planning to enjoy."

Paige glanced up from working the buttons on the green blouse. "Do you go out on assignment often?"

"Often enough."

"Always with David?" Despite her best efforts, she couldn't keep a faint trace of jealousy out of her voice.

"Not always." Maggie gave Paige a bland look. "But regularly enough to know what kind of a man he is."

Paige fought a little dart of resentment. The other woman certainly didn't make any bones about her intimate knowledge of someone else's fiancé. Former fiancé.

"And what kind of man is he?" she asked, a trifle coolly.

"The best," Maggie replied bluntly.

Paige's resentment melted, and she gave a small sigh. "I know."

Maggie nibbled on her lower lip for a moment, as if wanting to say something. But a glance at the ornate little clock on the dresser evidently made her decide not to share any further details about the man they both appeared to appreciate, if in vastly different ways.

"I'd better get out of here," she said, tossing a few items into a small overnight case. "I'm moving into the suite across the hall with Doc."

Busy with her packing, she didn't see Paige's shoulders stiffen.

"We've got a surveillance camera rigged that sweeps the hallway every few seconds. No one can get in or out of this suite without our knowledge."

She gave the bedroom a last, assessing glance, before turning back to Paige.

"You've got the compact in your pocket?"

"Yes."

"The gold halter is in your purse?"

"Yes."

"And the mascara?"

Evidently David wasn't the only member of this team who made lists. "Yes."

"Just be careful where you aim it, okay?"

With a final, encouraging grin, Maggie led the way out of the bedroom. "We've got our own bugs planted in each room. We can hear every word spoken anywhere in the suite. Just say the word, and we'll be here in three seconds flat."

Paige nodded, feeling a slight constriction in her throat. Now that the actual moment had come for her to begin her big adventure, she was a little nervous about it. More than a little. But she would've died rather than admit it to David.

She didn't have to.

He was too attuned to her, too sensitive to her every movement, to miss the sudden uncertainty in her eyes. Crossing the plush carpet, he curled a knuckle under her chin.

"You don't have to do this."

Paige stared up into his face, as if memorizing the handsome, regular features. The tiny lines at the corners of his gray blue eyes. The faint shadow that darkened his chin this late in the afternoon. The small, almost invisible scar on one temple that he'd never quite explained.

"Yes, I do," she replied quietly.

He expelled a slow breath. "I'll be just across the hall."

"I know."

Bending down, he brushed his mouth across hers. His touch was light. Warm. Possessive.

"I won't let anything happen to you."

"I know," she replied, sighing.

Long after the door had closed behind him, Paige felt the touch of that soft kiss.

Minutes slid into hours. The balmy breeze from the sea picked up a slight nip. The phone didn't ring.

Shadows slanted across the pale blue carpet as the afternoon faded into evening. No one knocked on the door, except Maggie once, to check on her, and David twice. Neither lingered more than a few moments. They expected a call from the contact at any minute. Or the chauffeur to show up at her door with another summons.

Growing more nervous by the minute, Paige called room service to order one of Cannes's famous *niçoise* salads. She paced the sitting room while she waited for it, arms locked across her chest. Every so often she slid a hand under her hair to touch the skin at the back of her neck with a light, questing finger.

The chip was there somewhere, she knew, but she couldn't feel it.

The discreet tap on her door a few moments later sent adrenaline shooting to her every extremity. Her shoulders knotted, her fingers shook, even her toes curled inside the Italian leather shoes, as she stared at the door.

David was watching, she reminded herself.

Maggie was listening.

Paige had insisted on this crazy scheme. She'd wanted to prove something to David. To herself. Yet for a moment, as she stared wide-eyed at the door, she couldn't for the life of her remember what it was.

Another discreet tap sounded.

Her feet dragging on the plush carpet, she crossed the spacious sitting room. With trembling fingers, she unhooked the heavy chain. A cold palm wrapped around the brass door latch.

"Your dinner, *mademoiselle*," a dark-haired young woman announced cheerfully as she wheeled a cart into the suite.

Paige sagged in relief.

After arranging the domed dishes on a small side table, the maid pocketed a generous tip and left.

The minutes crawled by as Paige picked at her salad. The tart dressing coated her empty stomach with an oily residue. To soak it up, she crumbled a crusty baguette and nibbled at its soft white interior. By the time she'd finished, crumbs lay scattered all over the table and a good part of the floor.

And still the phone didn't ring.

David came across the hall to tell her they'd had no luck yet tracing the yacht. Neither of the two owners of the silver Rolls kept a boat at Cannes with a registration number that included the digits 6, 1 and 3. Of course, the boat could have been rented.

"Or I could have mistaken the numbers," Paige admitted.

"Don't worry," he told her. "We'll find it."

When the sky outside the open balcony doors had darkened to a star-studded black velvet, Paige went into the bathroom to bathe and dress for the casino.

It was almost ten o'clock. No one in Cannes began the evening's pleasures until midnight, David had explained. The city's inhabitants played until the early hours, slept late, then took lunch at one of the elegant seaside hotel restaurants or strolled the Croisette or drifted on the azure sea in one of the fabulous yachts until it was time for a leisurely drink and dinner. Then the cycle began again.

Paige was a morning person. Her energy levels were highest then, her attention was sharpest, her senses were most alive, early in the day. The times she and David had made love in the early dawn, still warm and flushed from sleep, were among her most precious memories.

Yet, as she soaked in a sinfully rich bubble bath and slathered a creamy lotion on her skin, it seemed as though she were slowly coming alive in a way she'd never experienced before. Maybe it was the unaccustomed luxury of the enormous bath. Or the heady mixture of nervousness and excitement that tripped through her veins. Or the knowledge that David was going to see a different Paige tonight. A very different Paige.

After her bath, she brushed her hair back from her face in soft wings and let its shining length fall loosely down her back. She applied the expensive makeup Maggie had left with a heavier hand than usual, then reached for the small crystal bottle on the dressing table.

Just in time, she remembered Maggie's warning. A woman in Meredith's profession didn't use perfume on the job. Her clients didn't want to go home with a woman's scent clinging to their clothes or their skin.

Paige's fingers trembled as she tied the black velvet ribbon around her neck and felt the cool sting of the diamond-studded heart against her skin. When she finished dressing, she clutched her small evening bag to her chest and surveyed herself once more in the floor-to-ceiling mirrors.

This exotic creature in fuchsia and black looked as different from the shy, demure technical librarian who'd left L.A.—was it only a few days ago?—as it was possible to look.

With all her heart, Paige wished David was waiting for her in the sitting room. She wanted to sweep in, to show him this sophisticated side of herself that he'd never seen before. She wanted to take his arm and stroll out to enjoy the sights and sounds and serious pleasures of the Riviera.

She wouldn't be with David tonight, however. She'd be unescorted . . . until Meredith Ames's nameless, faceless contact finally met with her. Or a prospective client arranged for her services.

Gulping, Paige swept out of the bedroom in a rustle of taffeta skirts.

As the cab pulled away from the Carlton, she stifled the urge to twist around and check the rear window. Her mind told her Maggie wouldn't lose sight of her taxi. Her heart told her David wouldn't lose sight of her. Still, she had to swallow a lump in her throat when the cab turned onto the Croisette and left the stately hotel behind.

After a leisurely drive along the well-lit boulevard, the taxi swept up a curving drive to a gleaming vanilla villa on a high promontory overlooking the sea. A uniformed valet helped Paige out and escorted her inside, where a man who might have doubled for a Russian grand duke bowed over her hand.

"Good evening, *mademoiselle,*" he murmured in flawless English, having clearly identified her age, her marital status, and her nationality in a single glance.

"Good . . . good evening."

"Welcome to the Grand. May I have your passport, please?"

"Oh. Yes. Of course."

Fumbling in the evening bag, Paige dug out Meredith's hastily doctored passport. She checked to make sure the large-denomination bill Maggie had tucked inside it was still in place. It would signal her profession to this sophisticated head croupier more clearly than a printed announcement. Her fingers trembled as she handed the small leather-bound passport over.

With an unruffled savoir faire, the duke pocketed the bill and placed Meredith's passport in an old-fashioned walk-in safe, then gestured her inside with a charming old-world bow.

"Good luck this evening, *mademoiselle.*"

"I beg your pardon?"

"At the tables."

"Oh. Thank you."

That was it! Her first . . . business contact as Meredith Ames. A little dazed by the smoothness of it all, Paige stood at the top of a wide, curving marble staircase and tried to still her fluttery pulse.

Maggie had explained in detail how these matters were arranged among the elite. A note passed to a maître d', or in this case the head croupier. A murmur here, a whisper there. A glass of champagne, if she wished it. Perhaps a chip or two tossed onto one of the felt-covered tables. Then either the client himself or perhaps the croupier would approach her. To request her companionship. To arrange a meeting later. Only if *mademoiselle* wished it, of course.

It was all so civilized. So polite. So seemingly safe.

At this moment, the uglier aspects of Meredith's profession seemed to belong to another world. The somewhat shocking description of the various services a woman in her business might be requested to provide took on a hazy, surreal distance.

Paige stared at the sea of hushed elegance below her, trying to absorb the impact of its opulence. The sounds that drifted up the stairs were far different from those that had assaulted her ears in the Las Vegas casino David had taken her to one weekend. There was no raucous clatter of coins hitting the trays of slot machines. No exultant shouts and delighted exclamations. No loud music blaring from a lounge band to distract the gamblers.

Here, music from a string quartet floated above the low murmurs of laughter and muted conversation. Fine crystal champagne flutes tipped against each other with melodious clinks. The only discordant note was the subdued rattle of little wooden balls in the roulette wheels, and even that was muted by the plush carpeting and the acres of thick felt on the tables.

Paige swallowed, wondering if Meredith's contact was among the glittering crowd that swirled through the high-ceiling room. Gripping her small black evening bag with both hands, she started down the stairs.

Two hours later, she ached in every bone.

She'd never realized how much effort it took to appear relaxed when every muscle and tendon in her body was tight with tension. Her mouth hurt from keeping it curved into a small, provocative smile, and her eyes felt dry and strained from trying to search the crowd without appearing to. She wasn't sure whether she'd spent more time looking for David or for her prospective contact.

She hadn't seen either one.

She'd been approached several times, however.

Once by a rather florid-looking man in a tux and a stand-up collar that appeared to be choking him. Her heart had nearly jumped out of her chest when he stared at her from across a felt-covered table, but she'd managed what she hoped was a seductive smile. To her secret, infinite relief, he'd been detoured at the last moment by a chesty woman with short-cropped iron gray hair and a steely glint in her eyes. The man had sent Paige a regretful glance over one shoulder as he was led away.

Another potential client had materialized at her elbow not long after that. Bowing over her hand, he'd presented her with a fresh flute of champagne. After a few moments of murmured conversation—smooth on his side, somewhat stilted on hers—he'd brushed a knuckle down the curve of her cheek and asked if she included a certain rare skill in her repertoire. Paige had stared at him blankly. Smiling, he'd elaborated. When she finally understood exactly what skill he referred to, she could barely contain her shock.

Speechless, she'd shaken her head. Maggie had definitely not included that particular vice on Meredith's list of offered services. With a murmured expression of regret, the disgusting pervert had moved away.

At that moment, the glamour had faded from Paige's grand adventure. For the first time, she'd understood the darker side of this mission. And the danger if she didn't do just as David had instructed.

Her fingers had trembled as she slid them to the back of her neck, searching in vain for the tiny embedded chip. Suddenly her electronic tracking device felt less like a leash and more like a safety line. Only the knowledge that David was here, close by, a part of this glittering, swirling crowd had given her the courage to lift the crystal goblet to her lips and continue the charade.

Although there were no clocks anywhere in the casino, Paige guessed it was now close to 3:00 a.m. She was feeling the effects of one of the longest, most emotional days of her life. She couldn't believe that just this morning she'd pulled off onto a little overlook and gazed down at the Mediterranean for the first time. That just this morning she'd choked back tears as she slipped David's ring over her knuckle.

Since then, she'd lost her purse, her ring, and a little of her timidity. In return, she'd gained a new wardrobe, a new identity, if only for a short while, and an eye-opening insight into—

"Mademoiselle?"

Paige jumped. Delicate pale gold champagne splashed onto her chest. Blotting it with her palm, she stared at the man she'd labeled the grand duke.

"Yes?"

"One of our guests much admires your charm."

"He . . . he does?"

"He does. He comes to us well vouchered, you understand? Very well vouchered."

Paige understood. This unnamed patron represented the elite of the elite.

"Do you wish to meet him?"

So sophisticated, she thought. So polite. Unable to speak, she nodded.

"At your hotel? Within the hour?"

She swallowed, trying to find her voice.

"Within the hour, *mademoiselle?*"

Her powers of speech had completely deserted her. She could only stare at the duke and nod.

Chapter 7

Paige scarcely drew a full breath during the long drive back to the Carlton. The aching exhaustion that had racked her just moments ago was gone. In its place was a shimmering, shivering excitement.

She'd done it! By God, she'd done it!

Paige Lawrence, full-time technical librarian and sometime mouse, had just successfully passed herself off as Meredith Ames, woman of the world.

The gentleman who'd requested her company might not be Meredith's contact, she reminded herself. If he showed no interest in a certain microdot, he might have to be eased out of Meredith's suite, using the ingenious plan David devised earlier.

But then again, he just might be the individual trying to acquire stolen technology that would allow him to transfer millions and millions of bits of data at twice the current capacity. If he was, David would have identified his target, and Paige would have participated in the adventure of her life.

By God, she'd done it!

As the taxi swept along the broad, brightly lit boulevard, a gathering tension gradually replaced her initial spurt of exultation. She wasn't quite home free, she reminded herself. The adventure wasn't over yet.

When the Carlton's caramel-and-cream facade came into view, she quivered with a combination of nervousness and anticipation. Stiff black skirts rustling, she slid out of the taxi and fumbled in her bag for some francs to pay the driver. While the doorman sorted through her wad of notes and bent down to negotiate a respectable fare, a small, slight figure detached itself from the shrubbery along the curved drive.

"So, *mademoiselle,* you have recovered from your swim in the sea, no?"

Startled, Paige swung around. "Henri?"

"Yes, it is me."

Sauntering forward, the boy hooked his thumbs in the waistband of his rumpled shorts and looked her up and down. A long, low whistle drifted across the night air. "Of a certainty you have recovered."

"What in the world are you doing here? It's almost four in the morning. You should be in bed."

"Me, I do my business at night," he announced with a cheerful insouciance. His red brows waggled. "As do you and your friend, no? The one with the so lovely legs."

"What? Oh, yes."

"Is this boy bothering you, *mademoiselle?*"

The deep voice at her shoulder made Paige jump. She turned and hurriedly assured the frowning doorman that, no, the boy wasn't bothering her. Rocking back on his heels, Henri waited while the dubious doorman gave her the change, then moved away to assist another patron into the cab. Even at this late hour, a steady stream of limousines and taxis glided along the wide curved drive in front of the hotel, picking up and discharging passengers. Paige wondered if one of those vehicles held David. Or Maggie. Or her prospective client.

Nervously, she turned to bid the boy good-night, only to have him forestall her with a shrewd assessment.

"You have the customer, no?"

She nodded, her face heating. This youngster's frank knowledge of the world astounded her.

Henri smirked and rocked back on his heels. "It is the big man who takes you in his arms this afternoon, no? Of a certainty, he has the passion for you."

Arrested, Paige stared at him. "Really? You saw that, did you?"

"*Mais oui!* He will be generous, that one, as much as he desires you. You must make sure you ask a proper fee."

"Fee? Oh. Yes. Yes, I will."

A look of complete disgust crossed his freckled face. "Do not say you failed to establish the price before you make the assignation with him?"

"Well, I . . ."

"Just how long is it that you do this type of work, *mademoiselle?*"

"Not very long."

Paige couldn't believe she was standing outside one of the world's most elegant hotels, discussing such matters with a grubby-faced boy.

"Look, I have to go inside," she said, a little desperately. "It's late and I, uh, have to get ready."

The boy planted himself before her. "No, no, you must not. Not until we decide your fee."

"We?" she echoed weakly.

"But of course. Unless you have the manager to do this for you?"

"Er, no."

The boy frowned. "One can tell you need someone to assist you, *mademoiselle*. One who knows the value of the service you provide."

He looked her up and down once more, then suggested a figure that almost made Paige gasp. Just in time, she remembered she was supposed to be among the best of the best.

"Yes, that's about what I had considered. Well, good night."

"Wait. You must pay me fifty francs, *mademoiselle*."

"For what?"

"For my consultation."

Sure that David would come along at any moment and ask what the hell she was doing, Paige fumbled in her purse. She dragged out a note and thrust it in the boy's hand.

Clucking, he shook his head. "It is too much. Of a certainty, *mademoiselle,* you have need of the manager."

He reached into a pocket of his shorts and pulled out a fat roll of bills.

Paige blinked in astonishment. "Do your parents know you carry all that money around with you?"

His lips pursed in concentration, he counted out her change with careful deliberation. That done, he stuffed the roll back in his pocket and gave a nonchalant shrug.

"Me, I have no parents. This money is not mine. I deliver it for certain patrons who wish to place the bets with Antoine." He gave her a cheeky grin. "Antoine, he breaks my legs if the money does not arrive intact, you understand."

Paige stared at the boy incredulously. She wasn't exactly sure, but she thought he'd just admitted that he was a runner for the local bookie. Among other things, it soon appeared.

"So, *mademoiselle,* shall I be your manager?"

"No! No, thank you, Henri." Flustered, Paige knew she had to end this incredible conversation. "I'm, um, an independent."

With that, she bade him a quick good-night and hurried inside. Her nerves, already strung taut by the interminable ride back to the hotel, were now stretched to their limits.

As the wrought-iron elevator cage creaked and groaned its way to the fifth floor, Paige forced herself to repeat over and over the list of instructions David had prepared for just this situation. Still muttering under her breath, she unlocked the door to the suite and stepped inside.

First, sweep the suite for any devices that might have been planted in her absence.

She fumbled with the hairbrush handle for a moment, twisting it this way and that, then waited until a small red dot glowed in its end. With a sob of relief, she tossed the brush on the dressing table. No hostiles, as Maggie had termed them, only the devices she herself had planted.

Second, test friendly system.

"This is Jezebel," she whispered to the bedroom at large. "Can you hear me?"

"We have you covered, Jezebel," a feminine voice assured her.

Startled, Paige glanced up at the cherubs atop a high carved chiffonier. One of the plump little angels on the chest of drawers seemed to have spoken directly to her.

"Is . . . is Doc there?"

"He's on his way up."

"Okay."

"Just stay calm."

If she hadn't been rather shy by nature, and speaking to an angel, Paige might have made a very rude response to that comment.

Third . . .

Oh, Lord, what was the third item on David's list? Or had she already done the third? What was the fourth?

Frantic, Paige searched her mind. Oh, yes. She was supposed to leave the lights dimmed, to keep her client from seeing the nervousness in her face.

And leave the door to the suite unlocked.

David had stated calmly that he could take the door down without much difficulty, but he didn't want even that much of a barrier if Paige needed him. Her skirts swishing, she hurried into the sitting room and turned off all but one lamp. That done, she took the chain off the door.

When someone rapped softly against the door a few moments later, the knowledge that David was watching and listening and waiting just across the hall was the only thing that kept her knees from crumpling under her.

''Come in,'' she called out, her heart thumping.

The tall oak panel opened with agonizing slowness.

Throat tight, fists clenched in the folds of her full skirt, Paige stared at the figure silhouetted against the glow of the crystal chandelier in the corridor.

He wore a black tuxedo that shaped his broad shoulders like a mantle of night. The diamond studs in his white dress shirt caught the chandelier's light. He stood unmoving for a long moment, yet Paige sensed immediately the coiled power in his tall, muscled frame.

''David?'' she whispered.

With an unhurried calm, he locked the door and walked into the sitting room. In the dim shadows, he loomed large and reassuringly solid.

Paige did a quick mental inventory of the possible contingency plans he'd made her memorize. His presence in her suite when the contact arrived wasn't one of them.

"What are you doing here? I thought I was supposed to meet my—" she swallowed "—meet Meredith's client alone."

"You are."

She glanced at the clock on the mantel. "He should be here at any moment."

David shrugged out of his tux jacket and tossed it on one of the chairs. "He's here."

"What?"

"I saw how tired you were, and decided to pull you out of the casino," he told her, tugging at one corner of his white tie.

Stunned, she stared at him. "But... but I..."

"No buts, Paige." He dropped the tie on top of his tux. "The situation is too dangerous for you to muddle through with drooping eyelids and sagging shoulders."

Stung, Paige recalled the knife-edged tension that had racked her during the interminable drive back to the hotel. The buckets of adrenaline that had pumped through her veins. The wild exultation at the thought that she, timid little Paige Lawrence, had actually been mistaken for someone like Meredith Ames.

"I thought I did a little better than muddle," she retorted. "And you might have asked me if I was ready to leave before making a unilateral decision like that."

Curbing both his impatience and his mounting need to crush Paige in his arms, Doc slipped his Smith & Wesson Model 39 out of the holster at the small of his back. Specially bored and made with an alloy frame, the gun was light and flat and incredibly accurate. While Paige watched, wide-eyed, he checked to make sure a round was chambered, then laid the weapon aside.

In the little silence that followed, Doc walked over to the cabinet that housed the suite's bar. From his own years of experience, he knew she needed time to work the tension out of her system. Time to decompress after being plunged into an alien and unfamiliar world.

And he needed a drink, badly. He couldn't remember the last time he'd been so tense, so wired, during an operation.

After following Paige into the casino, he'd taken a seat at one of the chemin de fer tables, which were set on a raised dais that gave an unobstructed view of the casino floor. Normally, Doc would've been able to engage one part of his mind in the complicated high-stakes card game while another kept track of his target.

Tonight, he'd found it impossible to concentrate on anything but Paige. He'd watched her every move as she wandered hesitantly through the casino. He'd counted every sip of champagne she took. He'd tensed at every male who looked at her with more than passing interest. And he'd just about lost it completely when one of the jet set's better-known perverts sauntered to her side.

She'd handled that little encounter well. Doc had to give her that. Still, the idea of Paige, *his* Paige, being exposed to a man like that made his gut twist.

Although, he thought savagely as he splashed a generous amount of cognac into a crystal snifter, she sure as hell didn't look much like his Paige tonight. Christ, that pink thing she had on had just about destroyed his ability to function at all. He'd felt himself harden when he first glimpsed her full, rounded breasts plumped up above that heart-shaped bodice and saw the shimmer of light on her pale, golden hair. What was more, he'd stayed hard as a rock most of the night. She'd looked so seductive, yet so fragile, that it took all his control not to sweep her out of the casino and into his bed.

Which was what he intended to do. As soon as they settled a few things.

Turning, he held out the snifter. "Do you want a drink?"

When she shook her head, Doc took a long, satisfying swallow. Liquid heat curled in his stomach, fueling the tiny flames of desire he'd kept banked all afternoon and evening. He waited until the heat had distributed itself more evenly throughout his body, then dealt with Paige's indignation at his decision to pull her out of the casino.

"Let's review the bidding one more time," he said evenly. "This isn't a committee. You don't get a vote on each course of action."

She stiffened. "Is that so?"

"Yes, it is. You're in over your head here. Way over your head. I allowed you to continue the charade against my better judgment, but I'm not going to let you take any unnecessary risks."

"You know, David, I'm discovering that you have a rather nasty autocratic streak under that protective layer of yours."

"I do, where you're concerned."

"I'm beginning to wonder just what other traits you've hidden from me these past months."

Doc cradled the brandy snifter in one palm. This discussion had to come. He knew that. They hadn't been alone for more than a few moments since she'd stumbled into the suite this afternoon, half-naked and wholly wet. He hadn't had a chance to work through the desperate fear that had gripped him when he learned she'd been taken. Or the surging relief at her safe return. Or her sudden doubts over their marriage.

They'd work them through now, he decided with grim determination. The way they'd worked through their minor differences in the past. With a calm meeting of their minds and a slow, sweet joining of their bodies. Anticipation curled low in his groin as he took another swallow, then set the snifter aside.

Without taking his eyes off Paige, he lifted his chin and spoke over his shoulder. "You can switch off the cameras and the microphone, Chameleon. I'll send you an emergency signal if I need you."

"You sure, Doc?"

Paige gave a little start as Maggie's voice floated out of the bronze bust of some long-dead Roman emperor that sat on a pedestal by the foyer.

"I'm sure." Doc's shadowed gaze drifted over the woman facing him. "I'll provide Jezebel cover for the rest of the night."

After a slight pause, Maggie murmured, "Right."

Doc signed off, watching with silent amusement the bright wash of color that flooded Paige's delicate face.

"If that means what I think you meant it to mean," she said, wrapping both arms around her waist, "you're getting way ahead of yourself, David. We need to talk."

Doc's brief amusement disappeared as her movement caused her creamy breasts to swell above that damned pink-and-black thing. He'd never considered himself a particularly possessive or primitive type, but Paige's repeated appearances in Meredith's working clothes were stirring some deep, surprisingly atavistic urges. This was the twentieth century A.D., not B.C., he reminded himself savagely. He couldn't just sling her over his shoulder and carry her off to his cave. Not until they'd had their talk, anyway.

Paige drew in a slow breath, unaware that the simple act ripped away one more layer of Doc's civilized veneer. Swearing under his breath, he reached up to loosen the top stud on his dress shirt.

"I'm not going to sleep with you, David," she announced, in a small, determined voice. "Not until I know who you are."

"You know who I am."

"No, I don't! Until a few hours ago, I thought you were an engineer."

"I am an engineer. I've never lied to you, Paige. Except by omission."

"Well, you omitted a few rather significant details. A whole secret identity, in fact. A life completely apart from me. How could you do that, David? How could you deliberately exclude me from this part of yourself?"

She searched his face, her green eyes cloudy with the need to understand. "Didn't you trust me?"

"It's not a matter of trust."

"Then what? Have I been indiscreet? Am I too stupid? Were you afraid I might give you away?"

"No, of course not."

"Then what?"

Doc raked a hand through his hair, knowing that he owed her an explanation. "I wanted to keep you separate from this side of my life. It's too dark. Too dangerous."

She hugged herself more tightly.

Doc gritted his teeth as the creamy flesh swelled higher.

"I . . . I see," she said. "So you divided your life into nice neat compartments labeled Engineering, Undercover Work, and, oh, yes, Paige."

"That's one way of putting it."

"I see," she repeated in a small voice.

He waited while she struggled with the hard, undeniable truth. There was a part of him he'd withheld from her. A part he would always withhold.

Even if he'd wanted to, Doc wasn't cleared to tell her about his work with OMEGA. About the dark, twisted people he dealt with. The lonely days and weeks in the field, when an agent lived on the knife edge of danger, with only his wits and his skills to keep him alive. He couldn't even tell her about the debt he owed Adam Ridgeway, who had personally recruited him for OMEGA.

That debt originated far back in their navy days, when Doc had commanded an underwater demolition team and Adam had flown carrier-based jets. Most of the world assumed the wealthy Bostonian had simply been pulling a well-publicized stint in the military before dabbling in politics. Yet Doc could recall in vivid, minute detail the day his team had come under hostile fire while clearing a mine field in the Persian Gulf. Although low on fuel, Adam had coolly disregarded orders to return to his ship. Single-handedly he'd held the attacking small boats at bay until reinforcements arrived and a rescue helo was able to pluck the demolition team out of danger.

Since the attackers were at that time supposedly U.S. allies, frantic diplomatic efforts had hushed up the incident. All participants were sworn to secrecy. But Doc would never forget those moments when bullets had sliced through the waters all around him and a lone navy jet had repeatedly dived out of the skies overhead.

He couldn't speak of that day to Paige, any more than he could tell her about the missions he'd undertaken since joining OMEGA. Not just because she wasn't cleared for such information. Because he didn't want her to know.

Maybe he'd been wrong to try to shield her, he acknowledged silently, studying her pale, set face. Maybe he shouldn't have tried to protect her. But she symbolized all that was good and pure and innocent in his life. He hadn't wanted to contaminate that purity with what he did for OMEGA.

Not that she looked particularly innocent at this moment, he thought wryly. Not in that blasted pink contraption.

As she stared at his shadowed face, Paige tried desperately to contain her hurt. Even now, even after her brief foray into his world, David wanted to shut her out. To shield her from the man he really was.

Maybe she should let him, she thought with a touch of despair. Maybe she wouldn't even like the unknown David once the layers of his varied identities were peeled back to reveal the man beneath.

No! No! She couldn't spend the rest of her life wondering, unsure of him or herself.

As she grappled with her hurt and confusion, Paige tried to find a way to bridge the gap between the David she knew and the stranger he seemed to be. Maybe, she thought hesitantly, she had to show David a side of herself he'd never seen before he would risk opening those closed, secret compartments of his. Maybe he needed to discover she wasn't all sweetness and light. Maybe she needed to discover it herself.

"Look at me, David," she whispered.

A faint half smile curved his lips. "I'm looking."

She wet her lips. "What do you see? Who do you see? Paige? Or Meredith?"

The smile faded.

"Maybe I'm not quite the woman you thought you knew, either."

She was.

And she wasn't.

Until this moment, Doc had believed he could identify Paige in a crowded room by her scent alone. That he'd explored every nuance of her personality. That he'd discovered all her strengths. Accounted for all her weaknesses.

Yet now, as his gaze slid down her throat to the narrow velvet ribbon that banded it, he saw a tiny vein throbbing just beneath the circlet of black. He'd never noticed that vein before, and he'd sure as hell never felt anything as potent as the raw need that slammed into him as he watched that fluttering pulse.

"Do you want me, David?" Her whisper held a nervous, totally erotic huskiness. "You can have me...if you can afford me."

"What are you talking about?"

"Are you willing to pay for your pleasures?"

Afraid she was going to lose her nerve, Paige turned away. Her eyes sought his rigid figure, reflected in the huge Italian giltwood mirror that hung above the table directly in front of her.

"You can have the woman you see in this mirror," she told his shadowy image. "For a fee."

She stated the staggering figure Henri had suggested just moments ago. At least she hoped it was the figure. The swift narrowing of David's eyes made her fear she might have mixed the numbers up.

For long moments, he didn't move. Didn't speak. Then he moved slightly, and the light from the single lamp illuminated his face.

At the expression in his eyes, Paige felt a sudden tiny dart of sensation. Not fear, exactly. Not apprehension. Just a shivery, nerve-tingling ripple of something similar to it.

He slid one hand into his pants pocket. Without speaking, he tossed a neat fold of notes onto the table.

"That should cover it."

Henri would be proud of her, Paige thought wildly. She'd negotiated her contact and even been paid in advance. Or was about to be.

Moving slowly, David came to stand behind her. Her pale hair and bare shoulders gleamed in soft contrast to the stark whiteness of his shirt. The only color in the shadowed scene portrayed in the huge mirror was the deep rose of her bodice. Paige stared at his image in the silvered glass, sure he would say something. Anything.

Instead, he placed his hands on the curve of her waist.

It was such a simple gesture. Such a small touch. But so warm, even through the layers of satin and stiff boning. So firm. So familiar.

This was David, her heart cried. *Her* David, at least as much of him as he allowed her to possess. She stared at the big, blunt-tipped fingers that shaped her waist, then lifted her eyes to his.

The man who stared back at her wasn't her David, she realized with a shock. His face was taut with a need she'd never seen before. His eyes glittered with an intensity he'd never shown her before. His hands, those strong, safe hands that had caressed her so tenderly in the past, now tightened around her waist like an iron band.

Paige had wanted to discover what lay beneath the assured, loving exterior David had always shown her. She saw it now in the mirror. And her pulse leapt in wild, unfettered response to this stranger's blatant desire.

His fingers splayed downward, following the V-shaped bottom edge of her corset. The taffeta skirt whispered a protest as he spread his hands over her stomach and pressed her back against the rock-hardness of his body.

Then his hands, those sure, strong hands, moved to the bottom hook on the stiff-boned bustier. The hook gave with a soft snicker of sound.

"You're every man's secret fantasy in this thing," he growled, his warm breath stirring the fine hairs at her temple.

The second hook separated, and his hands slid up to the third.

"Your waist is so small."

Unconsciously Paige sucked in her breath to make it even smaller.

The third hook gave.

"That pulse in your throat is driving me crazy."

He bent and brushed her neck with a kiss.

Another hook came open.

"And your breasts, my sweet, seductive Jezebel, your breasts have made me ache with wanting you all night."

The last hook came undone, baring her from the waist up. She kept her arms stiff, her fists buried in her skirt as he eased the stiff corset from between their bodies. It dropped to the carpet, unheeded.

Her breath suspended, Paige watched him watching her. Their images seemed to blur. To merge in the dimness.

Her nipples peaked, either from the cool air or from the fierce masculine hunger in his eyes.

She thought he'd touch her then. She wanted him to touch her. She arched her back a little, offering herself.

Yet when his hands reached for her, they flattened against her midriff. With slow, sure strokes, he soothed the red marks left by the bodice's stiff ribs. His touch was gentle, so gentle, and erotically possessive.

Then his fingers brushed the underside of one breast, and she shivered.

"David . . ."

His name on her lips was a sigh. A plea. A promise.

"No, little Jezebel," he told her, bending down to nuzzle her neck once again. "Not yet."

His mouth and teeth and tongue played with the soft skin of her throat. His breath was warm and moist in her ear, his lips were firm. Fires curled in her belly. When she thought she would go wild from wanting more than just his lips, he kissed the spot at the base of her hairline where the tiny chip had been inserted, then moved back half a step.

Paige felt his fingers at the small of her back. The skirt's buttons slipped free, and then the taffeta slithered to a black pool at her feet.

Embarrassed and more than a little shocked by the image in the silvered glass, Paige fought the urge to close her eyes. Never, not even in her most secret fantasies, had she imagined herself standing before David clothed only in sheer black bikini panties, a black lace garter belt, thigh-high stockings and a velvet ribbon around her throat.

His palms planed her hips, her bottom, then slid around to her stomach. One moved up to cup her breast and played with the stiff, throbbing nipple. The other moved down to shape her mound. Paige felt the heat of his hand through her sheer panties.

''Open for me,'' he ordered softly.

Laying her head back against his shoulder, she eased her legs apart. He tugged the nylon aside, exploring her, preparing her. The pressure of his fingers against her core sent hot, liquid desire spiraling through her loins. She gasped and pressed her bottom back against his rampant arousal.

Was this really her? she wondered wildly. Was she really standing here like a . . . like a high-class call girl, in diamonds and velvet and black lace, while this shadowy stranger played with her body?

''I told you we might not recognize ourselves when this is all over,'' David murmured, as if reading her mind.

His fingers probed deeper, and suddenly the thought that a stranger was touching her so intimately frightened her. Suddenly she didn't want to uncover any more of the man in the mirror. She wanted David. *Her* David.

Twisting around, Paige flung herself against him. The diamond studs cut into her flesh as she dragged his head down. Her mouth was demanding, insistent, anxious.

With a low, savage sound, he wrapped his arms around her waist. She strained into him, both relieved and excited by the faint tremor in the muscles of his shoulders as he fought to control his passion. Whoever she might have seen so briefly in the mirror, this was *her* David.

She felt his rigid member against her stomach. She tasted the raw hunger in his mouth. She was gasping with need when he swept her into his arms and carried her into the bedroom. He dumped her on the wide bed with a noticeable lack of his usual gentleness and ripped off her panties.

She didn't stay prone for very long, however. As he yanked at his shirtfront, she scrambled to her knees. Her fingers tore at the studs while he shrugged out of the white suspenders. Tiny diamonds flew in all directions, followed in short order by his shirt, then the rest of his clothes.

When he tumbled her onto the satin coverlet and covered her body with his, Paige was ready for him. More than ready. The flesh between her legs was hot and slick and tight with anticipation.

He filled her, as he always did. And stroked her. And fanned the flames higher and higher.

But this time, his careful control slipped its bonds. For the first time, he let her feel the full weight of his body. For the first time, he lifted her hips clear off the bed with the force of his thrusts.

And this time, for the first time, when she arched her back, groaning with the force of her climax, he slammed into her with a shattering force and spilled himself into her.

Chapter 8

Restless and edgy, Maggie wandered out of the darkened sitting room and onto the small balcony. Although this suite faced the mountains instead of the sea, the view was almost as magnificent, especially in these last few hours before dawn.

Cannes slumbered peacefully, its subdued lights glowing like yellow diamonds against the inky blackness. In the distance, the city climbed upward at a sharp angle, clinging to the steep slopes of the Maritime Alps. The golden lights grew sparser there and appeared at higher and higher intervals, until a scattered few seemed to hang freely in the night sky.

Maggie wrapped both hands around the balcony's wrought iron railing and stared up at those distant pinpoints of light. Those were the villas of the ultrarich, she knew, sumptuous turn-of-the-century mansions that clung to the high hillsides or perched atop almost inaccessible peaks.

Her fingers tightened on the railing. In one of those villas resided Victor Swanset, the reclusive English expatriate whose classic films and right-wing political views had made him legendary in the thirties. He descended from his hilltop aerie only on rare occasions, Claire had reported. When he did, it was in a silver Rolls-Royce like the one that had whisked Paige off this afternoon.

Of the two possible suspects Claire had identified, Swanset was the only one whose location they had a fix on right now. The French banker, Gabriel Ardenne, had gone underground somewhere in this glittering city.

As she studied those soft, flickering lights, Maggie toyed with the idea of taking a little night reconnaissance trip into the hills. She knew the aging film star's private fortress sat in isolated splendor atop one of those high peaks. Unfortunately, Claire had ascertained that the villa was accessible only by helicopter or via a narrow, winding mountain road guarded with state-of-the-art security surveillance systems. Without Doc's backup, Maggie didn't dare try a reconnaissance.

And Doc was otherwise occupied.

Providing Paige close cover.

A rueful smile tugged at Maggie's lips as she recognized the source of her late-night restlessness. Ever since she'd turned off the cameras and listening devices, she'd alternated between a hope that Doc and his fiancée would work through their differences and a sneaking, silent envy that they had differences to work through.

It wasn't that Maggie was lonely, exactly. Her life was too full, her career too challenging, to allow time for loneliness. Nor did she lack for male companionship when she desired it. In addition to the circle of friends she'd established in her civilian life, she'd met one or two men during her missions for OMEGA who desired something far more intimate than friendship. A certain drop-dead-gorgeous Central American colonel made it a point to call her whenever he was in Washington. And a brilliant, somewhat clumsy young physicist was still pestering the president to have Maggie permanently assigned to the United Nations nuclear-site inspection team he headed.

Yet she had no desire to share this balmy night with either of those two men. She closed her eyes and breathed in the heady scent of primroses and cyclamens and tamarisks that drifted from the lush gardens below. Instantly, a vivid mental image rose of just the kind of man she'd like to have beside her on this small balcony.

Someone who could move easily amid the rarefied atmosphere of a city like Cannes, yet enjoy a quiet moment in the still hours before dawn.

Someone who combined a powerful masculinity with an inbred elegance that was all the more potent for being understated.

Someone like Adam Ridgeway.

A stab of pure physical desire tightened the muscles low in Maggie's stomach. Startled, she opened her eyes.

Damn! She was going to have to do something about her growing preoccupation with OMEGA's aristocratic director. Soon. She wasn't sure exactly what, since both she and Adam were too professional, too dedicated to their work, for either of them to step over the invisible line between boss and subordinate. Of course, Maggie admitted with a wry grin, she wasn't above bending the rules on occasion, but Adam . . .

No, not Adam Ridgeway.

None of the dozen or so OMEGA agents were privy to the exact details of their director's past, but they trusted him with their lives. His cool, ruthless logic and absolute authority were legendary. Maggie knew Adam would never allow personal considerations to color his judgment or his decisions when directing his agents. What was more, she valued her independence in the field too much

to give him any more control over her activities than he
already possessed. They'd had some rather strenuous
differences of opinion in the past over her somewhat un-
orthodox solutions to problems she encountered in the
field.

Still, if she could've chosen one man to stand beside
her on this tiny balcony and breathe in the heady, perfumed air, she knew darn well who it would be.

It was this city, Maggie decided as she surveyed the
dim, glowing lights. This center of sybaritic luxury.
Cannes saturated the senses with its breathtaking vistas,
pristine white beaches and fragrant air, not to mention its
unapologetic devotion to pleasure. In a place like Cannes,
it was easy to fantasize and forget such things as working relationships and—

Maggie stiffened, her fingers clutching the railing.
There was another side to Cannes, she reminded herself.
One that rarely pierced the consciousness of the plea-
sure-seekers. A small army worked behind the scenes to
keep those beaches so white. Fishermen got up before
dawn to drag from the seas the mussels and bream and
other local delicacies that appeared on the linen-covered
tables each night. The crews manning the yachts had
families tucked away in the old town who depended on
their wages.

A whole population of city dwellers out there actually
worked for a living, Maggie reminded herself. What was
more, those workers maintained an informal intelligence
network that operated at warp speed. Word had probably already circulated among the dockworkers about the
American tourist who'd fallen off the gangplank of a
yacht this afternoon. Those workers would know the
name of that yacht, and its current location.

Shedding her unaccustomed lethargy like a butterfly
sloughing off its cocoon, Maggie headed for the small
briefcase that housed the master communications unit.

She hated to do this to Doc, but duty called. Biting her lower lip, she punched in his code.

The ultralow-frequency hum emitted by the elegant gold cigarette case he would've placed within easy reach would wake him, but not Paige, Maggie knew. It was tuned to the absolute end of the spectrum of sounds he could hear.

"Doc here," he replied after a few moments. "Go ahead, Chameleon."

If she'd pulled him from sleep—or from any other bedroom activity—she couldn't tell it from his voice. He sounded calm, and wide-awake.

"I'm going out for a while, Doc. Down to the wharves. To see what I can learn about our unidentified yacht. Can you, ah, cover Jezebel for the rest of the night?"

"I'll do my best," he replied dryly.

Maggie grinned.

"Try the rue Meynadier first," he added. "It's in the heart of the old city. The town's wealthier merchants have their establishments there. Then the Vieux Port, particularly the quai Saint-Pierre. That's where the ship chandlers who sell everything from fishing nets to diesel engines are located."

Maggie blinked in surprise. "When did you gather all this information?"

"This afternoon, when you were packaging Meredith's product."

She might have known! While she and Paige were sorting through bustiers and ball gowns, Doc had been at work on one of his lists.

"Pretty good packaging, wasn't it?" she asked lightly.

He hesitated a moment before replying. "Let's just say it was very effective."

Grinning, Maggie signed off and headed for the bedroom she'd appropriated from Doc when she moved out of Meredith's suite. She dug through the items in the hastily packed overnight case, with little expectation of finding what she needed. There wasn't much in the wardrobe she'd brought on this assignment suitable for a late-night excursion to the old town. She tapped her foot for a moment, thinking, then reached for the phone.

The concierge assured her that he would have someone from housekeeping bring her fresh towels immediately.

Twenty minutes later, Maggie left the suite wearing a beige-and-white-striped maid's uniform. It hung a little loosely over her hips, but otherwise fit perfectly.

The housekeeper had departed just a few moments ago, having exchanged the spare uniform she'd fetched from a supply closet for a thick wad of notes. The worldly Frenchwoman had been most sympathetic to Maggie's desire to don a disguise and slip away from an overbearing husband to meet a young and most virile lover.

After a quick glance at the closed door across the hall, Maggie stifled another small pang of envy and hurried toward the stairs.

Behind that closed door, Doc stood unmoving. He'd pulled on his slacks and padded barefoot into the sitting room to acknowledge Maggie's signal, not wanting to wake Paige.

Now he needed to think through his partner's late-night excursion. He and Maggie had planned to operate independently during this mission, as they had on past assignments, so her decision to go down to the old town this late didn't surprise or particularly concern him. Maggie Sinclair wasn't the type to sit quietly by and wait for events to unfold.

Nor was he, normally. Since Paige's appearance on the scene, however, Doc had had to modify both his cover and his method of operation. He wouldn't be making more than a token appearance at the international symposium of engineers that was his cover for being in Cannes. He'd already dropped a subtle hint or two in a phone conversation with one of his colleagues that he'd found something more stimulating than the sun and the beaches to occupy his days and nights on the Riviera.

Paige didn't know it yet, but she wasn't going to be doing any more advertising. She didn't need to. When Meredith Ames left the casino tonight, she'd accepted more than just a onetime client. She'd entered into an exclusive contract for the duration of her stay in Cannes. Whoever wanted to claim the microdot from Meredith would have to work around Doc's visible presence. Now he just needed to find a way to let Paige know about the change in her professional status. She'd been surprisingly stubborn this afternoon, and again this evening, about her involvement in this operation.

He turned to head back to the bedroom, and a splash of deep rose pink snagged his attention. Doc smiled to himself as he moved toward the assorted articles of clothing still scattered across the plush carpet. Scooping up the stiff-boned top, Doc admitted that Paige had shown several new facets to her personality tonight.

He'd never seen her explode with quite that wild abandon before. Or felt himself drawn over the edge like that with her. He'd never quite lost all control with her before.

As he fingered the smooth satin, his smile faded.

With a painful honesty, Doc forced himself to acknowledge that until tonight he'd deliberately tried to fit Paige into one of those nice neat compartments she'd complained of. The day he met her, he'd formed an image of her in his mind that he'd both cherished and tried to perpetuate. An image that didn't allow for either her stubborn insistence on carrying out this dangerous mission or her unsettling appearance tonight as Meredith Ames.

It disturbed Doc, as a man and as an agent, to realize that he'd underestimated her.

"David?"

He turned, still clenching the thick satin.

The waning moon cast a silvery glow over Paige's pale hair and delicate features. Her makeup was gone. Her hair was tousled. Her skin was flushed from sleep. She'd wrapped a sheet around herself, toga-style, and Doc thought he'd never seen anything more beautiful in his life. Or more erotic. He loosed his grip on the pink top and tossed it aside.

"What is it?" she asked, her voice anxious. "Is something wrong?"

"No. I just got up to take a message from Maggie. She's going out. To do some surveillance."

Paige hitched the sheet up and padded into the room. "This late?"

"This early, you mean. She's going to try to catch the fishermen and dockworkers before they begin their day, to see what they know about your yacht."

"Won't they think it odd that an American woman is up before dawn, asking questions like that?"

"I doubt they'll know she's American," Doc replied. "And depending on the disguise she uses for this little outing, they may not even know she's a woman."

The mingled affection and respect in David's voice didn't trigger any of the jealousy Paige had felt earlier. Thinking about it, she wasn't surprised. Not after what had just passed between her and David. Not after she'd shared, even in a small way, some of the stomach-twisting tension of their mission.

Still, she wouldn't mind hearing a little of the same quality in his voice when he talked to her. Gathering the folds of the voluminous sheet, she sat down on the sofa and tucked her knees under her.

"What do we do if she finds the yacht? What's my next assignment?"

She wasn't sure, but she thought she caught a glimmer of amusement in his eyes. That wasn't quite what she'd hoped to generate, but at least it was better than the cold disapproval he'd displayed earlier this afternoon. Deciding she wanted to see his face during this discussion, she reached up to snap on the lamp.

When the light bathed him in its soft golden glow, it took Paige a while to raise her eyes to David's face. They seemed to snag at the level of his waist and get stuck there. She'd seen David half-dressed before, of course. She'd seen him wholly undressed before. But now, observing the play of the soft light across his stomach and chest, she realized she'd never quite appreciated the reasons for his sleek, muscled power.

Paige had always assumed he exercised so rigorously every day from an innate sense of discipline. She now knew he did so to hone his physical and mental faculties for this secret life he led. And well honed they certainly were.

The lamplight played on the bare skin of his upper torso, casting it in subtle shades of bronze and tan. A light sprinkling of reddish-brown hair dusted his chest and curled around his flat nipples. She'd always considered David handsome, but seeing him now, with his slacks hanging low on his lean hips and his pectorals bulging slightly as he crossed his arms, Paige made a startling discovery. His body turned her on. Totally. Completely. In a way she hadn't thought much about before. In a way she didn't have to think about at all. Her body was responding with no input from her brain whatsoever.

Beneath the swaddling sheet, her nipples peaked, and a gush of damp heat moistened the juncture of her thighs.

"Your next assignment will depend a great deal on what Maggie uncovers," David said casually, leaning one hip against a marble-topped sofa table.

Paige dragged her eyes from her intense contemplation of his navel.

"If she gets a lead on the boat you were taken to," he continued, "we'll arrange a meeting with whoever's on board. We'll have to make it seem accidental, but . . ."

"We?"

"We. As you pointed out this afternoon, you're part of this team, whether I like it or not. Until the contact is made, anyway."

He paused, his lips crooking in a rueful smile. "But I can't take another night of watching you make yourself available to the highest bidder."

"You can't?"

"No, I can't. So I think we should alter your status a bit. From available merchandise to reserved stock. For private enjoyment only."

At the look in his eyes, the moist heat between Paige's legs grew hotter, wetter.

"What about the contact?" she asked around the sudden tightness in her throat. "How will he get to me if you're . . . privately enjoying the stock?"

"Meredith indicated that the women who acted as couriers were free to indulge their own pursuits before and after delivering the merchandise. We'll just let word leak out that you've entered into an arrangement for the period of your stay in Cannes. Whoever wants that microdot is resourceful enough to work around an apparent lover."

"Apparent?" she echoed. Her gaze slid down the broad expanse of his chest as she recalled just how far beyond *apparent* they'd gone tonight. The memories made her clamp her thighs together.

Really, this adventure business was a sort of an aphrodisiac, she decided. The danger, the excitement, the experience of playing a role so different from life's ordinary routine, all contributed to a sense of heightened awareness, a feeling of being intensely alive. No wonder James Bond had such a devoted following, Paige mused as she slid her legs off the sofa and rose.

Hitching the wadded sheet under her arms, she walked over to stand before him. While one hand held the material more or less in place, the other reached out to touch the warm steel of his skin.

"We shouldn't have too much difficulty playing the role you just described," she murmured, tracing a whorl of hair lightly with one finger.

A flicker of regret crossed David's face. His hand closed over hers, stilling the small movement.

"It might be more difficult than you imagine. It has to be only a role."

Sure that she hadn't heard him correctly, Paige tugged at her hand. David held it captive against his chest.

"Listen to me, sweetheart. I lost control tonight, which is dangerous for someone on a covert mission, not to mention stupid as hell for us personally."

"Wh-what?"

"I didn't use anything," he reminded her softly. "I forgot all about the need to protect you."

"Wait a minute. There were two of us in that bed tonight, as best I recall. I think I deserve a little of the credit or the blame, whichever it is you're apportioning here."

"There were two," he agreed, with a wry twist of his lips. "But from now on, sweetheart, there will only be one."

Paige knew very well that her sudden surge of irritation had nothing whatsoever to do with the fact that David still assumed responsibility for her "protection." Although the status of their engagement was somewhat fuzzy at this particular point, in her heart of hearts she wanted desperately to have his children.

What rankled was his unilateral decision to put their sexual activities on hold. Especially now, when just the sight of him had her feeling so damn . . . aroused.

"Fine," she told him, hanging on to her dignity, and the sheet, with both hands. "I've got the bed. You can take the sofa."

So much for James Bond, she thought in disgust, trying hard not to slam the bedroom door behind her.

Chapter 9

Maggie hid a smile as she glanced around the small, crowded bistro, the third one she'd visited since slipping out of the hotel less an hour ago. So much for the glamorous, deliciously decadent undercover role she'd thought she was going to play while in Cannes.

Instead of breakfasting at one of the linen-draped tables in the Carlton's palatial dining room, she was wedged into a tiny café filled with a few oilcloth-covered tables and an astonishing number of people. She shared a narrow bench with a red-faced fisherman who exuded the pungent aroma of his trade and a voluble gray-haired woman who stabbed her croissant into a small cup of café au lait, then waved the soggy pastry in the air to emphasize every point. Maggie didn't mind the enforced intimacy in the least, however, since the woman beside her possessed just the information she'd been seeking.

"But no!" the sweater-clad woman exclaimed. "No, I tell you. The boat you seek is gone."

Maggie ducked as drops of coffee flew in all directions. Despite her evasive action, several more splotches appeared on the once pristine front of her beige-and-white-striped dress.

The various occupants of the bistro had recognized the Carlton's distinctive uniform immediately, of course. With gruff good cheer, they'd squeezed closer together to make room for another working woman. Just as cheerfully, they'd answered her careful, casual questions.

"This boat," the woman beside Maggie declared with another dramatic wave of the croissant, "the one the American tourist falls from yesterday, was docked at the marina where my Georges works. He operates the fuel station, you understand. Georges filled the tank not long after the woman falls, and the boat slipped its mooring."

"How unfortunate," Maggie murmured in soft, idiomatic Provençal. French—and its related but quite distinct sister dialect of the south of France—were among her favorite languages, and she hadn't needed any refresher training to prepare for this mission.

"The woman is staying at the Carlton," Maggie continued with a small shrug. "She lost her purse when she fell into the sea. She hopes perhaps someone aboard the boat might have fished it from the water."

"Not with the tide that swirls around those docks," the man beside her pronounced, reaching for a crock of creamy butter. "Her purse is halfway to Africa by now, you may take my word for that."

He slathered the butter onto a brioche, then popped the whole confection into his mouth. The lift of his arm sent an overpowering waft of fishy air in Maggie's direction. Her eyes watering, she leaned back against the stone wall and breathed in rapidly through her open mouth. When she had herself under control again, she addressed the woman on her other side.

"Do you think your Georges could give me the name or registration of this boat? So *mademoiselle* may contact its owner to ask about her purse, on the off chance it was found? I will share whatever reward she gives me for this information."

The gray-haired woman patted her hand. "But of course. I'll phone my husband. He's at the docks already."

Chair legs scraped the bare tiles to make room as she weaved her way through the close-packed tables. Maggie edged sideways on the bench in an attempt to put as much distance as she could between herself and the fisherman. Reaching for one of the feather-light croissants in a napkin-draped basket, she watched the woman duck under a row of cheeses dangling from the low ceiling and drop a coin into a pay phone. A few moments later she returned.

"It was the *Kristina II,*" Georges's wife announced. "She's owned by an agency that rents pleasure craft to the tourists. Or to those who don't wish to maintain their own boats. Georges didn't know who rented it yesterday."

Maggie concealed her sharp disappointment. Whoever had arranged to use the yacht as a place to meet with Meredith Ames would be too smart to leave a trail through a rental agency.

"Thank you," she murmured. "I will tell *mademoiselle* she must speak to this agency. Is it perhaps the one owned by Gabriel Ardenne?"

Maggie's question was a pure shot in the dark. Although the well-known tycoon and international jet-setter had a finger in a great many pies, not all of them legitimate, Maggie had no idea if he operated a yacht rental business.

Evidently he didn't. Maggie's companion shook her head.

"Gabriel Ardenne, the banker? No, I don't think he owns this agency. Georges has never mentioned him to me."

Hiding her disappointment, Maggie took a bite of her pastry. Across the table, a little man in a gray sweater and a black beret gave a snort of disgust.

"Ardenne? Ha! That one wouldn't own boats, even through a rental agency. I've never seen anyone so afflicted by *mal de mer*. He lost his dinner twice when I ferried him to Saint-Agnès last month, and the bay was as smooth as glass."

The woman beside Maggie stabbed a croissant into her cup once more, then sprayed the assembled crowd with both coffee and her opinions.

"These Parisians! They live such lives of dissipation, then come here seeking relief from their sins. To think our blessed saint's own island has become a sanctuary for men such as Gabriel Ardenne!"

At that point a lively argument broke out concerning the relative levels of degradation of Parisian bankers and the international film stars who flocked to Cannes each spring. When Maggie squeezed her way out of the bistro sometime later, excitement sang along her nerves. She now knew that the last time Gabriel Ardenne visited Cannes, he'd been ferried to a small island near the western arm of the bay. This island, named for the virginal, saintly recluse who'd retreated there in defiance of the Romans' ban on Christian practices two millennia ago, was now the site of a very secluded and very expensive spa.

As she walked through the narrow, still-dark streets of the old town, Maggie formulated a quick plan of action. The island was only ten minutes away. She could hire a boat, do a quick reconnoiter, maybe gain access to the current list of guests, and be back before the sun rose.

If she ascertained that Gabriel Ardenne was among the guests, Maggie would then get together with David and Paige to plan their next step. If he wasn't, she decided with a grin, she would've had a pleasurable early-morning boat trip to a scenic little island.

First, however, she needed to change uniforms.

She turned off the narrow lane into a back alley that threaded through the residential area. Peering over crumbling stone walls into tiny gardens and yards, she soon found exactly what she needed. A few moments later, she pinned several high-denomination franc notes to a clothesline with a plastic clothespin and tucked a bundle of dark garments under her arm.

Maggie's first indication that she might have underestimated the difficulty of her task came when she cut the engine of her small boat and drifted toward the island's only wharf. To her intense interest, she saw the jetty was flooded with light and guarded by two health spa attendants with suspicious-looking bulges under their right armpits. Thoughtfully Maggie tugged the billed cap she'd appropriated earlier down over her forehead and continued around the island, as though heading past it for the far arm of the bay.

Out of sight of the guards, she cut the engine and drifted slowly on the rolling swells. The sharp scent of pine and fragrant eucalyptus floated toward her from the tree-studded island as she studied its steep, rocky shoreline.

If she wanted to move about Saint-Agnès unescorted, she'd have to anchor the boat in one of the small coves that dented the island and swim ashore. Now that she'd seen those guards, Maggie's sixth sense—the tingling inner instinct that made her one of OMEGA's most effective and least orthodox operatives—told her she definitely wanted to move about Saint-Agnès unescorted.

Punching in a code on the digital watch that she'd substituted for the gold compact Paige now carried, Maggie waited for Doc to answer. Much as she hated to disturb him yet again, she needed to let him know she was going in.

Maggie's brief communiqué disturbed Doc, but not in the way she'd envisioned. Instead of rousing him from Paige's side in the gilded bed that dominated the luxurious bedroom, her call brought him instantly awake and off the hard sofa in the sitting room.

Massaging the crick in his neck with one hand, Doc listened intently to her brief report. His hand stilled as she outlined her plan to swim ashore and scout out the spa.

"I don't like it," he told her quietly. "Why don't you wait until control can get us some information on this operation?"

"There's still an hour or so until dawn. I might as well have a look around. I have a feeling that our boy's here."

Doc frowned, but refrained from any further protest and signed off. Maggie was a skilled operative, with as much experience in the field as he himself possessed. Like all OMEGA agents, she was trained to operate independently, and didn't take unnecessary risks.

What was more, Doc had a healthy respect for her instincts. Her intuitive approach to a mission represented the opposite end of the spectrum from his own deliberate, problem-solving approach, yet both had proven equally effective in the past.

Still, he didn't like the idea of Maggie going in to Saint-Agnès blind. Nor, he acknowledged with a flicker of irritation, did he like the idea of his partner going into action while he sat idle. If Paige hadn't insisted on involving herself in this mission, he wouldn't be tied to this hotel suite right now. Maggie could have handled Meredith's role without requiring this kind of close cover, but Paige didn't have the skills or the training to protect herself if things turned nasty.

A dozen ugly scenarios immediately sprang into his mind. The thought of Paige in any one of the situations he envisioned added considerably to Doc's gathering tension. Driven by an uncharacteristic edginess, he began to pace the sitting room.

Dammit, he shouldn't have let himself be swayed by Paige's arguments. He shouldn't have overruled his own common sense and allowed her to stay. There was a reason he'd kept the various parts of his life separate and distinct from each other, he told himself in disgust, and this was it!

Several hours later, Doc's mood had not noticeably improved. He'd dressed in a pair of tan slacks and a red knit shirt retrieved from the suite across the hall and had worked with Claire to compile a working dossier on the Saint-Agnès Health and Wellness Center. His pen tapping impatiently against the secretaire, Doc reviewed the information they'd painstakingly gathered.

There wasn't much. A list of the world-renowned physicians and health experts who consulted at the spa for astronomical fees. A brief description of the physical facilities, which included everything from cedar saunas to marble ice pools. And the names of its more notable clients, including one Gabriel Ardenne, but no accompanying information on the state of his health or wellness as documented by the doctors at Saint-Agnès.

Frowning, Doc stared down at Ardenne's name. The banker had made several secret trips to the spa in the past year. It appeared likely that he was currently on the island. At this point, Doc wasn't sure which worried him more. The fact that Maggie's instincts had proven correct, or the fact that she'd hadn't checked in yet.

She hadn't signaled for help. Hadn't requested his assistance. She was good, he reminded himself. Damn
good. Still, he'd give her another hour, max, and then
he'd take a trip to Saint-Agnès himself. Which meant
he'd have to secure Paige in the suite before he—

"Good morning."

He slewed around at the somewhat stilted greeting and
felt his jaw tighten in annoyance. Christ, wasn't there
anything in Meredith Ames's wardrobe that covered more
skin that it showed?

The beaded see-through white vest Paige was wearing
plunged to a deep V between her breasts. Strategically
placed pearls covered their tips, but not much else. The
top was paired with a long white skirt that looked conservative enough at first glance. It was only when she
moved across the room that Doc discovered it was slit
clear up to her thigh on one side. She'd pulled her hair
back from her face in a high braid that showed off both
her delicate features and a pair of huge, butterfly-shaped
white earrings that *his* Paige would never have tolerated.

Doc found himself admiring this seductive creature
and at the same time missing the familiar, comfortable
woman who usually bundled herself in bright plaids and
ankle-length jumpers and never bothered with jewelry.

Once again he experienced the unsettling sensation of
seeing the lines he'd drawn so carefully around his different lives blur past all distinction. His voice had a testy
edge to it when he responded to her greeting.

"Good morning."

Paige blinked, clearly taken aback by his curt tone.
"What's the matter?"

His pen tapped on the desk for a moment. "I've been
waiting for Maggie to check in," he said at last, forcing
the words out. His rational mind acknowledged Paige's
need to know, but it was tough to overcome both his desire to shield her and a deep-seated, conditioned reluc-

tance to discuss OMEGA matters with anyone outside the agency.

"Check in? Where is she?"

"I'll brief you about it at breakfast."

Doc recognized his response as the feeble attempt to delay the inevitable that it was. Rising, he grimaced and rolled his shoulders to ease their ache.

"Didn't you sleep well?" Paige asked sweetly. Too damn sweetly, in Doc's opinion.

"No, I didn't."

"Good. Just remember whose brilliant idea it was to keep our sleeping arrangements separate. Among other things."

With that, she headed for the bedroom to get her purse.

She wasn't in a much better mood than he was this morning, Doc acknowledged wryly. Shoving his hands into his pockets, he leaned against the desk and waited for her to reemerge. This wasn't shaping up to be a good day.

Where the hell was Maggie? And how was he going to explain to Paige without ruffling her feathers further that he'd have to shorten her leash considerably if he needed to make a quick trip to Saint-Agnès?

Not long after they were seated at one of the wrought-iron tables on the Carlton's sun-drenched terrace, Doc heard a low, resonating hum. He'd just filled Paige in on Maggie's early-morning excursion, so she was as relieved as he when he palmed the gold cigarette case and saw that he had a message from Chameleon.

Although most of the other tables on the broad terrace were unoccupied, Doc wasn't taking any chances. With a murmured admonition to Paige to stay put, he went to find some privacy.

Struggling to contain her curiosity, Paige watched the waiters nod deferentially as David weaved his way through the wrought-iron tables. She had to admit he carried himself with an air of authority that commanded respect. His red knit shirt emphasized the straight set of his shoulders and his lean, tapered waist. Paige hadn't seen those expensive-looking tan slacks or those loafers before. With a small shock, she realized that David must maintain a complete separate wardrobe for his various missions.

Frowning, she spooned a bite of the raspberries and cream she'd ordered, then leaned back in her cushioned chair. The flower-decked terrace overlooked the Croisette and gave a spectacular view of the sea beyond, but she was too tightly wound to appreciate the scenery this morning.

She nudged the purse tucked securely beside her on the chair with one thigh, just to reassure herself it was still there. How in the world was she supposed to pass the gold mesh halter inside the purse to this French banker, who might or might not be Meredith's contact and might or might not be locked away on some secluded island?

"So, *mademoiselle,* you are up early, no?"

Paige swiveled around to see a pug-nosed, freckle-faced boy leaning his disreputable moped against one of the palm trees that lined the boulevard just beyond the terrace. With casual aplomb, he sauntered up the broad stone steps.

"Henri! What are you doing here?"

At Paige's startled exclamation, one of the nearby waiters turned. A scowl marred his features when he spied the boy's grubby shorts and ragged sweater. He hurried over, and a rapid, rather heated exchange in French followed. Only after Paige's repeated assurances that she knew the boy did the waiter retire, still scowling.

Henri occupied the seat David had just vacated and poured himself a cup of thick black coffee. Flooding it with cream, he took several satisfying swallows.

"I see you breakfast with the too-large gentleman," he commented smugly. "I told you he had the passion for you. He hires you for the entire night, then?"

Heat crept up Paige's throat, but before she could decide how to answer, he gave her a stern look.

"I just hope you collect the appropriate fee."

She thought about the thick fold of notes David had tossed on the table last night, and the heat spread across her cheeks.

"I appreciate your interest in my, ah, business affairs, Henri, but I don't think I should be discussing such matters with—"

Her voice faltered as the boy reached across the table to snag a croissant from the linen-covered basket. In the process, the sleeve of his sweater rode up, revealing vicious, swelling bruises on his bone-thin forearm.

"What happened to you?" she gasped.

"Pah!" Henri got out around the pastry he'd stuffed in his mouth. "Antoine, he tried to take the commission you paid me last night."

Shocked, Paige searched her memory for a moment before she recalled that this Antoine was the man Henri carried money for.

The boy devoured the rest of the croissant, then grinned at her. "It appears I shall have to find a new business partner. You're sure you don't wish the manager, *mademoiselle?*"

Paige felt her heart constrict at that brave, irreverent grin. She swallowed, noting how his skin stretched across his sharp cheeks and how his thin, narrow shoulders were hunched under the baggy sweater.

"I'm sure," she said slowly, pushing David's untouched bowl of raspberries toward the boy.

She chewed on her lower lip as he attacked the berries with unabashed gusto. The entire bowl of fruit disappeared in less than a minute, as did the thick cream, which Henri slurped noisily from the silver spoon.

"Maybe there's some other service you can provide while I'm here...." she said hesitantly.

Tugging the pastry basket closer to examine its remaining contents, the boy nodded enthusiastically. "Most assuredly, *mademoiselle*. I shall be your guide, yes? I know shops that carry dresses with the labels of Saint-Laurent and Givenchy—but not the price, you understand. And perfumeries that sell scents for a third what you pay on the Croisette." His red brows waggled. "Not even your so-large gentleman will know it isn't Arpège you wear, and we will split the difference in price, no?"

"No," Paige said hastily.

Good Lord, was there anything this youngster wasn't into? She took another look at his pinched face and swallowed the impulse to ask.

"Look, why don't I order you breakfast and you can...you can tell me about Cannes, and some of the famous people who live here? Like Gabriel Ardenne," she added in a flash of inspiration. If anyone knew about the international jet-setter, she suspected this boy would.

"The banker? Pah, you don't want to waste your time on that one, *mademoiselle*. He is a pig."

"He is?"

Her heart thumping, Paige summoned a waiter. After ordering half the items on the menu, Henri recited a list of the banker's astonishing excesses, some of which he knew for a fact to be true, he swore.

He ran out of information at precisely the moment the first covered dish arrived at the table. His brown eyes alight with pleasure, Henri cut off a chunk of sizzling sausage and popped it into his mouth.

By the time she caught a flash of a red knit shirt out of the corner of one eye, Paige had extracted a few more interesting bits of information from the boy, including one or two about the reclusive film star Victor Swanset. She wondered if David knew that Swanset made private visits to the wing he'd endowed in the huge convention hall that was home to Cannes's famous film festival. According to Henri, his silver Rolls-Royce had been spotted parked at the back of the Palais des Festivals several times of late.

Anxious and excited, Paige scanned David's face as he wound his way through the scattered tables. At the silent, reassuring message he telegraphed to her, she sagged in relief. Wherever Maggie was at this moment, evidently she was all right.

When David approached, he caught sight of the diminutive figure ensconced in his seat. The array of empty dishes in front of the boy sent his brows soaring.

"Do you remember my friend Henri?" Paige asked.

"Of course." David eyed him thoughtfully. "Do you breakfast at the Carlton often, or was there some purpose to this visit?"

"I came to inquire how *mademoiselle* fares, of course. And to see if she has reconsidered my offer to act as her business manager."

"Her business manager?"

At David's startled glance, Paige shifted guiltily in her seat. She'd been so overcome by nervousness last night, she'd neglected to inform him of Henri's previous offer to act as her agent.

The boy scooted back the heavy iron chair and rose. Hooking his thumbs into the waistband of his shorts, he rocked back on his heels. "I fear *mademoiselle* has not the head for numbers. She needs someone to watch out for her and protect her interests."

"I won't argue with you there," David drawled.

"I've explained to Henri that I am *not* in the market for a manager right now," Paige put in. "Of any kind. But I'm thinking of engaging his services as a guide."

David's frown told her he didn't think much of the idea.

"He's been sharing some very interesting information with me. About Cannes, and some of the people who live here," she added, hinting heavily.

"He has?"

"I have, *monsieur*. Just to entertain *mademoiselle*, you understand, since you leave her unattended for so long." There was no mistaking the disapproval in Henri's voice, or the implication that he would manage Paige's time far more efficiently.

"Thanks for watching her for me," David responded in a dry tone. "I'll take over from here."

Paige didn't particularly care for this turn in the conversation. She felt like a pet poodle being passed from keeper to keeper.

"*Bon!*" Henri announced. "I will go, then." Contrary to his words, he rocked back on his heels and waited expectantly.

David's mouth twisted in a small smile. "Let me guess. I owe you another fifty francs."

"*Oui.*"

"For what?"

"For my time, of course. Like *mademoiselle*, I am paid by the hour."

With a shake of his head, David reached into his back pocket and pulled out his wallet.

Henri made an elaborate show of folding the bill and tucking it into his pocket. Then he brushed past David to give Paige a gallant little bow.

"If you wish me to show you the Palais des Festivals, *mademoiselle*, you have only to come to my headquarters. The telephone kiosk at the corner of the Croisette and the Allées de la Liberté," he added, at her blank look.

"Yes, of course."

"*À bientôt.*" He took a jaunty step toward his moped.

"Henri?"

"*Oui, monsieur?*"

"I'd like my wallet back before you leave."

Paige gasped, and a look of wounded innocence filled the boy's brown eyes.

"Your wallet, *monsieur?*"

"It's in your left pocket, I believe."

Henri's freckled face scrunched in disgust as he dug into his shorts. "Me, I am losing my touch."

Her jaw sagging, Paige watched him hand over the wallet, then saunter down the steps to his moped. With an unrepentant wave, he was off.

Calmly David took his seat and signaled for the check. During the brief interval while the waiter cleared the table, he scribbled a few quick words in a small leather-bound notebook.

Still struggling to recover from her shock at the attempted larceny, Paige craned her neck and saw that he'd jotted down the location of Henri's telephone kiosk.

"You're not going to have him arrested, are you?" she asked anxiously as soon as the waiter moved out of range. "I'm sure he just needed the money for food. He was so hungry."

David slid the notebook into his pocket, then eyed the five-digit total on the check. "*Hungry* isn't the word for it."

He caught Paige's anxious look and scrawled his name and room number across the bottom of the bill.

"I'm just going to have Control check him out," he told her, rising. "Come on, let's go upstairs. Maggie's on her way back to the hotel. She's discovered some rather interesting information about our friend Gabriel Ardenne."

"That one, he's a pig," Paige murmured, unconsciously imitating Henri's scornful tone. At David's quick glance, she lifted her chin. "Maggie's not the only one who can do a little extemporaneous sleuthing. Did she discover that Ardenne's into drugs, big-time?"

"She did," David said, holding the heavy door of the elevator cage. "But not the kind you think, perhaps."

The door clanged shut, and the elevator began to wheeze upward. Ignoring the panoramic vista of the Carlton's gilt- and palm-strewn lobby, Paige turned to the man beside her.

"What do you mean? What kind of drugs is he into?"

"Experimental ones. Very experimental, and as yet unsanctioned by most medical authorities. The clinic at Saint-Agnès is one of the few places in the world that will administer them."

"Why? What's he being treated for?"

"It appears Ardenne is in the last stages of AIDS. According to Maggie, he's on a respirator and IVs. He won't be leaving Saint-Agnès again."

Paige swallowed. "So...so it couldn't have been Ardenne who was waiting for me on that yacht," she said after a moment.

"No, it couldn't." David's jaw tightened. "Which means the only lead we have at this moment is Victor Swanset. And he's locked away in that impregnable fortress of his."

"No, he isn't! At least, not all the time."

The elevator clanked to a halt, but David didn't reach for the heavy lever that operated its door.

"What are you talking about?"

A thrill of excitement shot through her at the thought that she, plain little Paige Lawrence, had uncovered a nugget of information that this powerful secret agency David worked for hadn't.

"Victor Swanset recently endowed a wing at the Palais des Festivals," she said smugly. "The word on the street is that he visits it occasionally."

Chapter 10

After a debrief with Maggie in the suite across the hall, Paige and David left her to catch up on a few hours of much-needed sleep. They'd hit the Palais des Festivals around noon, they decided, unless the individual seeking the microdot made contact with "Meredith" sooner.

"There's still that possibility," Doc reminded a restless, pacing Paige.

She turned, and her skirt swirled open to reveal a length of satiny thigh.

Doc drew in a quick breath, then suggested casually, "Why don't you get changed while I work out our approach?"

She chewed on her lower lip for a moment. "Good idea. I'd better wear the halter, so the contact can identify me."

Doc stifled a groan as she pulled the slinky thing out of her purse and headed for the bedroom. He experienced a pang of real regret for Paige's plaids and bulky jumpers, which he suspected might now be a thing of the past.

He pulled out his notebook and flipped to a clean sheet to compile a list of items he wanted Control to check for him.

A—the exact physical layout of the Palais des Festivals.

B—the hours it was open to the public.

C—this wing Swanset had reportedly endowed.

Doc tapped his pencil against the notebook, studying the neat, precisely printed letters. A crooked grin tugged at his mouth as he recalled Paige's smug disclosure about Swanset's supposed visits to the Palais. She was so pleased with herself for having uncovered that bit of information. As she should be.

Unless . . .

Doc stiffened. His grin faded as he flipped back a page and stared at the address of the telephone kiosk.

Unless the information had been planted. By a certain grubby-faced boy.

They'd all assumed Henri's appearance on the scene after Paige fell into the sea was simple chance. Suddenly, Doc wasn't so sure.

Cursing under his breath, he ripped out a clean sheet of notepaper and began a new list. When it was done, he studied the four entries that documented the boy's involvement so far.

Henri had just *happened* to be in the right place at the right time to fish Paige out of the bay.

The chauffeur had accosted him outside the hotel, *supposedly* to find out where he'd taken the bedraggled woman.

Paige had reported belatedly that the boy had popped out of the bushes when she returned from the casino last night.

And now he showed up this morning, running up a breakfast tab roughly equivalent to the U.S. national debt while he cleverly fed Paige nuggets of information.

Christ! Doc shoved a hand through his hair, feeling like ten kinds of an idiot. They'd been sitting here all these hours, wondering just when Meredith's mysterious contact would try to approach her, and it was entirely possible that he had. Several times.

The boy could very well be acting as a courier for whoever wanted the stolen technology. If so, Henri would've grasped at once that Paige wasn't Meredith, when he plucked her from the sea. No wonder he'd been so obliging about delivering her to the Carlton. The boy wanted to find out exactly what Paige's relationship was to the real Meredith Ames.

David's unexplained presence in Meredith's suite must have confused him. Not enough to keep him from extracting his fifty francs, but enough to delay retrieval of the microdot from Maggie. What was more, Paige's emergence as Meredith Ames last night must have added to his confusion.

Anyone else would probably have abandoned his mission at that point. But not this kid, Doc guessed shrewdly. Not someone who lived by his wits and snatched at any chance to make a few francs. What was more, he could very well be too frightened to report failure to the individual who'd sent him. A kid like Henri was expendable. All too expendable, when the stakes were this high.

His face grim, Doc pulled his cigarette case out of his pocket and waited for Control to acknowledge his signal. Everything was conjecture at this point, he reminded himself. Their only recourse was to proceed with the plan to visit the Palais des Festivals this afternoon. But he was damn well going to know everything there was to know about a certain red-haired street rat before Paige set one foot out of the hotel.

Several hours later, Maggie slipped across the hall in response to Doc's signal. Her silvery-blond hair was still tousled from sleep, but her eyes were wide and alert.

Paige sat quietly on the sofa, thoroughly shaken by Doc's suspicions about the boy, while he briefed Maggie.

"Claire can't find out anything about the kid?" she asked incredulously.

Doc shook his head, frowning. "Nothing definitive. A child of his description was picked up for truancy a couple of years ago and returned to his foster home. The authorities suspected abuse, but the boy disappeared again before anyone could check it out. Since then, the local police have heard his name mentioned by several of the kids who work for a local thug by the name of…" He reached for his notebook.

"Antoine," Paige supplied in a small voice.

"Antoine," he confirmed. "The guy's a pretty rough character, from what Claire was able to piece together. He's a member of the Sicilian contingent here in Cannes. Specializes in drugs, prostitution and bookmaking. A few of his money carriers suspected of shorting him have been found strangled in back alleys."

Paige locked her arms around her waist. "Poor Henri."

"So far," Doc continued, "there's no known connection between Antoine and Victor Swanset, or Henri and Victor. I even had Claire check to see if there was any link to Swanset's missing cook, who, incidentally, was found a few weeks after he disappeared, floating facedown in the bay."

"Was there? Any link, I mean?"

"None," Doc admitted.

"If there is a connection, we'll find it," Maggie said. Maggie stretched, then tucked a stray curl behind one ear. "This telephone kiosk the boy mentioned is located on the Allées de la Liberté, isn't it? I'll nose around the area while you guys check out the Palais des Festivals."

"Be careful," Paige cautioned. "I saw the bruises this Antoine gave Henri."

"I will."

Paige's delicate features assumed a stern expression. "Check in with us if you stumble onto something. Don't try to take out this character by yourself."

Maggie snapped to attention and rendered her own, less than precise version of a salute. "No, ma'am."

"I'm serious!"

She abandoned her military posture and smiled at Paige. "I'll be careful. I promise. You just keep yourself covered at the Palais des Festivals."

That might take some effort, Doc thought wryly as the two women gave each other a little hug. The damned halter slithered sideways with the movement, baring a good portion of Paige's small, sweet breasts.

The sprawling five-tiered tan-and-white Palais des Festivals dominated the western end of the Croisette.

Crammed with every imaginable audiovisual device, the convention center had been designed as a permanent home for the film festival—which, Paige discovered from the guidebook Doc purchased for her at the front entrance, got off to a shaky start by opening on the very day in 1939 that Germany invaded Poland.

"'The festival reopened in 1946, when Ray Milland won the Best Actor award for *Lost Weekend,*'" she read aloud. "'Since then, this glamorous gathering each May has drawn greater and greater crowds and garnered worldwide attention, until Cannes now rivals Hollywood as a center for the serious study of cinematic art.'"

"I suspect the starlets cavorting on the beaches were as much of a draw as any of the films by Bergman and Fellini," Doc suggested with a grin, his eyes on the spectacular view visible through the floor-to-ceiling glass wall in the central rotunda.

It wasn't the panoramic seascape that had snared his attention, Paige saw at once. Her mouth dropping, she gaped at the generously endowed young woman who was using the Palais as a backdrop while she posed for a cluster of reporters on the beach below.

Paige recognized the girl at once. She was the star of a recent Czech release that critics in twenty different countries had raved about. She'd played an insatiable nymphet in the movie, and although Paige hadn't seen the film, she could understand why the critics said the girl had been born for the role.

As she draped herself over a rock on the beach in a series of shocking, suggestive poses, it became immediately obvious that her bathing suit lacked both top and bottom. It lacked everything, in fact, except a tiny twist of fabric that circled her flaring hips and dipped between her dimpled rear cheeks.

Paige gawked with the rest of the tourists gathered at the windows while cameras clicked and whirred and flashed all around her.

"The Swanset Wing is across the gardens," David reminded her, still grinning.

With a last glance over her shoulder at the starlet, Paige followed him through a set of glass doors into the formal gardens. Immediately the seductive scent of roses and a soothing peace enveloped them. After the chatter and the noise of the huge rotunda, the still, unruffled reflecting pools dotting the gardens offered a surprising tranquillity. Few tourists wandered the crushed-shell paths, and even fewer made it to the wing at the rear of the gardens.

In fact, other than a bored, sleepy-eyed guard, David and Paige were the only ones in the modernistic building, dedicated to the movies of the twenties and thirties. Black tile floors and stark white marble walls provided a dramatic backdrop for still shots from classic Charlie

Chaplin and Rudolph Valentino films. Screens set into the walls at various intervals flickered with scenes from old black-and-white melodramas.

"Look!" Paige nodded toward a room just off the main hallway. "This alcove's dedicated exclusively to Victor Swanset's films."

"So it is," David murmured, his eyes on the elaborately framed life-size portrait that dominated the far end of the alcove. It showed a brooding, intensely handsome man in his mid-thirties. He wore formal evening dress, with a dark cape flung over one shoulder and gloved hands curled around an ivory-headed cane. His glossy black hair was slick with brilliantine, as were his luxuriant mustache and his small, pointed goatee.

"This is a studio shot from *The Baron of the Night*," Paige reported, scanning the information engraved in marble beside the portrait. "Victor Swanset's first film, and one of two dozen he did for Albion Studios."

"Which he later purchased," David added, supplementing the engraved data with the intelligence he'd gleaned from Claire.

"He made his own movies?"

"He made his own statement," David corrected. "The films Albion Studios produced in the late twenties and thirties became vehicles for Swanset's increasingly vocal criticism of British foreign policy. He felt England and the United States should have entered the war long before they did."

"To stop Hitler?"

"To preserve the old, aristocratic order," David drawled.

Paige studied Swanset's striking features and arrogant pose. She wasn't surprised that his debut as the Dark Baron had catapulted him to immediate international fame. Or that he'd want to maintain the old order.

"The British government appropriated Albion Studios during the war," David continued, staring up at the portrait. "They used it to churn out propaganda films. Victor Swanset was so outraged by this bastardization of his art and his property that he refused to make another movie. He left England in the early fifties, and never returned."

Paige turned away, disturbed by the haunting portrait. As she wandered through the alcove, she had the uncomfortable feeling that Swanset's eyes followed her. Shrugging off the eerie sensation, she studied a series of framed black-and-white stills. Although Swanset appeared to have brought the same dramatic power to all his roles, from defrocked bishop to desert sheik, none of the stills held quite the intensity as the portrait of the Dark Baron.

David bent to examine a typed notice pasted to a bare spot on one wall. "It says that one of the stills was vandalized and has been removed for repair. I wonder which one?"

"The guard would know," Paige offered.

He nodded, then swept the quiet, empty alcove with a keen glance. "I'll go ask. You sit tight."

His heels echoed on the tiles as he retraced his steps to the entrance. Paige drifted to the black leather bench in the center of the small room. She perched primly on its edge, in a vain attempt to keep the high slit in the side of her skirt from showing more than just thigh.

Her gaze wandered to the marble pedestal beside the bench. A small sign invited her to press the black button, so she did. She half turned, expecting to see one of Swanset's films flicker to life on the opposite wall. Instead, a hazy beam of light focused on the portrait of the Dark Baron.

Surprised, Paige watched as the beam increased in both diameter and intensity. The brilliant light dazzled her and gave the figure in the portrait a slowly sharpening three-dimensional quality. The picture's background faded, blurred by the light. The walls on either side seemed to disappear, until there was only Victor Swanset, the Baron of the Night, standing before her.

Her heart thumping, Paige sat rigid on the leather bench. She was suddenly, ridiculously convinced that if she put out a hand she would touch cold flesh and hard bone instead of canvas.

She half rose, wanting out of the alcove, when the image moved. Paige gave a startled squeak and fell back on the bench a thump.

It was only a movie, she told herself. Some kind of enhanced video imaging or something.

Despite these hasty assurances, she couldn't hold back a small screech when the figure in the portrait smiled at her. He actually smiled at her!

Gasping in fright, Paige scooted backward on the bench. She couldn't breathe. Couldn't speak. Couldn't swallow past the huge lump in her throat. The Baron seemed to be looking right at her.

When the shimmering image hooked his cane over one arm, she scrambled back another few inches.

When he stepped out of the portrait, she toppled backward off the bench onto the black tile floor.

"Don't be alarmed, my dear."

The measured, mellifluous voice raised the hairs on her arms. Crabwise, Paige scuttled back, away from the approaching image. The high slit in her skirt parted as her sandaled feet sought purchase on the slippery tiles.

An appreciative gleam darkened the Baron's eyes, and his waxed mustache lifted in a small smile. Bending over her, he held out a gloved hand.

"Don't be frightened. Let me help you up."

"*Da-vid!*"

"Your friend will return momentarily, I'm sure. Please, allow me assist you."

Since the shimmering image was at that point hovering directly above her, Paige had to choose between taking his hand and lying on the floor quivering like the spineless, terrified blob she was. Her whole body shook as she lifted her arm, inch by agonizing inch, toward his outstretched hand.

Blinding light from the projector bathed her arm in the same eerie glow it did the Baron's. Paige thought she would faint when she touched the white glove and felt solid flesh inside. She gave a tiny whimper of abject terror, closed her eyes, and let him pull her to her feet.

"Oh, my dear, I'm sorry to have frightened you so. Please, forgive me."

When nothing violent happened immediately, Paige opened one eye. She wasn't quite sure, but she thought she detected genuine remorse on the Baron's handsome face as he led her back to the bench.

"Here, sit down while I turn off the projector."

Paige collapsed onto the padded bench. She would've tumbled right off it again a moment later, if total shock hadn't held her pinned in place.

When the Baron pressed the switch for the projector, the dazzling white light disappeared. So did Swanset's handsome, youthful face. His smooth skin lost its firm tone and sank into wrinkles. Liver spots darkened his forehead. His hair grew thinner, sparser, duller, and his tall frame seemed to shrink into itself, until the Baron of the Night became a stooped, thin man in a conservatively tailored business suit. Only his dark eyes retained their intense, penetrating quality.

Paige glanced from the man before her to the dramatic image in the portrait, then back again.

"How . . . how did you do that?"

He gave a small, self-deprecating smile. "It's a new process I'm working on. One which digitizes images and projects them onto living objects. When perfected, this process could revolutionize filmmaking."

"Well, it certainly revolutionized me," Paige admitted shakily. "But I don't understand how you walked out of the wall like that."

His smile deepened, and he lifted his cane. Its tip disappeared into the portrait.

"This is what we call a molecular screen," Swanset explained gently. "It's composed of air bubbles, not solid canvas, as are those in movie theaters. The Baron's portrait is projected onto the bubbles, or, at certain degrees of intensity, onto the object behind them."

"Onto you," Paige murmured.

"Onto me," he concurred with a rueful twinkle in his eyes. "I must ask you to forgive an old man's vanity, my dear. I shouldn't have done it, I know, but I simply couldn't resist the chance to appear before a beautiful young woman as I once was."

He gestured toward the spot beside Paige on the bench. "May I?"

At her small nod, he leaned both hands on his ivory-handled cane and eased down. Once seated, he studied her face. "Will you be all right?"

"I doubt if I'll ever be able to walk into another movie without swallowing a few dozen tranquilizers first, but aside from that, I'm fine."

Swanset gave a low, delighted chuckle. The sound rippled over Paige like deep, dark velvet brushing across her skin. Millions of women must have swooned when they heard that husky laugh, she thought in some astonishment. Particularly when it was accompanied by the heavy-lidded, blatantly masculine stare Swanset raked her with.

"You really are a most beautiful young woman," he murmured, his gloved hands curling around his cane. "That costume you're wearing enhances your charms quite deliciously, Miss—?"

Paige went very still as his gaze lingered on the gold collar of her halter. In the terror of the preceding few moments, she'd forgotten the reason she'd come to the Victor Swanset Wing of the Palais des Festivals in the first place. The reason came rushing back with soul-shattering intensity.

He cocked a brow, politely awaiting her response.

"Ames," she supplied, in a small, breathless voice. "Meredith Ames."

Oh, God! Was he going to ask her for the microdot? Frantically she tried to recall David's itemized list of instructions for just such a possibility.

First . . . First . . . Dear Lord, what was first?

The sound of approaching footsteps reined in Paige's spiraling panic.

David's deep voice preceded his arrival on the scene by a tenth of a second. "No luck with the guard. He doesn't have any idea—"

Both his voice and his footsteps ceased abruptly.

Paige swung around on the bench. She had never been more glad to see anyone in her life. She had never been more glad to see David, *her* David, in her life.

His red shirt and tan slacks stood out in startling contrast to the sterile white-and-black decor. As did his strong, athletic body and gleaming, steel blue eyes. There was nothing sterile about David, Paige thought in a rush of relief. Nothing ephemeral, like the shimmering image of the youthful Victor Swanset. David was real. He was solid. He was hers.

The instant communication she felt with him at this moment went deeper than mere visual identification. With the heightened instincts of an animal for her mate,

Paige knew that she would recognize David even if he stepped out of a molecular screen wrapped in the body of Michael Jordan.

Unfortunately, her brief flash of absolute identity with, of belonging to, this man vanished when he caught sight of Victor Swanset on the bench beside her.

David, *her* David, disappeared in an instant. In his place stood the stranger she'd seen last night in the mirror.

Only someone as attuned to him as Paige was could have noticed the switch. It was so swift, so subtle. She caught the almost imperceptible tightening of his jaw. The slight shift in the planes of his face. The hint of menace in his walk as he strolled into the alcove.

"Ah," Victor murmured. "Your gallant returns."

Rising to his feet with the aid of his cane, he nodded politely. "You are this delightful creature's David, are you not?"

"I am," he replied, laying a light hand on her bare shoulder. Neither Paige nor Swanset missed the significance of his possessive gesture. He might be hers, but there was no doubt that she was also his.

This time Paige had no objection whatsoever to being claimed like a lost toy poodle. Even by this stranger, who was almost, but not quite, her David. In fact, she would've been more than grateful if he'd tugged on her electronic leash at this very moment and walked her right out of this bizarre situation.

A life of adventure, she decided, wasn't all it was cracked up to be.

"I fear I frightened your lovely companion," Swanset said, with a charming, apologetic glance at Paige.

Frightened wasn't quite how she would have described it, but she never used the kind of words that sprang into her mind at that moment. Not in public, anyway.

"I couldn't resist the opportunity to demonstrate a new technique I'm working on," the aging star explained.

"The Swanset visual imaging ionization process?"

Victor's smile broadened to one of pure delight. "You're familiar with my work?"

"I'm an electronic engineer by trade. My firm is very much involved in preparing for the transition to the information highway. Your pioneering work in visual imaging will ease that transition."

"Ah, yes, this information highway one hears so much about. An interesting concept, is it not? Channeling all information, whether written, visual, or audio, through a single network, into millions and millions of homes around the world."

Victor looked into the distance, his dark eyes gleaming with a vision of a world he might not ever see. A world that would explode with ideas, images, sounds. One that would exploit the new technology encoded on a tiny sequin attached to Paige's glittering gold collar.

Swallowing, she resisted the urge to lift her hand to her throat and cover the gold band.

With a tiny shake of his head, Victor recalled himself to the present. "May I be permitted to make amends for frightening your lovely companion so? Perhaps you both might join me for dinner, Mr. —?"

"Jensen."

His dark eyes widened. "But of course! Dr. David Jensen. I've read the paper you presented at the international symposium this week. It's brilliant, quite brilliant."

If David was surprised that this aging recluse had obtained a copy of the highly technical paper that provided his cover for this mission, he didn't show it.

"Please," Swanset insisted. "You must join me for dinner. To allow me to apologize for discomposing Miss Ames so, and, perhaps, to discuss further your paper."

David glanced down at Paige, as if politely seeking confirmation of her wishes.

"Dinner would be wonderful," she managed with a small smile.

"Fine. Shall we say tomorrow evening? My car will pick you up at the . . ."

"The Carlton."

"The Carlton. At eight o'clock, then."

With a gracious bow to Paige and a nod to David, he strolled out of the alcove.

When the clicking of his cane on the tiles had faded, David slipped a strong hand under her elbow. "Come on, let's get out of here."

Paige wasn't surprised to find that her knees were still shaky. Grateful for both David's support and for the opportunity to put some distance between herself and the Baron's portrait, she clutched at his arm as he led her back out into the gardens. In the rose-scented arbor, he swung her around and curved a hand around her neck. Tilting her face up to the light, he scanned it anxiously.

"Are you all right?"

"More or less."

His fingers curled into her skin. "I just about lost it when I walked in and saw Swanset sitting next to you."

"I did lose it."

With a small, embarrassed laugh, she described the abject terror that had toppled her onto the floor when the star made his dramatic appearance.

"Damn!" David muttered, resting his forehead against hers for a moment. When he lifted his head, his blue eyes gleamed down at her with a combination of resignation and reluctant admiration.

"You have your own inimitable style, Jezebel, but you do get results."

Paige basked in the glory of his praise for all of twenty seconds, then sighed.

"I'd take full credit for this coup, except for one small detail," she said gloomily. "We really don't know if Victor Swanset invited us to his villa to get his hands on my microdot or to pick your brain about your brilliant paper."

Chapter 11

When she walked out of the Palais des Festivals, Paige experienced a sharp sense of disorientation. With all that had happened, it seemed as though she and David had been inside the huge convention center for hours, if not days. Yet the sun still hung high overhead, and bright diamonds sparkled on the bay. The scent of spring drifted along the Croisette, and even the traffic moved more slowly, more politely, as though the drivers were taking the time to enjoy the balmy afternoon.

"Do you mind walking a bit?" David asked as they approached a rank of waiting taxis. "We can have lunch at one of the beach cafés, then, if you're up to it, take a stroll through the Allées."

At the mention of the Allées, the nervous tension still gripping Paige shifted focus. She shoved aside the lingering jitters generated by her meeting with the Baron of the Night and instantly started worrying about Maggie's meeting with Antoine the bookie.

By the time this great adventure of hers was over, she thought, she was going to have an ulcer.

"I could use some fresh air," she said truthfully.

David smiled and slipped on a pair of aviator-style sunglasses. "Me too."

At any other time, Paige would have delighted in the spectacle that presented itself as they strolled along the palm-lined boulevard. If ever a city had been made for people-watching, it was Cannes, especially at this time of day. The previous night's revelers were just emerging for a late brunch. All along the Croisette, the idle rich rubbed shoulders with camera-laden tourists. On the white, pebbly beaches, northerners who'd come to escape the cold, drizzly wet stripped down to string bikinis, or less, and displayed their pale bodies beside those of tanned sun worshipers. Paige managed to refrain from gawking the way she had at the well-endowed starlet posing on the beach at the Palais.

They chose a small seaside restaurant run by one of the huge hotels on the other side of the Croisette. The tiny open-air café was dotted with gaily striped umbrellas and tubs of pink geraniums and white primroses. The aroma of hot bread and mouth-watering sauces made Paige suddenly aware of the fact that she hadn't eaten anything since her breakfast with Henri.

Was that only this morning? She sank into the chair the waiter held out for her, feeling as though she'd aged several years since then.

After ordering crabmeat salad and a carafe of wine, David stretched out his legs and folded his hands across his stomach.

He looked so at ease, she thought with a touch of mingled wonder and resentment. She was still tied up in knots from her encounter with Victor Swanset, and David appeared so relaxed. And so darned handsome.

She hadn't missed the looks he'd attracted as they strolled the Croisette. No wonder. That red shirt deepened the hue of his skin to a polished oak and brought out the mahogany tints in his thick brown hair. What it did to his powerful, well-sculpted body made her squirm in her seat.

Strange. Paige had never thought of herself as the kind of woman who could regard a man as a sex object. In fact, she hated the TV ad that showed a bunch of women gathering at an upper-story window every morning at a specified hour to watch some hunk in a hard hat peel off his shirt. She'd always considered the ad sexist and demeaning to both men and women.

Since last night, however, she'd come to the conclusion that she might just be more susceptible to a man's body—to this particular man's body, anyway—than she'd ever realized. And he, in his infinite, irritating wisdom, had decided this wasn't the time to indulge in some serious body wrapping.

Wrenching her gaze, if not her thoughts from David, Paige stared out at the shimmering azure bay. The dazzling, dancing pinpoints of light reflecting from its surface hurt her eyes. She wished she had the deliciously gaudy star-shaped sunglasses Maggie had given her, but they were at the bottom of the bay, with her purse. And her engagement ring.

"Don't you think you should call Chameleon?" she asked, turning back to face David.

"No. Not yet. She's probably still nosing around the Allées. With any luck, we'll run into her there."

"You don't seem nearly as concerned about keeping tabs on her whereabouts as you do mine."

"Maggie's a pro," he replied with a small shrug. "And I'm not engaged to her."

"You're not engaged to me, either, remember?"

"Are you ready to talk about that?"

Paige rubbed her thumb across the base of her bare ring finger, feeling strangely naked without the familiar white-gold band.

"I'm sorry I lost the emerald, David."

"I'm sorry you felt the need to take it off."

She gnawed on her lower lip, remembering the wrenching unhappiness and insecurity that had caused her to slip the ring over her knuckle.

"I sensed that you were holding something back from me," she told him slowly.

"Now you know I was."

Paige forced herself to articulate the feelings she'd been too shy, too timid, to discuss with him before. "I'm not talking about this secret life you lead, although I'll admit that was a bit of a shock."

"Then what?"

"You were always so much in control, even when we made love. You never seemed to lose yourself. All of yourself." Heat crept up her cheeks, but she met his eyes. "Until last night."

"Did I hurt you?" he asked, frowning.

"No!" She shook her head, her face fiery now. "I liked it. A lot. I liked thinking that I was woman enough to push you past the limits you set on yourself. On us. I like what I do to you when I'm wearing satin and sequins."

"Dammit, Paige—what you wear doesn't have anything to do with what I feel for you."

She cocked a brow.

"Okay, so maybe seeing you in Meredith's working uniform has given me a slightly different perspective."

"Ha!" She placed one elbow on the table and leaned forward. The golden halter drooped enticingly.

"A very different perspective," he conceded, with a small grin. "But doesn't that disprove your doubts about us? Evidently I still have as much to discover about you as you think you do about me.''

''What if—what if we never really find the real us, David?''

''I'm not sure anyone can ever know all there is to know about another person. We're too complex, too changeable. But isn't that what marriage is all about? Long years of learning what works, what doesn't. What pleases you, or irritates me. What makes you sneeze or makes me lose control. Think about it, Paige. Think of all those days and nights of exploration.''

She was still thinking about those days and nights— particularly the nights—when they strolled through the Allées de la Liberté, a series of delightful avenues shaded by wide, leafy plane trees.

The Allées teemed with color and humanity. During balmy afternoons such as this, the natives gathered to sip kir, a white wine spiced with black currant liqueur, at open-air cafés or stroll the flower-filled markets and squares.

Her arm looped through David's, Paige paused to watch a lively game of *boules*. The players tossed the heavy, palm-sized balls into a sandy gravel pit some distance away, gesticulating and arguing so vociferously after each throw that she couldn't tell if the object of the game was for the balls to touch or not touch each other when they landed. David was trying to explain the rules when she caught a flash of carroty red hair out of the corner of one eye.

Paige glanced across the small square, then gripped David's arm. ''Look! Isn't that Henri?''

''So it is.''

As they watched, the boy hurried toward a circular booth plastered with colorful posters advertising everything from toothpaste to what was billed as the most extravagant transvestite nightclub act in Cannes.

"That must be the kiosk he uses as his headquarters," Paige murmured.

When David didn't reply, she glanced up at him. With a small shock, she saw that her relaxed companion of a moment ago had vanished. In his place was another man, not quite a stranger anymore but not one she felt entirely comfortable with.

Eyes narrowed, David watched the boy dig through his pockets, then begin shoving coins into the phone with a frantic disregard for their denominations. Even from across the square, they could see the controlled desperation on his young face.

"Come on."

Paige didn't need David's terse order. She was already heading across the tree-shaded plaza, the gravel crunching under her sandals with each quick step.

When the boy caught sight of them, a look of relief flashed across his freckled face. He slammed the receiver down and rushed to meet them.

"*Monsieur!* I try to call you!"

"Why?"

"*Mademoiselle*'s friend, the one with the so-lovely legs. She offers me fifty francs to take her to Antoine's shop. I tried to dissuade her, but she insists."

"Why did you try to dissuade her?"

Doc kept his voice even, allowing no hint of his suspicions to color it. His muscles tightened as he noted the worry that sharpened the boy's thin face. If Henri was acting, Doc thought grimly, he was doing a damn fine job of it.

"Antoine, he is a pig. He has the weakness for beautiful women, but they do not always return his regard." The boy hesitated. "Not without some persuasion, you understand?"

Doc's jaw hardened. "I understand."

"I cannot go inside the shop, since Antoine and I have severed our business relationship, but I point it out to *mademoiselle*. She goes in some time ago, and does not come out."

David ignored Paige's small gasp. "Where is this shop?"

"Two streets over. I will show you."

In the space of a single heartbeat, Doc ran through a short mental list.

A—this could be a setup, an attempt to separate him from Paige so that Henri could retrieve the microdot.

B—Maggie could be engaging this Antoine in idle chitchat while she scouted out the place.

Or C—she could be in serious trouble, even though she hadn't signaled an emergency or requested backup.

Given the very real possibility of A or C, Doc wasn't about to let Paige out of his sight, and he sure as hell wasn't going to waste any more time.

"Let's go."

Without another word, Henri turned and darted off.

Doc took Paige's arm with one hand and slipped the other into his pocket to activate the transmitter in the gold cigarette case, preset to Maggie's code. If she responded to his signal before they got to Antoine's shop, good. If she didn't, Doc would take it from there.

Henri led them down a narrow lane and across an intersection clogged with afternoon shoppers. He turned right at the next cross street, then skidded to a halt halfway down a block lined with shops and pizzerias. Keeping to the shadows, he pointed across the pavement to a narrow facade near the corner.

"It is there, that *tabac*."

Enough afternoon sunlight filtered through the tall windows to illuminate the tabacco-and-sweet shop's interior. Even from this distance, they could see that it was deserted. A sign hanging crookedly on the front door announced that it was closed until four o'clock.

His jaw tight, Doc surveyed the shop. "Is there a back entrance?"

"*Oui.* Through the storeroom. But Antoine, he's very cautious. He keeps the door locked at all times."

"Show me."

By the time Henri had led them down a narrow alley studded with malodorous garbage cans and grocer's boxes overflowing with wilted vegetation, Doc knew he was going in.

He'd spent enough years in the field to recognize when something had gone wrong with an operation, and this situation had all the hallmarks of a major disaster. Maggie would've responded to his signal by now—if she could. Doc still suspected Henri's motives, but he didn't believe the boy was lying or trying to lead them into a trap. Not with that scared expression on his face.

Adding to Doc's worry over Maggie was a gut-wrenching need to shield Paige from what he feared he might find inside the tobacco shop. Every protective instinct in him was on red alert, but he didn't dare take the time to send her to safety.

Edging around an overturned wooden crate spilling soggy, rotting tomatoes onto the cobbles, he glanced down at the woman beside him. She picked her way carefully through the muck in her open-toed sandals, her nose wrinkled and her face pale. Under her evident disgust and natural nervousness, however, was a strength of purpose every bit as strong as his own. Seeing the determined set to her chin, Doc suspected she wouldn't leave the alley even if he dared send her back out onto the street alone.

With a sheer effort of will, he forced himself to accept the fact that Paige, his sweet, delicate Paige, was beside him in this foul-smelling alley. He couldn't shield her

from this side of his life any longer. Besides which, she
didn't want to be shielded.

Nevertheless, he halted her a safe distance away from
the back entrance to the tobacco shop.

"You and Henri stay here," he instructed in a low,
clipped tone.

"But, *monsieur!*" Henri hissed. "You have need of
me! To pick the lock."

Somehow Doc wasn't surprised that the boy included
breaking and entering among his many talents.

"I need you to stay right here, with Mademoiselle
Paige."

The boy frowned, then nodded a reluctant agreement.
"*Oui*, someone must protect her."

"Take him with you, David," Paige whispered. "I'll
be all right. I've ... I've got my weapon with me."

"What weapon?"

She fumbled in her purse for a moment, then held up
the mascara tube.

"Paige!" Doc shoved her hand to one side. "Watch
where you aim that thing."

"I will stay with her," Henri said, shaking his head.
"You need not worry. Me, I have the knife."

He unfolded one grubby fist to display an innocuous-
looking pocketknife. Curling his fingers around the
handle, he pressed some hidden mechanism. With a
deadly click, a thin stiletto blade slid out of the handle.

Doc didn't need to ask if Henri knew how to use the
switchblade.

"Both of you, get back in the shadows and stay there."

Paige pressed backward and tried not to shudder as her
bare skin made contact with a dank stone wall. God only
knew what was growing between the cracks in the stone.
Henri scooted back, as well, gouging one of his bony
shoulders into her ribs.

"If I'm not out in two minutes, or if you hear shots, get the hell out of here, understand?"

If he wasn't back?

Terror clawed at Paige's chest. Any lingering vestige of excitement or adventure was stripped away at that moment. Her fingers dug into Henri's shoulders.

"I won't leave you here!" she whispered frantically.

"You will if you want to summon help for Maggie and me. Get in the clear, and as soon as it's safe, send the emergency signal 311. Got that?"

"David..."

"Three-one-one. Say it, Paige."

"Three-one-one. What does it mean?"

"Agent down, request immediate extraction."

"Oh, my God."

"Say it again."

"Three-one-one. David..."

"I love you. Say it again."

"Three-one-one, dammit. I love you, too."

Incredibly, he grinned. A crooked, slashing grin that showed his white teeth and his heart-stopping handsomeness.

"We'll finish this discussion later."

"Right. Later."

He leaned over Henri to give her a swift, hard kiss. "Three-one-one, Paige."

"I have it! Just... just be careful."

Her heart hammering with a painful, erratic beat, Paige watched David move down the alley. He stopped a few feet away from the green-painted door.

He seemed to draw in a deep breath, then threw his shoulders against the wood panel. It crashed open on the first thrust and bounced inward against the wall.

Through the opening, Paige caught a glimpse of a short, heavily muscled man frozen in place beside a figure slumped over a table. Aghast, she saw a cascade of white gold hair spilling across the table.

"Antoine." Henri spit out the name, just as David launched himself at the man with a snarl of animal fury.

In the shattering moments that followed, Paige discovered yet another David, one she'd never suspected lay beneath his surface. Gone was all trace of the brilliant engineer. Nothing showed of the skilled, considerate lover. What she saw was a powerful, enraged attacker who mowed down his victim with all the finesse of a Mack truck.

This battle wasn't like those in the Karate Kid and Steven Segal movies Paige had seen, in which the good guys moved with a sort of balletic grace, their arms and legs swinging in slow-motion arcs.

There wasn't anything balletic about the fist David slammed into the man's face. Nothing graceful about the blow he delivered to the bookie's stomach. They were brutal powerhouse punches, thrown with every ounce of strength David possessed.

Blood spurted from Antoine's nose with the first hit. He grunted and doubled over at the second, only to connect with David's upthrust knee. Paige heard a sickening crunch, then a gurgle as he collapsed in an untidy heap.

Forgetting David's admonition to stay put, she and Henri ran forward. They rushed through the door just as David gently raised Maggie's face from where it lay amid a litter of cloudy glasses and bottles on the rickety table.

"Oh, my God..." Paige whispered, stumbling to a halt.

David went on one knee beside the slack woman. "Chameleon, look at me. Look at me."

Her eyes wide and unfocused, Maggie stared at him blankly at for a moment, and then her head lolled back limply, like a rag doll's.

"Son of a bitch." David slid an arm around her waist and dragged her up out of the chair.

"The pig!" Henri turned and spit on the comatose Antoine. "He has given her the drug."

"What kind?" David snapped at the boy. "What kind of drugs does he use?"

"That one? Anything and everything."

"Son of a bitch." With visible effort, David reined himself in. "Chameleon, can you hear me?"

Maggie made a pathetic attempt to lift her head from his shoulder. Her dilated pupils tried to line up on David's face, but couldn't seem to focus.

"Get out your compact," he snapped at Paige.

Still clutching the mascara tube with one hand, she tugged at the clasp of her small white shoulder bag and dug inside. After a few frantic moments, she found the diamond-studded compact.

"Open it and press the center stone," David ordered. "Once to transmit, twice to receive. Once, Paige! Once."

"Nuuu..." Maggie's protest was so weak and indistinct, they almost missed it.

David shifted her weight in his arms to look down into her face. "Chameleon! Can you hear me? Do you know what he gave you?"

Maggie tried to swallow. It was a slow, agonizing effort, painful to watch.

"Nuuu..." she mumbled. "Nhat drrr...." Her hoarse whisper trailed off.

"Press the stone again," David growled at Paige. "Once to transmit, twice to receive."

She squeezed the diamond as hard as she could and shouted into the compact. "This is Jezebel! Can you hear me?"

David began to pace the small room, forcing Maggie to walk with him. "Try again," he told Paige.

"This is Jezebel. Is anyone there?"

"*Mademoiselle!*" Henri reminded her. "You must press the stone twice to hear."

"Oh. Yes." Paige juggled the mascara to her other hand and squeezed the stone twice in rapid succession.

"This is Cyrene," a woman announced calmly. "Go ahead, Jezebel."

Her fingers slick with sweat, Paige engaged the diamond once. "I'm with Doc and Chameleon. She's been drugged. We need an ambulance."

Paige stared at the compact, waiting for a response. Any response.

"Press the stone, *mademoiselle!*" Henri shouted. "Twice!"

As soon as she hit the stone twice, she heard Cyrene's steady voice. "I repeat, Jezebel, give me your coordinates."

Paige sent David a helpless look. "What are my coordinates?"

"Reach into my left pocket," he instructed Henri. "Pull out the small flat pocket calculator."

The boy's nimble fingers quickly extracted the device that the waiter-surgeon had passed David after inserting Paige's little tracking chip.

"Press the switch in the upper left corner," David told the boy. "Now read the numbers on the screen aloud. Slowly!"

His faced scrunched up in fierce concentration, the boy started to call out the numbers.

At that moment, Maggie's head lolled sideways. Her eyes seemed to focus for an instant on something over David's shoulder.

"Daf-fid!" she groaned in warning, just as a blood-spattered figure lumbered out of the shadows.

His battered face twisted into a snarl, Antoine charged toward David.

Without thinking, without hesitating, Paige dropped the compact, aimed her mascara and fired.

Chapter 12

His face blank with astonishment, Antoine stumbled back against the rear wall. He looked down at the bright red blood blossoming on his thigh, and then at the unidentifiable object in Paige's hand. His legs bowed, and he slithered down the wall until his butt hit the floor with a solid *whump*.

"You shoot me?" Dazed, he stared at Paige. "With that?"

"Yes, and I'll do it again, you pig."

She kept the tube pointed at his chest, which took some effort, considering how badly her hand was shaking. For the life of her, she couldn't remember whether the weapon carried more than one projectile, but she figured Antoine wouldn't know, either.

With a savagely controlled gentleness, David eased Maggie into one of the chairs.

"I'll take it from here," he told Paige. A feral light glittered in his eyes as he swung toward Antoine.

He crossed the room in two strides. Reaching down, he wrapped his fists in the man's shirt, hauled him upright, and slammed him back against the wall, with no regard for either his battered face or his bleeding thigh. The powerful muscles in David's shoulders bunched as he pinned the heavyset Antoine to the wall, several inches off the floor.

"You've got five seconds to tell me what you gave her."

"I gave her nothing!"

"Four."

"*Monsieur!* I swear!"

"Three."

Blood and sweat rolled down the grooves beside the man's mouth and dripped onto his gore-stained shirt. "She comes into the shop! We talk. She smiles. I invite her to the back room to drink!"

"Two."

"I swear, *monsieur!* I swear. We drink the *pastis!* Together! Look, there is the bottle." He gestured wildly toward the middle of the room.

Keeping the man pinned to the wall, David slewed his head around. His narrowed eyes took in the cloudy bottle and glasses that still littered the table beside Maggie.

With a curse that made Paige blink in surprise—she had no idea engineers used such graphic terms!—David dragged Antoine over to the table. He kept a stranglehold on the man's shirt with one hand while he lifted the bottle with the other and sniffed at it.

From her position across the table, Paige sniffed, too, but couldn't detect anything over the strong, tobacco-y aromas that emanated from the boxes stacked haphazardly around the storeroom. She wasn't sure, but she thought *pastis* was some kind of a liqueur or local drink. She'd seen it on the menu at both the Carlton and the seaside café where they'd had lunch.

"It is *pastis!*" Antoine choked, clawing at David's hand. "Only *pastis*, I swear. She took but a sip, then her throat closes like...like an overstuffed sausage, and she struggles for the breath."

"Let's see what it does for your throat," David snarled. Twisting the man's collar even tighter, he poured the remainder of the bottle's contents into his open, gasping mouth. He loosened the pressure enough to allow Antoine to gasp and gag and swallow some of the liquid.

For long, tense moments, the only sounds in the small room were Maggie's shallow, rasping breath and Antoine's frightened pants.

"You see?" Antoine sobbed. "Nothing. There is nothing in the bottle, nothing but *pastis*."

"Daf-fid." Maggie's weak call jerked everyone's attention to her.

"What did this bastard give you?"

"Naaht...drugs. He...had...same. Ho-tel. Take me...ho-tel."

With an utter lack of compunction, David smashed a fist into Antoine's jaw. The burly, heavyset man crumpled to the floor.

Scooping Maggie up in his arms, David strode toward the door.

"Come on." He threw the words at Paige over his shoulder.

She stepped over the unconscious body and hurried after him. "Come on," she called to Henri.

The boy spit on Antoine one final time. "Pig!" he muttered as he followed Paige out the door.

The day and night that followed were the longest Paige had ever spent.

David threw a wad of bills at the driver of the taxi Henri flagged down and told him to move it. During the kamikaze ride along the Croisette, Paige fumbled with the compact and managed to give Control a whispered recap of what had happened. Promising to get a doctor to the hotel immediately, Claire signed off.

Maggie was still dazed and struggling for breath when David laid her on the satin-covered bed.

"Doc," she gasped, and clutched at his arm. "I... The drink..."

"I know," he murmured, brushing the tangled hair back from her temples. "Just hang on, Maggie. The doctor's coming."

As Paige watched David stroke his partner's face, she felt a huge lump forming in her own throat. This was the man she knew. This was the side of his personality he'd always shown her. Tender, gentle, caring. She felt a wash of love for him so strong it overwhelmed her. Sinking down on the other side of the bed, she took Maggie's hand and murmured soft reassurances.

When David smiled at her across Maggie's prone form, Paige's heart melted. The contrast between this David and the one who had tenderized Antoine's face just minutes ago was extraordinary. And almost beyond her comprehension—until she remembered that she, timid little Paige Lawrence, had shot a man. With a mascara wand, it was true, but she'd actually shot someone.

David was right, she thought. No one could ever know every facet of another person's personality. Or even one's own.

She glanced at the man on the opposite side of the bed. His short, usually neat hair now stuck up in uneven patches. His red knit shirt carried a variety of stains. And his hands, those incredible, gentle hands, sported bruised, split knuckles.

She didn't need to know anything more about him, Paige decided in that instant. It was enough that he was David, *her* David.

* * *

The doctor arrived a few moments later. Not the little waiter-surgeon this time, but a tall, chic woman in a two-piece navy blue Chanel suit and an Hermès scarf. Paige recognized the scarf. She'd seen one similar to it during her brief foray into the boutiques of the Croissette. The price tag had nearly put her into cardiac arrest.

Paige and David, with Henri hovering in the background, stood to one side while the doctor examined Maggie.

"Anaphylactic shock," she announced almost immediately. "It is a severe allergic reaction, similar to what some people experience from bee stings. What has she eaten or drunk?"

"Pastis," David said tersely.

"Ah, yes. It is made from anise, which has carminative and aromatic qualities some people simply cannot tolerate."

At Paige's blank look, the doctor folded her stethoscope and tucked it into her purse.

"Anise, or aniseed, as some call it, is an herb of the carrot family. It's grown locally, and used to make this potent liqueur."

"I...hate...car...rots," Maggie murmured. "Make...me...gag. Al...ways...have."

"Yes, so I would imagine. It's best if you don't talk for a while."

The doctor extracted a hypodermic syringe and a small vial from her purse.

"It will take at least twenty-four hours for the paralysis of the throat to lessen to where it is not painful, but this will help relax the muscles so you can breathe more easily."

Paige shut her eyes as the doctor swabbed Maggie's arm and slid the needle in.

"Someone must stay with her at all times," the woman instructed a few moments later. She drew a package of pills out of that seemingly bottomless pit of a purse.

"She may have water, only a sip at a time, and soft food when she can eat it. And one of these caplets every three hours."

David nodded. "We've got it covered."

"Oui, madame," Henri concurred, reaching gallantly for her bag. "We shall manage. May I escort you out?"

David gave him a warning frown. "I'm sure *madame* can manage her purse."

Henri's small face assumed a wounded look. *"Monsieur!* You don't think I would steal from her?"

"I don't?"

Paige intervened hastily. "Why don't you come with me while I show the doctor out, Henri? You can check the room-service menu and decide what to order for Maggie. And for yourself, of course," she added quickly as his eyes lit up.

Just after midnight, Paige walked through the tall double doors of the bedroom into the sitting room. She was limp with weariness, but relieved that Maggie seemed to be getting back her color, if not her voice.

Inside the sitting room, she leaned tiredly against the wall and crossed her arms over the little beaded vest she'd changed back into earlier. It wasn't the most appropriate sickroom attire, perhaps, but it was comfortable and allowed her ease of movement while tending to Maggie. When he saw it, David had muttered something under his breath about plaids and jumpers, but Paige had been too busy to pay much attention.

Between them, they had worked out an hourly schedule to take care of their patient. During her shifts, Paige helped Maggie into the bathroom and fed her soup or the smooth, exotically flavored ice creams Cannes was famous for.

During his shifts, David administered ice water and the medicines and sat in an armchair pulled up to the little dressing table while she slept. He'd occupied the quiet hours making lists, Paige supposed.

Throughout all shifts, Henri had offered encouragement and advice. Enthusiastically pursuing his duties as procurer of sustenance for the patient, he'd established a personal hot line to the kitchens, sampled everything that came up and gradually stuffed himself into a stupor.

He was now curled up on the sofa, one fist tucked under his cheek and a litter of empty plates on the floor beside him. Paige smiled at the sight and wandered over to tug a light blanket up over his bony shoulders. He'd certainly gotten enough to eat tonight. A steady stream of waiters had knocked on the door of the suite, bringing dish after dish, delicacy after delicacy.

The last had left a pot of rich black coffee and a silver bowl of ripe strawberries. Paige studied the bowl for a moment, then picked out a huge, luscious berry. She took a nibble from the tip and was savoring the sweet flavor when another knock sounded on the door.

Throwing Henri an amused look, she wondered what else he'd ordered before falling asleep. They'd gone through every item on the menu, plus a few he'd requested that the chef improvise. She ambled to the door, nibbling on the ripe berry.

The man who stood on the other side looked like no waiter Paige had ever seen. He was tall and tanned and carried himself with an air of unshakable authority. A faint trace of silver threaded his black hair at the temples, giving him an aristocratic touch. Although he carried a leather flight bag in one hand, his knife-pleated dark slacks and tailored blue shirt were smooth and crisp, as though they wouldn't dare do anything as undignified as wrinkle during travel.

Paige stood rooted to the floor, her mouth pursed around the fruit, her eyes wide.

He took in her surprised expression, her half-eaten strawberry, and her beaded see-through vest. A smile creased his tanned cheeks, and he descended from the aristocratic to the merely devastating.

"Jezebel, I presume?"

If he knew her code name, he was one of the good guys. She hoped. Reminding herself that David was only a scream away, she pulled the fruit out of her mouth and fumbled for an answer.

"Er, I'm not sure. I mean, isn't there some kind of a code or something you're supposed to give first? So I know who you are?"

The smile widened. "I'm Thunder. Adam Ridgeway. We spoke yesterday."

"Oh. Yes."

Paige remembered Mr. Thunder all right. This was David's boss in his secret life, the one who'd given her the choice of being fitted with an electronic leash or being bundled out of Cannes on the next available plane. She eyed him a touch of dislike.

"You know, you have a rather nasty manner over the..." She made a small circle in the air with the strawberry, not quite sure what that diamond-studded compact was. "Over the radio," she said.

"So I've been told." He walked into the suite and deposited the leather flight bag on an armchair. "Where's Maggie?"

Paige gestured toward the high double doors. "In the bedroom. David's with her. You can go—"

He didn't wait for her permission.

There couldn't be any mistake. This was definitely Mr. Thunder. Brows raised, Paige trailed after him as he opened the doors. He stopped on the threshold, his eyes fixed on the still figure in the bed.

"Adam!" David kept his voice low, but his face registered total surprise as he rose from the armchair. "What are you doing here?"

Adam Ridgeway's intent gaze didn't leave the unmoving Maggie. "I had planned to come for your wedding, anyway. I decided to move the trip up a bit."

David sent Paige a quick look.

"How is she?"

Adam's question betrayed no emotion, but there was a quiet, almost indiscernible intensity to it that made Paige glance at him quickly.

"She's going to be fine," David assured him. "I gave Claire hourly status reports. Didn't she keep you posted?"

"She did. I got the last report during an in-flight refueling over the channel." His jaw worked. "It appears that Chameleon has a near-fatal aversion to carrots."

"Distilled carrots, anyway. We've been with her every moment, Adam," David said, his voice gentling as he studied his boss's face.

Well, well . . . Paige thought.

"The doctor says she shouldn't have any lingering aftereffects from the reaction, other than a sore throat as the paralysis wears off. She's supposed to talk as little as possible for a while."

Paige thought she detected a slight softening of the stark lines around Adam's mouth, as if in relief—or was it amusement? Whatever it was, it was gone when he turned to face David.

"I'll take over here," he said with cool authority. "You and Paige had better go across the hall and get some sleep. I understand you have an appointment this evening. With Victor Swanset."

Shock rippled down Paige's bare arms. Good grief, she'd forgotten all about the Baron of the Night and his invitation to dinner!

At that moment, she wanted nothing more than to tell both David and his boss that she was abandoning her role as Meredith Ames. She no lo ger cared who got the blasted microdot. Or how. Or when. She'd had enough.

In the past twenty-four hours, a world-class pervert had sidled up to her in the casino and offered her an unbelievable amount of money to do things she was sure were anatomically impossible; she'd been frightened out of her wits by an eighty-year-old man who stepped out of a wall wearing his thirty-year-old body; and she'd capped off the day by putting a mascara-wand bullet through Henri's former business partner. What's more, David, *her* David, had made her repeat over and over again an emergency code to be used in the event he didn't return.

Paige had had more than enough excitement and adventure to last her the rest of her life. She wanted to go home, and she wanted to take David with her.

Unfortunately, he grinned at her then.

It was that slashing, crooked grin he'd given her earlier, just before he went in to make hamburger out of Antoine's face. The grin that finally, unreservedly, said they were in this together. They were a team. Equal partners.

Paige swallowed a sigh and pasted a weak answering smile on her face.

"That's right," David answered, turning to Adam again. "We have an appointment with Swanset tonight. If everything goes as planned, we're going to wrap this mission up, and then..." His glance swung to Paige once more. "And then we're going to arrange that wedding you came for."

She didn't say anything. She didn't have to. David saw the answer to his unspoken question in her eyes. His grin softened into a smile that was for her and her alone.

For a moment, there was just the two of them in the quiet room, Paige and David. Jezebel and Doc. Meredith and...whoever. At this point, Paige was too tired to sort out their growing cast of personalities. All that mattered was the tender smile in David's eyes.

That smile stirred a slow, delicious heat just under her skin. While David gave Adam concise instructions on Maggie's medication, Paige shoved aside her weariness and made a mental list of her own.

First, a bath.

Second, find something sinful enough in Meredith's wardrobe to make David forget both his caution and his control.

Third... Well, she'd improvise on items three through ten.

After all they'd shared today, there was no way in hell she was going to let David occupy the sitting room sofa tonight. Not if he was going to throw emergency codes at her that suggested he might not be around to occupy anything else in the near future. Not if they were getting married.

Which they were. As soon as they could arrange it. As soon as they wrapped up this mission. She'd shed the last of her doubts and insecurities about herself and David somewhere in a dank, garbage-strewn back alley.

Feeling far more determined about the upcoming evening with Victor Swanset than she had a few short moments ago, Paige tucked her hand in David's as they left the bedroom and walked through the sitting room. They were halfway to the door when she caught sight of the small figure curled up on the sofa.

"David! We forgot about Henri."

"So we did."

Turning, he walked back to the door to the double doors of the bedroom.

"The kid on the couch is Henri," he informed Adam. "If he wakes up, make sure you keep one hand on your wallet at all times."

"Roger."

Back in Meredith's suite, Paige ran hot, steaming water into the claw-footed tub. She'd washed her hands and face before tending to Maggie, of course, but there was no telling what her bare back had made contact with in that alley. And her feet . . . Ugh!

Her plans for the rest of the night definitely didn't lend themselves to dirty feet.

Sweet, tingling anticipation fought its way through her layers of exhaustion. Smiling, she dumped an extra measure of bubbling, perfumed oil into the tub. Tonight, she wasn't worried about Meredith's client walking out of the suite with an unfamiliar scent clinging to his skin. Tonight, Meredith's client wasn't walking anywhere.

Shedding her vest and skirt and white lace panties, Paige sank into the hot water with a groan of pure pleasure. She let the water run until the bubbles reached the tip of her chin, then turned off the old-fashioned ceramic handles with one foot. Leaning against the high, sloping back of the tub, she went completely, bonelessly limp.

She'd soak for ten minutes, she told herself. Then she'd pull on the erotic lace teddy she'd dug out of the wardrobe and demonstrate to David its unique construction. The sinful little scrap of pale lemon lace was designed, she'd discovered to her somewhat embarrassed delight, for immediate carnal copulation.

Doc found her in the bathroom fifteen minutes later, sound asleep. She'd slipped down in the tub until the water lapped at her lower lip. Her slow, deep breathing fanned the bubbles dotting the water's surface into small circles.

Smiling, he bent and scooped her out of the tub.

Naked and wet, she burrowed against his body, seeking his warmth. "David?"

"I'm here, sweetheart."

"I want to go to bed," she muttered grumpily.

"Me too."

Supporting her bare bottom on one knee, he reached up to turn off the bathroom lights, then carried her into the darkened bedroom.

Chapter 13

A chorus of chattering, chirping starlings woke Paige the next morning. The birds were perched on the wrought-iron balcony railing, noisily commenting on the glorious sunshine or the availability of insects in the lush gardens below or whatever it was that birds chattered about at the ungodly hour of...

Paige lifted her head and squinted at the painted porcelain clock on the bedside table.

Ten o'clock? That couldn't be right.

She blinked a few times to clear the sleep from her eyes and checked again.

Ten o'clock.

Flopping back down, Paige studied the ornate plasterwork overhead and wondered what had happened to her normal morning energy. Usually, she jumped out of bed at dawn, eager for the day ahead. Except, of course, on those mornings when David was lying beside her.

Which he was not doing this particular morning, she acknowledged. Her hair slithered on the pillow as she turned her head to survey the empty space on the other side of the bed. She couldn't tell whether or not David had abandoned the sitting room sofa last night. The covers on his side were neatly smoothed, the way they always were when he rose before she did.

A flash of pale lemon yellow just beyond the bed caught her attention. Paige sighed, eyeing the lace teddy she'd laid out in such anticipation. If any carnal copulation had occurred in this bed last night, she'd slept right through it.

Of course . . . there was always this morning. And this afternoon. And most of the evening, before they were to go to Victor Swanset's villa for dinner.

At the reminder of the Dark Baron's invitation, Paige slipped deeper under the covers. After her surge of determination to see this thing through last night, in the bright light of day she was having second thoughts. And third. And fourth.

Despite his gallant, old-fashioned charm, the Baron gave her the creeps. She'd be glad when her brief association with him was over.

Of course, they still didn't have proof that Victor Swanset was the man they were after. Until and unless he showed his hand, they had to maintain their cover. Paige would be Meredith for another day and night, at least. David would be the engineer who had engaged her services for his own private symposium.

More adventure.

More excitement.

Paige groaned.

Mumbling under her breath about being careful what she wished for in future, she pushed the covers aside. She needed to go to the bathroom, badly, and she wanted to check on Maggie. She was sure Adam Ridgeway had provided their patient excellent care last night, but there were some things a woman would just as soon not have a man do for her. Especially a man who looked at her the way Adam had looked at Maggie.

Paige had one bare foot on the carpet when a brisk knock sounded on the bedroom door. She slid back into the bed and yanked the covers over her naked form once more. Maybe Maggie wouldn't mind waiting a few more moments, she thought, her pulse leaping.

She cast a quick glance at the lace teddy, but it was too far out of her reach. She'd just have to make do without it, she decided, injecting a note of sleepy-sultry huskiness into her voice.

"Come in."

The double doors were nudged open. A heavily laden cart trundled in, followed immediately by a bright, freckled face.

"*Bonjour, mademoiselle.*"

Paige clutched the satin coverlet higher. "Good morning, Henri."

"*Monsieur,* he tells me to order you the breakfast, which I have done. Me, I have eaten already, but I will join you. Just to keep you company, you understand."

A collection of domed dishes and an elegant silver coffeepot rattled as the boy rolled the cart to the edge of the bed.

"We have here the brioches and the croissants," he informed her, lifting the lids for her inspection. "And sausage and fresh fruit. And a seafood quiche of a quality that is not quite what one expects of the Carlton, but it will do."

He plucked a fat pink shrimp from the dill-and-lemon garnish atop the quiche and popped it into his mouth.

"Yes, it will do."

Dragging the dressing-table chair over next to the cart, he plopped down on it and beamed at her expectantly. "So, *mademoiselle,* which shall you have first?"

Paige's need to go to the bathroom had transitioned from urgent to desperate. Moreover, she didn't think it entirely appropriate for her to breakfast naked with this child, as precocious as he was. But the covetous sidelong glance he gave the sizzling sausages tugged at her heart.

"Why don't you pour me a cup of coffee?" she suggested. "I'll start with that and wake up a bit while you, uh, test the dishes for me."

Tucking the coverlet under her arms, she puffed the pillow up behind her back and accepted the milky coffee Henri prepared for her.

With unabashed gusto, he piled a dish high with delicacies and dug into them.

"Where is *monsieur?*" Paige asked after a moment, trying to catch the boy between mouthfuls.

"He goes across the hall, to confer with the other gentleman and your so-lovely friend."

Tilting his head, Henri eyed her shrewdly. "Your friend is not in the business I thought, yes? Nor are you, *mademoiselle.*"

Paige took a sip of coffee, hiding behind the cup until she decided how to answer.

"Why do you think that?" she finally asked, stalling.

"Because the so-large gentleman who has such a passion for you tells me I must stay here, where he can keep the eye on me. But I am not—under any circumstances, you understand—to discuss fees and prices with you."

"Oh."

"And me, I am not stupid."

No, he wasn't stupid. Pitifully thin and bruised, perhaps. Definitely dirty. But not stupid.

"So, *mademoiselle,* what is it that you do here? And what is it that we must do tonight that puts the so-serious look in *monsieur*'s eyes?"

"We?"

"But of course, we."

If David had been reluctant for Paige to join the OMEGA team, she could just imagine his reaction to the news that Henri was volunteering for an active role in their mission. She was trying to find a way to let the boy down gently when he gave her a cheeky grin.

"I will stay here with you for a while, no? I cannot go back to the Allées, you see. Not for a while. Antoine, he sees me with you before you put the bullet through him. Now he will break my head, as well as my legs, if he catches me."

"The pig," Paige muttered.

Although Maggie had managed to confirm that there wasn't any connection between their operation and Henri's former business partner, Paige now wished David had put the thug away permanently, instead of just pulping his face.

Henri was not going back to the Allées, she decided grimly. Not today. Not next week. Not ever. Paige wasn't exactly sure where he *would* be going, but she'd get David to work something out. Or Adam Ridgeway. He could put all that inbred authority of his to work on Henri's behalf.

"Why don't you roll the cart into the sitting room?" she suggested to the boy. "Just leave me a brioche and some coffee. We can finish this discussion after I get dressed."

She waited until Henri had closed the bedroom doors, then made a dash for the bathroom.

Ten minutes later, she'd scrubbed her face, brushed her teeth and her hair, and pulled on a black knit tank dress held up by narrow spaghetti straps that crossed over her bare back. The deceptively simple little dress—what there was of it—clung to Paige's body like a second skin.

Slipping on a pair of strappy black sandals with thin cork soles, she grabbed a few essential supplies for Mag-

gie and stuffed them in her purse, alongside the gold
halter, then hurried across the hall with Henri. While
waiting for a response to her knock, she rested a hand on
his shoulder. The light touch caused the boy to blink up
at her in surprise, as though he weren't used to human
contact.

Paige smiled down at him reassuringly, although the
sensations conveyed from her fingertips to her brain
shocked her. She registered both the threadbare quality
of the navy sweater the youngster seemed to live in, and
the thinness of the shoulder it covered. She'd make an
excursion to the hotel's gift shop this morning, Paige decided, her mouth settling into a determined line. Henri
needed clothes, as well as nourishment.

When David opened the door a moment later, her inner tension and nervousness eased perceptibly. This was
the David she knew. Calm, solidly handsome, his brown
hair combed, his gray shirt tucked neatly into a pair of
dark slacks. His eyes showed no trace of the so-serious
look that Henri had noticed earlier.

"So you've finally decided to rejoin the living," he
said, with a small, teasing smile.

Warmed by the intimacy of that half grin, Paige followed Henri into the suite. "You should've wakened
me."

"I tried," he murmured, for her ears alone. "Several
times. You were unconscious. Naked and sprawled over
most of my side of the bed, but unconscious."

"Try harder next time."

That settled the question of whether or not he'd abandoned the sofa last night. Unfortunately, it didn't tell
Paige whether he'd tried to wake her in an attempt to
abandon his self-imposed restraint, as well. Resolving to
put that scrap of lemony lace to work at the first opportunity, she headed for the bedroom, while Henri peeled
off to investigate a basket of pastries.

"How's Maggie?"

"Better. Her throat is still a little raw, but she's recovered her energy."

She'd recovered more than just her energy, Paige saw as soon as she walked into the bedroom. Her face had lost its deathly pallor, thank goodness. Her eyes, a deep nutmeg brown without their disguising contacts, sparkled with a combination of rueful humor and relief.

"Morn...ing," she rasped.

Paige had heard bullfrogs with more melodious voices. "Good morning. Sorry I slept so late. Certain people failed to wake me."

"That's probably my fault," Adam volunteered. He pushed back his chair, one of two around the graceful Italian table that had been dragged in from the sitting room and placed next to Maggie's bed.

A total absence of sleep certainly hadn't lessened Adam Ridgeway's air of command, Paige thought. His blue shirt wasn't quite as crisp as last night, and the crease in his dark slacks had all but disappeared, yet he showed no other visible signs of his long night, except the dark stubble shadowing his cheeks and chin.

"Doc and Maggie were bringing me up to date on the operation," he explained.

Paige glanced at the papers and drawings littering the table's tooled-leather surface.

"So I see."

Her respect for the other woman edged up another notch. As sick as Maggie was last night, she'd recovered enough to participate—nonverbally, Paige hoped—in a mission briefing.

"Control came through with a detailed description of Swanset's villa," David told her. "The place has thirty-six rooms, including the servants' quarters. I've drawn out a floor plan for you to memorize before we go in."

Her jaw sagged. "You want me to memorize thirty-six rooms?"

"You can't go in blind."

"No, of course not," Paige said weakly. Good God, while she was sprawled blissfully across the bed, David had been sketching out thirty-six rooms for her to memorize!

He pulled a folded sheet of notepaper out of his shirt pocket. "We've revised the emergency codes, as well."

"New codes?" she asked, her heart sinking. "I've got them down, at least the important ones. One-one-three for emergency assistance. Two-three—"

She stumbled, trying desperately to remember the digitized signal for "Agent in place, backup requested".

"The numeric system allows too much possibility of error during translation at headquarters," Adam interjected smoothly. "We've switched to a selection of code words that allow immediate voice recognition."

"Voice?" Paige threw Maggie a doubtful look.

The patient grinned. "Only...one...word. Can't... mistake...it."

Paige knew darn well that this small, select committee had made the switch from numbers to words for her benefit, not because of any translation problems at headquarters. She was grateful, relieved, and just the tiniest bit annoyed that she hadn't been consulted in the matter.

"I'll study the codes and the floor plan later," she told David. "Why don't you and Adam take a break and go into the sitting room?"

He flipped through his little notebook, frowning at the neat lists. "We've got a lot of work to do here."

"We can do it later," Paige said firmly.

Adam rolled his shoulders a bit, finally demonstrating a little human weariness, but seconded David's opinion. "If Maggie's up to it, we should go on."

"La . . . ter," the patient croaked.

Paige ushered the two men out and shut the door behind them. Her shoulders sagging, she leaned against it.

"Are they like always this on the job?"

"Doc . . . is."

"And Adam?"

"Don't . . . know. Am . . . finding . . . out."

Paige caught a flicker of what looked like intense, personal satisfaction in the other woman's brown eyes. She was dying to ask how the long night had gone with the impeccable Mr. Thunder waiting on Maggie hand and foot, but she respected her privacy too much to pry.

Levering herself away from the door, she walked over to the bed and dumped the contents of her purse onto the satin coverlet.

"I brought some essential sickroom supplies," she announced. "Perfumed bath oil. Meredith's complete makeup kit. Silk panties. And your little lavender kimono, guaranteed to make the wearer feel like a million dollars and the observer loose his cool completely."

The private satisfaction in Maggie's eyes went very public. She stroked the short, silky kimono with the tip of one finger and gave Paige a wicked grin.

"You . . . doll!"

By late afternoon, Maggie's energy, Paige's ability to concentrate and Doc's patience were all wearing thin.

Even Henri's inexhaustible curiosity had petered out. He had stopped trying to listen in while they conferred, and had taken up residence in front of the armoire housing the entertainment center. A huge bowl of sweet black cherries kept him company.

"Let's go over the mission objectives one more time," Doc instructed.

"A—I pass the microdot," Paige parroted. "B—you convince Swanset to demonstrate his digital imaging technique, and in the process insert a virus into his system."

"Go on."

"C—we leave the villa, giving him time to play with the stolen information. You activate the virus by remote signal, thus destroying his system, and that of anyone who tries to access to the stolen technology."

Doc nodded. "Right. No heroics. No flashy stunts."

"No making hamburger out of Swanset's face," Paige added sweetly.

"And D—" Maggie croaked, her voice almost recovered, "OMEGA sweeps in for the kill."

Doc rubbed the back of his neck. Compared to many of his missions, this one sounded relatively tame. Passing a subtly altered microdot and slipping an electronic time bomb into a computer wasn't exactly the stuff of an Ian Fleming or Tom Clancy novel.

But this technology was on the cutting edge. Right now only a handful of international military and paramilitary organizations, like police and drug-enforcement agencies, were using its awesome, high-speed video and data imaging capabilities. If an outsider with his own agenda was to tap into or divert the flow of essential security information, he could hold some of the most powerful governments in the world hostage.

The psychological profile Claire had pieced together on Victor Swanset showed them he would be merciless with that kind of power.

It had taken most of the night and all of this morning to sort through Swanset's many dummy corporations and his tangled financial dealings, but OMEGA now knew that Victor Swanset himself had destroyed Albion, the studio he'd built from the ground up. Rather than see it produce what he felt were inferior films after the war, he'd anonymously reacquired large blocks of shares in both the studio itself and its major suppliers. In a ruth-

less move that sent shock waves throu~~gh~~
stock markets, he'd dumped the shares a~~nd~~
eral major entertainment corporations to fol~~d~~

He'd brought down two successive governm~~ent~~
well, all without leaving his mountain fortress
Cannes. Since then, his financial empire had spr~~ead~~
around the globe, until he gained controlling interests i~~n~~
several multinational communications-industry corporations.

The man felt no ties, no loyalty to any country, Claire
had emphasized. Nor to any other person. Only to himself. And to his art, which was now a thing of the past.

Or was it?

There was something missing in this picture of Victor
Swanset, international financier. Something that didn't
add up. Some piece of illogic that nagged at Doc, although he couldn't quite put his finger on it.

In his precise, methodical way, Doc had broken everything they knew about the onetime star down to specific categories of information and tied them together in
every possible combination. The trail always led back to
Albion. To Swanset's days of glory.

And to a dead cook.

The pieces of the puzzle didn't fit, and Doc was not the
kind of man to be satisfied until they did.

"Let's go over this again," he said.

Paige gave a small groan.

Even Maggie sagged back on the pillows, protesting.
"Doc! E...nough."

"We're missing something," he insisted.

"Maybe we'll see what it is if we come at it from a fresh
perspective later," Adam commented quietly.

It was a suggestion only, and Doc accepted it as such.
Adam had kept in the background throughout the long
afternoon, informing them that he had no intention of

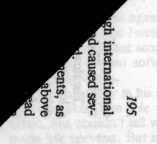

in the field. This was their

panied that remark had gone
ng Paige's attitude toward

...mpany, she still wasn't quite
...s too controlled, too enig-
...t he was thinking, and that
...could certainly understand
...him. Even after twenty-four
hours without sleep, he radiated an unshakable confidence, not to mention an undiluted masculine potency.

Paige knew that she could never handle a man like Adam Ridgeway, and she didn't want to. She had David. All twenty or so different versions of him.

She also had Henri, she remembered belatedly.

"Before we adjourn this meeting," she said, lowering her voice so that it wouldn't carry to the sitting room, "I have another item to place on the agenda."

David paused in the act of gathering his notes. "What's that?"

"Henri."

Frowning, David made an automatic check of his back pocket. Satisfied that his wallet was still in place, he glanced at the red head planted in front of the TV. "What about Henri?"

In her best David manner, Paige ticked off her short list.

"A—he needs clothes. B—he needs shelter. And C—he needs protection. All of which OMEGA is going to provide."

Adam sent her a cool look. "It is?"

"Yes," Paige replied. "It is."

Chapter 14

Henri glanced at the closed bedroom doors of Maggie's suite, then turned to glower at Doc.

"Me, I do not like this."

"So you've said. Several times."

The boy's face settled into stubborn lines. "I should go with you to this villa in the hills. I am the guide."

"Not this time, Henri."

"Someone must watch Mademoiselle Paige while you are busy," he insisted. "I will protect her, as I did last afternoon in the alley."

"I'll take care of her."

Henri's lower lip jutted out. "I do not like this." He stuffed his hands into the pockets of his new jeans, hunched his shoulders and began to pace the sitting room. It was a measure of his agitation that he walked right past a cart laden with silver dishes without giving it more than a passing glance.

Feeling almost as edgy as Henri, Doc glanced at Adam. Sprawled at his ease in an upholstered armchair, the di-

rector wore a thoughtful expression as he watched the
boy pace. Earlier this afternoon, while Paige and Doc
took Henri on an expedition to the Carlton's exclusive
gift shops to accomplish the first item on her list, Adam
had set Control to working on items two and three. Claire
wasn't quite sure what the French authorities would come
up with for the boy in terms of shelter and protection, but
she'd promised to get back to them as soon as possible.

Doc slid back the cuff of his white dress shirt to check
his watch. What in the hell were Maggie and Paige doing
in there? Swanset's car would be here at any moment.
Doc wanted to go over the contingency plan and the
emergency codes with Paige one more time before they
left.

As he stared at the closed doors, Doc found himself
wondering if he'd recognize the woman who would step
through them. Folding his arms across his chest, he considered just how much he'd learned about this incredible, complex woman in the past few days. Far more, he
guessed, than she'd learned about him.

His sometimes timid, usually sweet, Paige was showing an inner resilience and stubborn courage that alter-
nately irritated and amazed him.

She was as nervous as a cat about tonight, he knew.
She'd all but worn a track in the carpet with her pacing
during the mission brief. Her color had fluctuated with
each mention of Swanset's name, and she'd stumbled
more than once over the emergency codes. But she wasn't
about to give up on her damned adventure.

If everything went as planned tonight, Paige would
have her adventure. If not . . .

Doc felt his jaw tighten as the urge rose in him to call
off this part of the operation. Now, before Paige stepped
through those doors. Now, while they still had room to
maneuver and time to activate an alternate plan.

In the past forty-eight hours, however, he'd learned to accept the fact that this wasn't the fifteenth century, when a man could shut his wife away in a stone tower to keep her from harm or chain her to his bed, if he wanted to.

Not that this Paige would have allowed him either option, in the fifteenth or the sixteenth or any other century. What was more, Doc acknowledged ruefully, he couldn't have loved a woman who would allow it.

Although his need to protect his mate was as natural to him as breathing, either consciously or otherwise he'd chosen one as strong as he in her own way. One who would not sit quietly on the sidelines while others acted. Despite his reservations about her involvement in this mission, Doc felt a reluctant pride and silent admiration for Paige's determination to see it through.

Still, he admitted, glancing at his watch once more, the idea of those chains did hold a lingering appeal as the minutes until their meeting with Swanset ticked steadily by.

When the bedroom doors finally opened and Maggie walked into the sitting room, Doc straightened. Smiling, she gave him a thumbs-up, then stood aside.

The woman who stepped through the double doors after her was not quite Meredith Ames and not quite Paige Lawrence, but a fascinating combination of both.

A skilled application of Meredith's makeup had heightened Paige's delicate features. Shadows deepened the tint of mossy green eyes and added thickness to the sweep of her lashes. Her full lips were melon ripe and glossy and altogether too alluring for Doc's peace of mind.

The sophisticated Meredith had drawn the wings of her hair back from her face and pinned them up in some kind of elaborate braid, but the rest of Paige's silky mane hung down her back in a shining curtain of pale gold.

The gown she wore could have been designed for either woman. It was elegant, elaborate, seemingly demure and totally erotic. Doc didn't quite understand how a long-sleeved, floor-length creation that, for once, concealed more skin than it showed could engender immediate fantasies in his mind about peeling the thing off, but this one did.

Maybe it was the color, a deep olive green that added a glowing luster to her smooth skin. Or the fitted bodice that hugged her slender form like a glove. Or the tiny crystal beads accenting the gold trim at the neckline and waist and wrist. The beads shimmered and sparkled with each breath she took, each small movement she made, drawing Doc's eyes like tiny beacons of light.

Her only jewelry was a magnificent pair of drop earrings, made from the finest Swarovski crystal. Doc had purchased them this afternoon in one of the hotel's gift shops. Just an hour ago, the left earring had been fitted with a highly sensitive state-of-the-art wireless communications device. Paige had only to murmur the new emergency code words, and the earring would transmit them instantly to Maggie's receiver.

Between this miniaturized communications system and the electronic tracking device implanted under her skin, Paige wouldn't be out of contact for a moment. The knowledge should have reassured Doc, should have eased his knife-edged concern for her safety. But despite her dramatic appearance, this was Paige. *His* Paige. The small smile she'd plastered on her lips didn't disguise her nervousness. Not from him.

Fear was a healthy emotion for any field operative, Doc reminded himself as he walked across the room. It kept agents alert. Kept their senses tuned to the least fluctuation in the environment, the hidden nuances in a target's voice or behavior. Anyone who didn't experience fear was a fool.

Doc just didn't like seeing that particular emotion in Paige's eyes. He stopped in front of her and reached up to brush back a wispy tendril of hair with one knuckle.

"You take my breath away."

His quiet, confident tone seemed to reassure her far more than the compliment. Her shoulders relaxed a bit, and her mouth curved into a smile.

"You're having a very similar effect on my respiratory system."

In fact, Paige thought she'd never seen David look quite so devastating. It wasn't so much the crisp white dress shirt, or the stunning black tux that molded his wide shoulders. It was his assured air, his absolute mastery of the tension she knew must be gripping him as it was her. Paige could only marvel at the iron control she'd once resented and now drew strength from.

"You've got the microdot?" Maggie croaked from behind her.

"Yes, in my purse."

"And the mascara?"

Paige paled a little, but nodded. "Yes."

"Pah!" Henri snorted, coming across the room. "That toy! Here, Mademoiselle Paige. Take this."

Paige stared at the worn black knife handle resting on his upturned palm. She knew the deadly blade enclosed by that handle, and didn't want any part of it. But she also knew what it meant for Henri to offer the one possession he valued.

The knife was the only object he'd insisted on keeping after their excursion to the hotel shops this afternoon. He'd gleefully tossed everything else—his ratty sweater, the well-worn shorts, even his sandals and scruffy underwear—into the wastebasket. After a bath and a grooming session supervised by David, the boy had sauntered into the sitting room clothed in new Adidas, designer jeans, a jaunty blue-and-red-striped polo shirt with the Carlton's distinctive crest on the pocket, and a broad grin.

There wasn't any sign of the grin now, and his brown eyes carried a grim knowledge that made Paige's heart ache.

"You press the side of the handle, like so," he said with deadly seriousness. The blade slid out with a soft click. "Hold the knife low, *mademoiselle*, and go for the gut, like so."

He gripped the knife in one small fist to demonstrate, then bent the blade back into the handle, reversed it, and held it out to Paige.

Wetting her lips, she lifted it gingerly with a thumb and forefinger. "Thank you."

"Remember, *mademoiselle*, go for the gut."

"The gut," she repeated weakly, dropping the knife into her gold evening bag.

His freckled nose wrinkled. "I do not like this! Me, I should be with you."

The jangle of the telephone sent Paige's heart leaping into her throat and deepened Henri's fierce scowl. Fighting the sudden, craven impulse to slip back into the bedroom and lock the double doors behind her, she watched David move across the suite and lift the receiver.

"Yes?"

After a moment, he replaced the instrument in its old-fashioned cradle. His eyes met hers across the room, and then his cheeks creased in that slashing grin Paige was coming to both love and dread. The one that said she was his partner in what was to come.

"Ready?"

Paige swallowed. "As ready as I'll ever be."

Paige's secret, lingering hope that Victor Swanset was simply a charming, if eccentric, expatriate faded the moment David escorted her out the Carlton's columned main entrance.

As soon as she spotted the swarthy, dark-haired driver who stood beside the silver Rolls, she recognized him. She'd last seen him just before she tumbled off a gangplank into the oily waters of the marina. He'd been sent to pick up Meredith Ames, and had bundled Paige into the silver Rolls-Royce instead.

His face pleasantly blank, the chauffeur touched a gloved hand to his hat.

"Bonsoir, mademoiselle, monsieur."

David returned the greeting, which was just as well, since Paige's throat had closed completely. Her knees felt like unset Jell-O as the driver handed her into the back seat. She sank down with a grateful sigh and was immediately surrounded by soft gray leather and the heady scent of the white roses filling the silver vases attached to the frame on either side of the car.

Surreptitiously Paige wiped her palm on the green satin skirts of her gown. When David joined her, she inched her hand across the soft leather. His fingers folded around hers, warm and strong and infinitely reassuring.

"There is champagne and pâté, if you wish it," the driver informed them, sliding behind the wheel. "It will take perhaps an hour to reach the villa. Monsieur Swanset hopes you enjoy the ride and the view."

Paige did *not* enjoy either.

Her anxiety mounted with each whisper of the tires as the Rolls glided through the twilight traffic along the Croisette with silent, majestic grace. A few minutes later, it turned inland, and headed toward the mountains that rose behind Cannes like sleeping sentinels.

When they entered the foothills, the city gradually fell away. The road swirled and curved, backtracking on itself in an endless series of hairpin turns. Through gaps in the stands of fragrant eucalyptus and fir trees, Paige caught glimpses of a stunning panorama.

Far out on the bay, the last of the sun's rays painted a kaleidoscope of colors across the distant horizon. Brilliant pink, deep magenta and royal purple clouds all swirled together above an indigo sea. Lights strung from the masts of the yachts anchored in the bay bobbed slowly in the ebbing tide.

It was a scene she might have drunk in with wonder if she hadn't been clutching David's hand in a death grip and holding her breath each time the long, sleek vehicle swung around another of those impossible turns.

"This car is *not* designed for roads like this!" she gasped, staring into the stretch of dark, empty space just outside her window with the morbid fascination of a rabbit gazing into the wide-stretched mouth of a cobra.

David smiled a reassurance. "As a matter of fact, a car like this is much safer on these roads than a mini. With its heavy engine and armor plating, the Rolls has a center of gravity well forward of the driver's seat. It's not going to go over unless he loses control—or sends it over deliberately."

"Oh, that's comforting."

Paige closed her eyes as they swung around another curve and the vehicle's rear end seemed to hang suspended in thin air.

"Have a little champagne," David advised her. "It will help you relax."

Gently easing his hand from her clawlike hold, he poured a small amount into a gold-rimmed crystal flute. He poured some for himself, as well. Leaning back, he touched his glass to hers.

"To us."

He'd warned her that the Rolls would be wired with the latest in electronic listening and recording devices. In her role as Meredith Ames, his paid companion during his stay in Cannes, Paige couldn't answer his toast as she so desperately wanted to.

She couldn't tell him that she loved him with every corner of her heart and soul. That she knew all she ever needed to know about him. That when this night was over, she was marching him straight to the American consulate on the Croisette and forcing the first official they came across to marry them on the spot.

"To us," she replied, holding his eyes with hers. "And to tomorrow."

His teeth gleamed in the gathering darkness. "To tomorrow."

Paige took a sip of her champagne and willed herself not to doing anything as unadventurous as stain the underarms of her shimmering ball gown with nervous perspiration.

Just when she was sure neither the champagne nor the lingering effects of David's rakish grin would protect her or her gown much longer, the car's headlights illuminated tall stone pillars and a pair of massive wrought-iron gates. An ornate *S* in gleaming brass was entwined amid the iron grillwork on either side.

At their approach, the gates swung open and the Rolls swept through. Paige sagged in relief at leaving the narrow cliffside road behind, only to discover a moment later that she'd relaxed too soon. More hairpin turns followed as they climbed even higher. When they finally passed through the arch of what looked like a medieval gatehouse set into a high stone wall, her jaw sagged in sheer astonishment.

Victor Swanset's mountaintop villa looked like something right out of one of his movies. Which one, Paige didn't know, but it was too perfect, too stunningly beautiful, to be real.

A cluster of outbuildings roofed in red Mediterranean tiles circled a wide, cobbled courtyard. At the west end of the yard was a long building that had obviously been a stable in a previous century, but had been converted to a garage for Swanset's collection of vintage luxury automobiles. Another low building, connected to the central structure by a graceful arched walkway, housed the kitchens. That much Paige remembered from her study of the floor plan.

But it was the main residence that drew her awed gaze. Washed a pale yellow in the moonlight, the red-tiled villa boasted a central tower and two sweeping wings. Light spilled out of the many leaded-glass windows and illuminated a magnificent stone portico that might have been sculpted by Michelangelo himself. Muscular Roman gods stood with one arm upraised, supporting an arched pediment. Beneath the pediment was a set of massive timber doors that looked as though they could withstand any medieval battering ram ever constructed.

When the Rolls purred to a halt at the steps of the portico, the huge doors swung open, and more light cascaded onto the cobbles. A butler or majordomo or whatever the dignified individual in black tails was called came forward with a measured tread to open the Rolls's rear door.

Paige gripped her skirts in one damp palm and took his outstretched hand with the other.

"Good evening, Miss Ames. Mr. Swanset has been eagerly awaiting your arrival."

Paige wished she could say the same.

She mumbled something she hoped was appropriate and gave David a grateful smile when he tucked her hand into the crook of his arm to escort her inside.

How in the world could he appear so calm? she wondered. As though he were looking forward to nothing more than a pleasant evening with a gracious host.

Paige could only marvel at this David, so handsome in his white shirt and dinner jacket, so sophisticated and self-assured. Drawing in a deep breath, she strolled beside him as he followed the butler into a paneled library.

The huge, barrel-vaulted room took her breath away. Floor-to-ceiling bookcases lined the length of one long wall and were filled with leather-bound volumes. A fire blazed in a marble hearth at one end of the library, and a larger-than-life portrait of Victor Swanset dominated the other. Paige's fingers clenched spasmodically on David's arm when she saw the painting.

This one portrayed the film star in perhaps his most famous role, as a swashbuckling Elizabethan pirate who single-handedly sank most of the treasure-laden Spanish galleons plying the seas. One hand rested on his sword hilt with unconscious arrogance, the other held a white rose. He'd presented the rose to a beautiful, titled Spanish captive he'd plucked from one captured ship, Paige recalled, just before he ravished her.

"If Victor Swanset steps out of that portrait, I'm going to embarrass myself and ruin this dress," she whispered to David, uncaring what listening devices might pick up her comment.

He smiled down at her. "You can't embarrass yourself. Not with me."

That showed what *he* knew!

To Paige's infinite relief, Victor Swanset's appearance on the scene this time was far more conventional than the last. Leaning heavily on his cane, he entered the paneled library wearing his own body and a gracious smile. Crossing the polished parquet floor, he took her hand and raised it to his papery lips with a courtly flourish.

"Miss Ames! How elegant you look this evening." His trained, melodious voice rolled over Paige like smooth, dark velvet.

"Thank you," she murmured, impressed by his charm in spite of herself.

He relinquished her hand with a show of real regret and turned to David.

"I must tell you, Dr. Jensen, that I reread the paper you presented to the symposium earlier this week. I was impressed, most impressed, with your research into improved digital imaging techniques."

"Thank you. That paper was written some months ago, however," David commented casually. "We've gone well beyond the research stage, and are now into concept demonstration."

Swanset paused in the act of directing the butler to the crystal decanters arrayed on a massive sideboard. He turned back to David, his dark eyes filled with interest.

"You have?"

"We have. In fact, I developed an unclassified version of the concept to demonstrate at the symposium. It's quite simple, really. Basically a variation of the imaging process you yourself introduced a few years ago."

Swanset folded one hand atop the other on his cane. "My lab downstairs is rather well equipped. Perhaps you might demonstrate this variation after we dine?"

"I'd be delighted."

The distinguished gray-haired butler, or whatever he was, appeared at Paige's elbow, a gold tray in hand.

"Would you care for a glass of sherry?"

Normally she hated sherry. The few sips she'd tried in the past had been too sweet for her palate and coated her throat with a smoky almond flavor. At this point, however, Paige didn't trust her voice to request anything else. She grasped the fragile crystal stemware in one hand and listened to the increasingly technical exchange between David and Victor Swanset with a growing sense of wonder.

She hadn't expected it to be this easy.

Despite the rehearsals, despite David's endless lists of possible scenarios and Maggie's careful coaching and Adam's quiet observations, Paige really hadn't expected their plan to work so smoothly. Yet they'd been in the villa less than ten minutes, and David had already laid the groundwork for his part of the operation.

Now she had to do hers.

She gulped down a healthy swallow of the sherry, trying not to grimace at the taste, and waited for a lull in the conversation.

"Mr. Swanset..."

"Victor, my dear. You must call me Victor."

Paige returned his smile. "Victor. Would you and David excuse me for a few moments? I'd like to freshen up before dinner."

"But of course. How thoughtless of me to keep you standing here after that long ride. Please, let me show you to the first-floor retiring room. It's outfitted with the exact furniture and fixtures we used in *The Rogue of Versailles*. I think you'll find it quite delightful."

"I'm sure I will," Paige returned faintly.

He crooked an arm, inviting her to accompany him.

Clutching her evening bag, with its deadly mascara wand, well-worn switchblade and neatly folded gold halter in one hand, Paige placed the other on his bent arm.

Her heavy satin skirts swished in a hushed counterpoint to the tap of his walking stick on the parquet floor as he escorted her out of the library.

Chapter 15

"It doesn't feel right."

Maggie's raspy whisper hung on the cool night air that permeated the small operations hut. One by one, the black-clad team seated at the table turned their attention from the receiver nestled amid a litter of blueprints and scribbled diagrams and focused on their leader.

Maggie shook her head and repeated her murmured worry. "It just doesn't feel right."

Adam stood in the shadows at the rear of the hut, his arms folded, his expression neutral, as he watched the interplay between Maggie and her team. They were all pros, all highly trained and experienced, the best operatives France and the U.S. had to offer. Several of them had worked together in the past. All of them had volunteered for this mission. They'd assembled at this isolated airstrip outside Cannes earlier this afternoon, bringing with them their individually tailored equipment and their governments' full sanction for whatever action they deemed necessary.

During the long wait for Doc and Jezebel to move into position, they'd reviewed the villa's floor plans, studied ingress and egress points, and confirmed team assignments. Just moments ago, they'd presented their individual plans for Maggie's throaty concurrence.

They were ready.

Adam felt the steady thrum of adrenaline in his veins. It had been a long time, too long, since he'd been in the field, but he understood how this team felt. Controlled. Intent. Edgy with anticipation. Eager to swing into action.

Now Maggie's raspy whisper had given that anticipation a sharper edge.

A small, wiry man with a ginger mustache leaned forward into the light, his eyes narrowed on her face. "What doesn't feel right?"

Brows furrowed, she thrust a hand through hair that gleamed a pale silver.

"It's too easy," she muttered.

A silence descended, to be broken a few moments later by a gasp. All eyes turned to the receiver.

Her face taut, Maggie planted both palms on the table and leaned toward the source of the sound.

"Is that a throne?" The sensitive device magnified a hundredfold the stunned surprise in Jezebel's voice. "I mean, a real one?"

Victor Swanset's chuckle floated on the still air. "A foolish whim, is it not? But what better use for a discarded movie prop than to grace a bathroom?"

"I can't imagine."

The dazed reply brought a grim smile to Adam's lips. For all her delicate appearance and thinly disguised nervousness, Paige Lawrence had impressed him with her determination to see this operation through. He'd expected the woman who'd captivated Doc to be special. Paige, he'd decided, was several cuts above special.

A slight movement to his right caught Adam's attention. Henri shifted on the rickety straight chair he'd been banished to earlier and propped his elbows on the knees of his new jeans. His freckled face scrunched into a scowl as he listened to Jezebel's exclamations over Swanset's majestic retiring room.

The boy still hadn't forgiven Doc for not taking him along tonight. His fertile imagination had come up with a wide assortment of reasons why an engineer out for an evening with his very expensive hired companion would have a small redheaded boy in tow, none of which Doc would listen to. Adam had been forced to bring Henri with him to the team's rendezvous point tonight, sure that he'd slip away and find his own way up to the villa if he wasn't kept under close watch.

"I believe you have something which interests me, my dear."

Swanset's soft, cultured tones caused a ripple of immediate reactions.

Maggie sucked in a swift breath.

Adam's eyes narrowed to icy blue slits.

Henri hunched his thin shoulders and scowled ferociously.

The rest of the team froze.

Several miles away, and several hundred feet up in the rarefied elevations above Cannes, Paige stared at Victor Swanset's wrinkled face with the fascination a mouse might give a patient gray cat. His eyes met hers, as dark as obsidian, as inscrutable as death.

"The microdot? You have it with you, do you not?"

Paige nodded. The movement was reflected a hundred, or perhaps a thousand, times in the tall, gilded mirrors lining this wide antechamber. It was, Victor had told her, an exact, if somewhat smaller, version of Versailles's famed hall of mirrors.

At one end of the corridor was the most sumptuous bedroom Paige had ever seen, furnished as it had been for Louis XVI. At the other was a vast bathroom featuring an eighteenth-century throne with twentieth-century plumbing. Victor had graciously demonstrated the flush mechanism before returning with her to this hall of mirrors.

So nervous she could barely keep from shaking, Paige wanted desperately to banish Victor immediately and retreat to that throne. The knowledge that Maggie and Adam and half a dozen other assorted individuals were listening to every word of this conversation through the tiny transmitter in her earring held her in place. She couldn't chicken out now and let them all down. She wouldn't disappoint David. Or herself.

"Yes, I have the microdot."

Resting both gnarled hands on his ivory-headed cane, he regarded her benignly. "May I have it, my dear?"

"Of... of course."

Paige fumbled with the clasp of her evening bag. Her fingers shaking, she withdrew the slithery halter and passed it to him.

"Ah."

Intense satisfaction gave his voice a vibrant depth as he lifted the sparkling collar up. The shimmering gold sequins caught the bright glow of the lamps that marched at regular intervals along the hall. Flickering, dancing light swirled around and around in the endless mirrors, until Paige felt dizzy and a little sick. She swallowed hard against the nausea that gripped her stomach.

Just when she thought she might have to beat an undignified retreat to the throne and toss up the thimbleful of sherry she'd allowed herself, Victor lowered the collar. He folded the halter carefully and slipped it into his pocket.

"You will be suitably recompensed, of course," he murmured absently, as if such mundane matters as money were of little interest to either of them. "Please, take your time, my dear. We'll go in to dinner when you rejoin us."

The moment the mirrored door closed behind his stoop-shouldered form, Paige slumped against the opposite wall. Her heart was hammering so hard and so fast it hurt. She gulped in several deep breaths and willed her lungs to pump the air to the rest of her body. She was sure they hadn't operated at full capacity since Victor had led her from the library.

Slowly her eyes focused on the image in the opposite mirror. A pale, slender woman in a green-and-gold designer gown and crystal drop earrings stared back at her. A stranger. A sort of secret agent. An almost call girl. An honest-to-goodness, full-fledged adventuress.

She'd done it!

She'd passed the microdot to Victor Swanset!

The heady realization gave Paige the spurt of energy she needed to dash to the throne. Just in time, she rid her heaving, swirling stomach of the damned sherry.

Paige passed the next few hours in a blur of unimaginable, unabashedly sybaritic luxury. The butler seated her next to her host and across from David at a polished table half a mile long. She gazed at the forest of sparkling crystal stems in front of her with some consternation. After suffering from the combined effects of the champagne and sherry, she wasn't about to court any more trips to the throne room by working her way through that maze of wineglasses.

A small army of servants set course after course before her, each nestled on a baroque gold charger emblazoned with a scrolled *S*. Paige nibbled at each dish, contributed her share to the wide-ranging conversation, and resolutely stuck to sparkling water. To all intents and purposes, her part in this mission was over, but she didn't intend to start celebrating until she and David were safely back at the Carlton.

Later, she promised herself. They'd celebrate later.

A mental image of a scrap of lemon lace sent a sudden spear of heat through her belly. Half startled, half embarrassed by its intensity, she studied the man opposite her from beneath lowered lids.

If David was the least bit nervous about pulling off his part of this mission, Paige couldn't detect it. He lounged against the high back of his chair, one big hand loosely wrapped around a fragile crystal stem as he conversed with their host. The candlelight hid the subtle red tints in his dark brown hair, but Paige knew they were there. She'd seen them often enough in the bright light of day. She curled her fingers into fists, wishing with all her heart that this dinner was over and she could reach up to disturb the disciplined order of his hair.

She wanted to feel its springy softness. To taste his mouth on hers. To forget these nerve-racking hours and lose herself in the solid, soaring passion that David brought her.

Later, she promised herself.

After what seemed like two dozen courses, the parade of servers bearing new dishes finally dwindled to a trickle, then slowed to a halt. At the butler's murmured query, Victor gave his guests a choice.

"Shall we take coffee in the library, or would you like to see my laboratory first?"

David rose. "Your laboratory, by all means."

Victor's pleased smile softened as he turned to Paige. "Would you care to wait for us in the library, my dear? My little demonstration at the Palais yesterday was a bit unsettling for you, I'm afraid."

"A bit," Paige admitted dryly.

"I wouldn't want to startle you again."

"Now that I'm familiar with your propensity for stepping through walls, I think I can handle another demonstration."

He chuckled in delight. "Good. Good. Come with me, please."

His cane clicking on the black-and-white tiles, Victor led them through the central hallway, toward the rear of the main tower, and ushered them into a paneled elevator. In contrast to the Carlton's clanking wrought-iron cage, the doors to this one slid shut with silent efficiency and the elevator plunged downward.

Victor rested his hands on his cane. "We're descending to what used to be the dungeons. They were quite primitive, originally, as you might expect." His dark eyes glinted. "I've done some rather extensive modifications."

Without realizing that she did so, Paige nudged closer to David. For some unexplained reason, her euphoria at having completed her part of the mission dissipated with every foot they dropped downward.

"We're descend . . . what used . . . to . . . dungeons."

Swanset's voice fuzzed.

Maggie shot up out of her chair. "We're losing them!" she said, her voice a rasp.

"Done . . . mod . . ."

The entire team stared at the receiver as the broken transmissions degenerated into an indistinct hiss. A second or two later, even the hiss disappeared.

"Dammit, we've lost them."

Maggie yanked a folded blueprint out of the pile on the table and spread it out in front of her.

"According to these floor plans, the dungeons are approximately forty feet below the villa's ground floor. The communications folks swore that we'd be able to hear all transmissions from them.''

Frowning, she shoved a hand through her hair. ''Santorelli, get hold of the technician who inserted that device in Jezebel's earring. I want to know why that transmission failed, and fast!''

Paige held her breath as the elevator door hissed open at last. She expected another fantastic scene from one of Swanset's movies. An early version of *Frankenstein*, perhaps, or *The Prisoner of Zenda*.

But Victor's subterranean lair held little resemblance to either a mad scientist's habitat or a medieval dungeon. Bright fluorescent light bathed a large environmentally controlled chamber that contained only a few scattered armchairs with a table between them, a single computer workstation and a bank of small, innocuous-looking white boxes.

Paige had worked for a major defense firm long enough to recognize the logo on those boxes instantly. They were components of the most powerful, most sophisticated supercomputer in the world, one whose sale was rigidly restricted by the United States government and whose price hovered at about a hundred million dollars.

Her disbelieving eyes met David's. She could tell by the set to his jaw that Swanset's acquisition of this computer for private use was an unwelcome surprise to him, too.

''Please,'' Victor said, gesturing toward the armchairs, ''make yourself comfortable while I access my latest program. I think you might find the application interesting.''

Interesting wasn't the word for it.

Frightening came close.

Terrifying even closer.

But by the time Paige could recover her power of speech, it was too late to even try to categorize what she'd seen.

At Victor's invitation, Doc seated Paige and then himself in an armchair. For long moments, nothing happened. No walls moved. No swashbuckling pirates materialized before them. No sounds disturbed the stillness except the subdued clatter of the keyboard and the discreet whirring of the small white boxes.

When Swanset finished, he swiveled around on his chair and gave them a charming, apologetic smile.

"It takes a few moments to activate. Why don't I ring for coffee while we wait? Or cognac, perhaps?"

Doc eased the slight pressure on his gold cuff link. The tiny device implanted in it had recorded the audible clicks of Swanset's keyboard and translated them into digital impulses. With that translation, Doc could duplicate Swanset's computer access code at will.

"Coffee would be fine," he replied, his relaxed tone giving no hint of his gathering tension.

This was too easy.

It didn't feel right.

Swanset was playing with them. Had been playing with them all night. Doc knew it with a gut-deep instinct honed by years in the field. What he didn't know was why.

He found out moments later.

Both he and Paige turned as the elevator door hummed open once more. The stately gray-haired butler stepped out, the handles of a footed silver tray gripped in both hands.

"Put the tray on the table by Miss Ames, if you would, Peters."

The butler inclined his head and moved forward with a measured tread.

His every instinct on full alert, Doc heard the faint click of the keyboard. He turned his head and caught Swanset's bland smile.

Beside him, Paige gave a small gasp. Eyes narrowed, Doc swung his gaze back to the butler.

It was Peters. And it wasn't. Before Doc's eyes, the man's features blurred.

He heard another soft click of the keyboard.

The butler's gray hair darkened imperceptibly at first, then with deeper and deeper shading. His bushy eyebrows followed suit. A shadow appeared along his chin, then sharpened into a pointed beard.

Swanset pressed the keyboard once more.

Peters's faded blue eyes took on a dark hue.

"Oh, my God!" Paige shrank back in her chair as the Dark Baron approached her, silver coffee service in hand.

"Will you..."

The keyboard clicked, and Peters's pleasant tenor changed pitch, dropping with each syllable until it became Swanset's deliberate, dramatic baritone.

"...take milk and sugar with your coffee, Miss Ames?"

Her hands pushing against the chair's armrests, Paige strained away from the hovering butler and stammered an incoherent reply.

Doc rose and moved to stand between her and the attentive server.

"I don't think she cares for anything right now."

"Very good, sir."

Peters, in the living, breathing guise of a young Victor Swanset, turned aside to set the tray on the nearby table.

Even Doc, who understood the limitless, as yet untapped, power of virtual reality and image projection, had never seen anything like this. A cold sweat trickled down his spine, but the face he turned to Swanset held only professional approval and admiration.

"Remarkable."

Victor—the older, white-haired, liver-spotted Victor—chuckled in genuine delight.

"It is, isn't it? Quite remarkable."

Doc turned to the eerie image standing quietly, his hands tucked behind his back.

"I assume you ingested some kind of material that reflects the digitized images?"

Peters nodded. "Mr. Swanset assures me it's entirely harmless, quite like the dye a patient ingests before an MRI or CAT scan or similar procedure."

Doc searched the man's eyes. The pupils were the slightest bit out of focus, like a TV screen that needed a fine adjustment. "Why would you consent to an experimental procedure like this?" he asked slowly.

"For the money, of course. Even butlers need retirement funds. I shall exist quite comfortably on what I've put by these past few months."

"Assuming you exist at all," Doc murmured, turning back to his host. "Do you really believe he'll experience no ill effects from this transformation?"

Swanset waved a thin, veined hand. "None at all. The process is all but perfected."

Doc raised a brow. "*All* but perfected?"

The film star's brilliant smile dimmed a bit. "The ingested material is quite safe, I assure you."

"But?"

Swanset gave a small shrug. "But, as you can see from Peters's eyes, I've encountered annoying difficulties in the image transfer software. I must break the visual images down into minuscule particles, small enough to be projected from the lining of living cells. I've developed a scanner that does that. All I need now is a conveyor with sufficient capacity to handle the transfer of the millions of data bits involved."

The man's voice gained in dramatic fervor. "Think, Dr. Jensen! Just think what this imaging technique can mean! No more unsightly deformities. No pathetic wrinkles and sagging jowls. At least none that the eye can perceive. We can all look like—" he nodded toward the Dark Baron "—like that."

Good Lord! Swanset had just confirmed Doc's worst fears. This insane man had been experimenting with unproved technology in an attempt to project images onto living cells. No wonder the medical examiners had puzzled over the poor dead cook's tissue damage. And no wonder the aging film star had been so eager to acquire the fiber-optic technology.

He wasn't interested in the high-speed transfer of information via the burgeoning Internet. He didn't intend to tap into or divert military command-and-control networks. He wasn't out to expand his own communications empire.

He wanted the increased data transfer capacity to project his own image at will. To surround himself with himself. To relive his past glory every day of his life.

The implications of his process were staggering, even to Doc's trained mind. This was genetic engineering taken to its highest plane. Why wait for medicine or selective breeding to perfect the species? With Swanset's imaging technique, a click of a keyboard could change hair texture or skin tone or even speech intonation to more "acceptable" patterns.

Paige grasped the implications only moments after Doc. Her eyes wide and unbelieving, she pushed herself out of the armchair.

"You . . . you want to populate the world with dashing, youthful Victor Swansets?"

His smile encompassed her from head to foot. "My dear Miss Ames, not only with Victor Swansets. The world will also need women with your fresh, luminous beauty."

"Forget it." Doc rapped the words out. "You're not experimenting with her."

The star gave him a pained look. "I'm well past the experimental stage, I assure you."

"And I'm well past the diplomatic stage. Listen, and listen good, Swanset. You try any of your imaging techniques on her, and you won't live long enough to see yourself projected on anything."

"I was afraid that might be your attitude, Dr. Jensen. I can understand why you're taken with her. She's really quite lovely, isn't she?"

"She is, and she's going to stay that way."

Swanset folded his hands across his cane and heaved a dramatic sigh. "I had so hoped a man of your brilliant vision would be more receptive to my program, Dr. Jensen. In fact, I thought to persuade you to assist me."

"You thought wrong."

"I'm afraid I must insist," the older man said softly. "I haven't much time left. My heart, you understand, among other disgustingly feeble organs, is failing me."

His gaze shifted to Peters, to the image of himself in his prime. His eyes took on a glitter that raised the hairs on the back of Doc's neck.

"With your assistance, I can perfect this program. Then I will live forever. As I once was."

At that moment, the missing piece of the puzzle fell into place. Doc finally grasped the tiny bit of illogic that had nagged at his subconscious all afternoon.

Swanset hadn't invited them up here to retrieve the microdot from Paige. If that had been his sole objective, he would have found a way to accomplish it at the Palais des Festivals. He'd invited them to his villa because he wanted Dr. David Jensen's help in eliminating the last annoying bugs from the program that would ensure his immortality.

With sudden, chilling certainty Doc understood Paige's role here tonight. She was the leverage Swanset needed, the means to guarantee Doc's cooperation. Somehow, some way, the film star must have discovered her true identity and her relationship with David Jensen.

Her purse! Damn, the purse she lost when she fell off the gangplank! It had held her passport, her wallet. Swanset must have recovered the damned thing from the bay. With his vast communications empire, it would have taken him only a few moments to verify who she really was.

The man's next words confirmed Doc's gut-wrenching certainty.

"I'm afraid I must ask Peters to escort Miss Lawrence next door for a little while."

Miss Lawrence, Doc noted. Not Miss Ames. The wily bastard had known all along.

"Peters can give her a tour of the real dungeons," Swanset said, with a smile Doc ached to wipe off his face. "They're quite interesting from an historical perspective. You and I have work to do, Dr. Jensen."

Doc didn't need to turn around to know that Peters had a weapon trained on Paige. With the speed of Swanset's supercomputer, he composed a mental list of all possible options.

A—he could cooperate and wait for Maggie to bring in the extraction team. Without a second thought, he nixed that option. Paige wasn't going into any dungeon. Not while he was alive to prevent it.

B—he could try to talk Swanset out of his mad scheme, which wasn't really a viable option at all.

Or C—he could terminate the mission now and get Paige the hell out of here.

Chapter 16

The next few minutes contained enough excitement and adventure to last Paige through several lifetimes.

She was never quite sure what happened first. It might have been the sudden blow from David that knocked her sideways. Or Swanset's shout. Or the gunshot that exploded somewhere behind her and plowed into one of the white boxes with a sickening *splat*.

Whatever it was, Paige went flying. Her heel caught in her long skirt, and she went down on all fours. The chain of her evening bag twisted around her wrist as she reached behind her and wrenched frantically at the snagged material.

The skirt came free, and she pushed herself upright just as David sent Peters crashing to the floor. Across the room, Victor raised the tip of his cane.

Too late, Paige remembered a scene from *The Baron of The Night,* the one in which a dark, brooding hero brought down an attacker with the rapier hidden in his walking stick. Although the ivory-handled instrument

Swanset held clutched in both hands was similar to the cane in the movie, Paige suspected it now housed something far more lethal than a rapier.

"David!" she screamed as she lunged toward the console. "Look out!"

She didn't have time to dig either her mascara or the switchblade out of her bag. Instead, she used the small gold purse itself as a weapon. Swinging it by the chain, she slammed it into Swanset's outstretched arm with every ounce of strength she possessed.

The walking stick bucked in his hands a split second before Paige's purse connected. She glanced over her shoulder and gave a terrified sob as David crumpled to the floor.

"You bastard! You damned bastard!"

Raging with fury, she swung the bag once more. Swanset threw up an arm to block the blow to his head and jerked backward. He toppled over, just as Paige had during her first encounter with him, taking the console chair and the keyboard with him. The monitor teetered unsteadily on the console table for a second, then settled back with a thud.

Paige kicked the cane out of the fallen man's grasp, then whirled and raced across the lab. Ignoring the semi-conscious, twitching Peters, sprawled a few yards away, she dropped to her knees and dragged David into her arms.

"Are you all right? Where were you hit?"

She knew the answer as soon as her palm made contact with his shoulder. A sticky warmth smeared across her hand and oozed through her fingers. Her arms convulsed around David, who grunted and gave a little jerk.

"Stay still!" Paige panted. "Let me take a look at the wound."

"I'm—I'm all right."

"No, you're not! You're bleeding!"

Cradling him in her right arm, Paige stretched out her left to unbutton the black dinner jacket and peel it back. The spreading blossom of red on David's shoulder sent terror streaking through her every vein.

"Don't move!" she sobbed, clutching him even tighter while she grabbed at the hem of her gown and wadded it against his shoulder.

"I'm all right." He twisted upright in her arms, his voice slowly gaining in strength. "It's just a flesh wound. I'm all— Jesus!"

At the startled exclamation, Paige threw both arms around David and crushed his head against her breasts. She was determined to shield him at all costs from this new threat, whatever it was. Shoulders rigid, nerves screaming, she waited for the attack.

None came.

"Paige." His voice was muffled against her breasts. "Sweetheart. Let me go."

Reaching up, he pried loose her stranglehold and eased himself out of her arms. With another small grunt, he pushed himself up on one knee. The effort sent a ripple of pain across his face, and he paused, panting a little. Paige watched him, her heart in her throat.

Only then did she absorb the unnatural stillness in the lab. There was no sound but her rasping sobs and David's breath whistling through his clenched teeth. No movement other than the lift of his body as he forced himself to stand upright.

She twisted around on her knees, searching for the other two men. Peters she saw immediately. He was lying only a few yards away. His limbs were grotesquely rigid and outflung, as though he'd suffered some sort of electrical shock. A trickle of blood had traced a path from the corner of his mouth and pooled on the floor.

His jaw tight, David knelt beside the butler and searched for a pulse. After a moment, he reached up to close the eyes that would remain forever blurred.

"He's dead."

"How—?" Paige gasped. "What—?"

In answer, David swiveled on his knee and looked toward Swanset.

The aging film star lay sprawled where he'd fallen, his eyes fixed sightlessly on the ceiling, his lips blue. One bony hip rested squarely on the keyboard, depressing half its keys. On the console above him, a steady stream of electronic messages raced across the computer screen.

"Evidently his program wasn't as far past the experimental stage as he thought," David said grimly. "When he fell on the keyboard, he sent several million bits of visual imaging data pouring into Peters's cells. The poor bastard must have exploded internally."

While Paige watched, stunned, David crossed to the unmoving Swanset. Hunkering down in a stiff, awkward movement, he felt for a pulse. After a few seconds, he shook his head. Easing the keyboard from under the man's body, he set it on the console. The screen flickered, then went blank.

"Oh, my God," Paige moaned, burying her face in her hands. "I killed him. I killed them both."

David covered the short distance between them in a few strides. "No, you didn't."

"I did!" she cried, rocking back and forth on her knees. "I hit Victor in the head with my purse. I knocked him out, and he fell on the keyboard. I killed them both."

Using his good arm, David reached down and pulled her to her feet. It took some doing, but he finally managed to pry her hands from her face.

"Paige, listen to me. You didn't kill him. You didn't kill either one of them. Swanset had a heart attack. He was probably dead before he hit the floor."

She turned her tear-streaked face up to his. "What?"

"His lips are blue. He had a heart attack. A massive coronary, by the looks of it."

"Are you sure?"

Doc folded her into his arms. This wasn't the time to remind her that he was an engineer, not a medical examiner.

"Yes, I'm sure."

He held her until her sobs dwindled to watery hiccups. She lay against his chest for a moment longer, then jerked out of his arms.

"Oh, David, your shoulder! Let me look at it."

Doc stood quietly while she fumbled with the studs on his shirt and lifted the edge to peer at the wound. He'd had enough experience in the field to know that the hit wasn't fatal, although white-hot pain ripped through his shoulder with his every movement and bright red blood seeped from the wound. Paige's face whitened when she saw the ragged hole in his flesh, but she swallowed a couple of times and glanced around the sterile lab. Her gaze fell on the footed silver tray.

Shuddering, she stepped around Peters's rigid body and snatched up a handful of white linen napkins. Within moments, she had eased off Doc's dinner jacket and shirt and pressed the folded napkins against the bullet hole. While he held the compress in place, Paige dug Henri's switchblade out of her evening bag and sawed a long, ragged strip of green satin from her full skirt. Her brows knitted in fierce concentration as she brought the makeshift bandage under his armpit and wrapped it around his shoulder.

Doc gritted his teeth against the lancing pain and focused his concentration on Paige. This frowning, intent woman held little resemblance to the Paige he'd kissed and left behind in L.A. less than a week ago. This one looked as though she'd been through a small war. Which she had.

Her hair had tumbled free from its elaborate braid and hung in wisps about her face. Her brief bout of tears had left smudges of mascara under her eyes. When she buried her face in her hands, she'd smeared his blood across her cheeks, and one of her gown's tight sleeves had ripped at the shoulder seam when she swung her lethal little purse. Yet her hands were steady as she tied the edges of the green strip, and her eyes intent as she surveyed her handiwork.

"You're pretty handy to have around in a tricky situation, Jezebel," he told her, his lips curving into a smile.

"Yes, well, I'd prefer to avoid tricky situations in the future, if you don't mind. And don't grin at me like that! I know I insisted on being part of this team, but I do *not* want any more excitement like this. Not in this lifetime. Or the next! Or the one after that!"

Doc curled a knuckle under her chin and tilted her face to his. "As soon as we get out of here, my darling, we'll generate a whole different kind of excitement. Enough to last us through this lifetime. And the next. And the one after that."

When he bent to brush a quick kiss across her mouth, Paige almost forgot his bleeding shoulder and her slowly receding terror and the two still forms just yards away. His mouth was warm and hard and tasted of David. *Her* David.

She closed her eyes, savoring that brief kiss. An image of the man she loved imprinted itself on her every sense. She felt the strength and the gentleness in his touch. She heard his rasping, indrawn breath. She drew in the salty tang of his sweat, or perhaps it was his blood.

She didn't need any visual imaging wizardry to see him in the mirror of her mind. Tall and broad-shouldered and incredibly handsome, his brown hair disordered for once, his steel blue eyes filled with an emotion that set her heart thumping painfully. She ached with the need to hold him, to feel his body against hers, to arch her hips into his and take him into her.

She stepped back, breathing heavily.

"I was wrong," she admitted, with a ragged sigh. "I'm ready for whatever excitement you care to generate."

She couldn't know, of course, that she'd regret those rash words not two minutes later.

David planted another hard kiss on her lips, then strode to the console. "Let's insert that bug, then get the hell out of here. Swanset's too smart not to have at least one, perhaps more, backup systems. We don't want anyone accessing them before we can locate them and shut them down."

Still shivering from the force of her own reaction, Paige blinked at his swift transition from lover to secret agent. Half-naked, his bare upper torso streaked with blood and bound by a ragged strip of green satin, he looked like a character out of one of Victor Swanset's movies. The muscles in his shoulders rippled as he leaned over the console and punched one of the keys. The screen flickered back to life.

"Good. The program's still active. I recorded his access code, but it looks like I won't need it."

With swift, sure confidence, he keystroked in a series of commands. A few moments later, he straightened.

"There," he murmured in satisfaction. "Anyone who tries to—"

He broke off, his dark brows snapping together, as he studied the monitor. From where she stood a few feet away, Paige could see some kind of a message flicker across the screen.

"What?" she asked. "What's wrong?"

"There's a posthumous message here from Swanset."

"There is?" she squeaked.

"The bastard knew he was just a heartbeat away from a coronary. He must have coded in this message months ago and triggered it somehow just before he died."

David's eyes scanned the print that painted across the screen. "Damn it all to hell!"

"I don't think I want to hear this," Paige said in a faint voice.

He whirled and grabbed her hand. "Good—because there isn't time to explain. We've got to get out of here. Fast!"

Yanking her along behind him, he raced to the elevator. He stabbed the button, his breath harsh as he waited for the door to open. When nothing happened, he stabbed it again. And again.

When the door refused to open, David slammed the heel of his hand against the wood panel, listening intently.

"It's reinforced with some kind of alloy," he snarled. "The damn thing's sealed tighter than a drum. The whole lab probably is."

Spinning on one heel, he scanned the room. "Look for another exit. There has to be one."

"How do you know?"

"Swanset told Peters to escort you 'next door.' For a historical tour of the dungeons, remember?"

"Oh, God! Yes!"

His eyes met hers. "We have approximately ninety seconds to find that door and get the hell out of here."

They found it in less than sixty.

Actually, Paige found it. By the simple expedient of scraping her nails along the far wall as she ran the length of the lab. When she encountered a slight depression, she screamed for David. He was at her side in seconds. Endless heartbeats later, he uncovered a concealed latch. Yanking the handle upward, he slammed his shoulder against the panel.

Paige could imagine the pain that must have caused him. The green bandage darkened with a fresh spurt of blood as David turned and shoved her through the opening ahead of him.

Darkness and cold, dank air surrounded them like a smothering shroud.

These were definitely the dungeons. As they raced down the narrow corridor, Paige caught a glimpse of barred cells cut from solid rock. A rusted implement of some kind dangled from a hook on the wall. She almost tripped over a discarded tool, the use of which she didn't even want to *guess* at.

Panting with fear and exertion, Paige thought she caught a faint glow of moonlight ahead. She twisted around, intending to tell David, when an ominous rumbling sounded in the laboratory behind them.

"Run!" David shouted.

Paige ran.

The rumbling grew to a roar, then exploded in a blinding wave of light and noise. David threw himself against her, knocking her to the stone floor and covering her body with his. Her head smashed against the stone, and she must have lost consciousness for a few seconds or minutes or hours.

When her eyes opened, she was trapped between David's weight and the unyielding stone. Paige couldn't breathe, couldn't move.

Neither could David, she discovered.

He was unconscious. His breath rasped in her ear, and his body lay sprawled over hers. Paige felt his warm blood soaking through the back of her gown and wanted to scream with terror. Instead, she wriggled and scratched and snaked her way forward until she'd cleared enough of his weight to twist free.

With the last of her strength, she dragged at his good arm until she had him turned over on his back. She refused to cry, refused to let the blood seeping down his chest reduce her to the quivering mass of hysteria she knew she was.

Dragging the gold bag still chained to her wrist into her lap, she fumbled for the switchblade and sawed another ragged strip from her skirt. If—*when!*—they got out of here, she'd find some way to thank Henri for the gift he'd pressed on her. The knife had been his most valued possession. At this moment, it was hers.

Hands shaking, she folded the heavy satin over and over again, then pressed the pad against David's wound with both hands. She held it there for what seemed like hours, murmuring his name, pouring out her love.

When he stirred, she wanted to cry in relief.

When his eyes fluttered open, she did.

"Paige!"

She barely heard his raspy whisper over the sound of her own gulping sobs.

"Paige, send . . . signal."

"What?"

"Send . . . signal."

"To Maggie?" Paige wiped the back of her sleeve across her nose. "Can't she hear us?"

"Alloy . . . seal . . . lab. No emissions."

"You mean she couldn't hear us the whole time we were in the lab? She doesn't know what's happened?"

"Send . . ."

"David!"

His muscles slackened under her hand, and he slumped unconscious once more.

Moaning, Paige pressed the pad against his shoulder with one hand and reached for the crystal eardrop with her other. To her horror, it was missing.

Trying not to jar David more than she had to, she dragged him a few inches to the side. Frantically she brushed her fingers across the stone where she'd hit her head, sweeping the area over and over again.

She found the earring. Or what was left of it. The crystal drop had shattered upon impact with the stone, as had the tiny device it concealed.

Paige stared at the bits of glass and plastic in her hand in disbelief.

She wouldn't panic! She wouldn't!

She pushed herself to her feet. One glance told her she couldn't go back to the lab. It wasn't there. The explosion, or implosion, had dumped tons of stone into the subterranean chamber.

Her feet dragging, Paige turned and stumbled toward the opposite end of the dark tunnel. Toward the faint glow that she hoped, prayed, was moonlight.

It was.

"Thank God!" she whispered.

She wondered fleetingly why the small, square window wasn't barred, as the cells were. As soon as she leaned over the sill, she understood why.

Given her difficulty with numbers, Paige couldn't have said whether the cliff dropped for two hundred or two thousand feet straight down. She only knew that it was a long, long way to where the sea crashed against the cliff's base.

She twisted in the small opening, scanning the sheer rock on either side. There was no path, no ledge, no outcropping of stone of any kind. Nothing but a perpendicular wall of granite.

Her heart sinking, Paige realized that this tiny opening wasn't a window at all, but rather a ventilation hole. It didn't need bars. No one was going out through that opening. Not alive, anyway.

Slumping back against the wall, Paige felt her knees buckle. She sank to the floor in a dejected heap.

David seemed to think Maggie didn't know what had happened. Even if the OMEGA team stormed the villa, it would be days, maybe weeks, before they cleared the lab and found this narrow subterranean tunnel.

She couldn't wait, not for a day, not for hours. David needed medical attention. Now.

What was she going to do? Paige asked herself in desperation. What could she do?

She could send a signal, as David had instructed. But how? A fire, maybe. Or a flash of light from the other earring, when the sun came up. Or...

Paige's heart leaped into her throat. Scrambling to her feet, she ran back to where she'd discarded her little gold evening bag. Tearing at the clasp, she dumped the contents on the stone. The mascara. A lipstick. And the compact! The diamond-studded compact!

With the introduction of the crystal earrings, the compact had been retired from active service as a communications device, but Paige had kept it for its more mundane and utilitarian purpose. She'd powdered her nose with it only an hour or so ago in the throne room.

She snatched it up and raced back to the opening, fumbling for the square stone in the center.

Dear Lord, how did the thing work? Once to transmit, twice to receive? Or was it once to receive, twice to transmit?

And what was the damn emergency signal? One-one-three? Three-one-one? Three-two-two?

Paige swallowed a groan and reminded herself this was for David. *Her* David.

She could remember the code! She had to! All she had to do was concentrate. Think of the alley behind the tobacco shop, she told herself, emptying her mind of everything else. Think of David's instructions as he'd cradled an unconscious Maggie in his arms. Think of Henri hopping up and down on one foot in impatience as he repeated the instructions in a near shout.

Not half a mile away, a fleet of five black-painted helicopters skimmed the surface of the bay. Rotor blades whirring, they raced without lights or directional signals toward the high peak that housed Victor Swanset's aerie.

Maggie hunched forward in the copilot's seat of the lead aircraft, scanning the darkness though high-powered starlight-vision goggles. Beside her, Adam worked the controls with a skill that had astounded her when they first took off. She'd had no idea he could pilot a craft like this, but she hadn't wasted time arguing with him.

Maggie had made the decision to launch immediately after losing contact. Her instincts had told her that the broken transmission wasn't the result of any equipment malfunction. Wherever that elevator had taken Doc and Paige to had been shielded to prevent emissions. Although Doc hadn't signaled for help, hadn't called for backup, Maggie intended to be within range if and when he did.

They were only minutes away from the target area. Sheer cliffs loomed in front of them, looking much like a wall of chalk through the night-vision goggles. Adam pulled back on the stick and began a smooth climb to the central, highest peak.

Maggie spun the dial on the aircraft's digital radio, hoping, praying, for a signal. She'd tried every emergency frequency, every satellite channel, on the system at least a dozen times during the short flight.

She had just reached for the dial to spin to another frequency when static cackled through her headset. She froze, her hand in midair.

More static filled the earphones, then a voice filled with quiet desperation.

"...can't remember the code, but we need help."

"It's Paige!" Maggie shouted over the helo's intercom.

Adam lifted a hand from the controls to give her a thumbs-up.

Maggie pressed the radio mike to her throat to activate it. "Jezebel, can you hear me?"

Evidently not.

"...dead, and David's hurt," Paige continued, in the same desperate tone. "He said the wound wasn't bad, but he's bleeding heavily and unconscious. Uh, we're in a tunnel beneath the villa. It ends at the cliff face, in a small hole that overlooks the sea."

Maggie's heart sank as she peered through the helo's Plexiglas windshield at the endless stretch of chalky white cliffs below. Even with the goggles, it was going to be tough to locate a small opening in that indented, snaking wall.

Paige's voice faltered, then resumed. "I hope this is transmitting. I pressed the stone once, but I may have the sequence wrong, so I'm going to press it twice and try again."

"She's using the compact," Maggie breathed. "Do it, Paige. Do it! Press the stone twice, so I can talk to you."

A staticky silence hummed through the earphones. Maggie spoke slowly, clearly, into the mike.

"Jezebel, this is Chameleon. If you pressed the diamond twice, you should be hearing me. Now press it once, and acknowledge my transmission."

The helicopter swerved to one side, caught in a sudden updraft. Maggie ignored the violent movement and Adam's smooth corrective action. Her entire being was turned inward, focused on the mike pressed to her throat.

"Press the stone once," she repeated calmly. "Acknowledge my transmission."

"This is Jezebel. I can hear you!"

"Yes!"

Reining in her wild elation, Maggie jammed the mike against her throat.

"Search Doc's pockets, Jezebel. See if he has the receiver on him. The one that homes in on the tracking chip you were fitted with. It looks like a small flat calculator with a liquid crystal display."

Maggie held her breath until Paige replied.

"I've got it."

"Good! There's a small switch in the upper left-hand corner. Push it to the right, then read me the coordinates. Slowly!"

"Do you mean these numbers in the display? I—I can barely see them."

"Yes, those numbers. We need those coordinates to find you. Read them to me. Slowly!"

She did. Slowly and accurately, repeating them over and over until Maggie locked them into the helicopter's global positioning unit.

Within moments, Adam had the aircraft hovering two hundred feet above the crashing sea and a powerful searchlight trained on a small square opening in a sheer rock wall. With a skill learned long ago and kept finely honed, he held the platform steady while one of Maggie's team members fired a titanium-tipped steel anchor dart from a shoulder-held launcher. The dart shot through the night, trailing a snakelike nylon line, and buried itself in the rock just a few feet above the opening.

Adam kept one eye on the instruments while Maggie and the wiry Santorelli strapped body harnesses on over their black jumpsuits. Rushing wind whipped through the belly of the helo as they pulled open the side hatch.

"Have you used this rig before?" Santorelli shouted to her over the noise from the chopping rotor blades.

"No, not this one!" Maggie yelled back. "One similar to it, though!"

"Roger! Let's go!"

Adam made no comment as they rigged a lifeline to the specially designed lift that swung out over the open hatch. But his jaw was so tight it ached as Maggie snapped the lifeline to her harness and stepped toward the hatch.

"Okay, Jezebel," she said into the mike, her hoarse voice filled with a breezy confidence that made Adam's fist clench on the control stick. "We're coming in. And once we get back to Cannes, we'll have to hit the boutiques. Don't you have a wedding dress to shop for? I saw just the thing. All white silk and silver sequins."

Paige's shaky laughter floated over the headset. "No sequins. Please, no sequins."

Chapter 17

Paige sat at the ornate rosewood dressing table and
towel-dried her hair. While she rubbed the squeaky-clean
strands through the thick cotton, she went over the arrangement she'd made for the ceremony scheduled to
take place thirty minutes from now.

As weddings went, theirs would be a relatively small
affair. Only a handful of people would attend—just the
immediate wedding party, the deputy from the American consulate who'd act as an official witness, and the
French magistrate hurriedly contacted to perform the
ceremony.

Paige had refused to wait until more of their friends
and family could gather in Cannes. She was determined
to join her life to David's today, scant hours after swinging out of a dark tunnel and dangling hundreds of feet
above the sea while she was winched aboard a hovering
helicopter. Today, before Maggie and Adam got called
back to OMEGA for some crisis or another. Before she
and David flew to Paris with Henri to arrange his pass-

port and visa for an extended stay in the United States. Before any of them began any new adventures!

It had taken most of the night to sort through the aftermath of their mission. Luckily, Maggie's extraction team had included a skilled paramedic who patched David up so neatly that he was able to conduct a detailed debrief on-site with Maggie and Adam and the rest of the team. That done, they'd evacuated the servants, sealed off the villa and left guards in place until the French authorities arrived to excavate the laboratory.

Dawn had feathered the skies with gold and painted the sea a deep wine red by the time they returned to the hotel. Too wired from the night's events to sleep, they'd all feasted on the breakfast Henri ordered from his friend the head chef.

After that, Paige had taken charge. With a ruthless assumption of authority, she'd directed an amused but compliant Adam to use whatever influence was necessary to take care of the legalities. Henri was put in charge of the wedding supper. David was told to rest and recuperate. And Maggie... Maggie had gleefully accompanied her on the promised shopping expedition. They'd found exactly what Paige wanted in the first shop they entered.

Her senses tingling with delicious feminine anticipation, she swiveled on the dressing stool to gaze at the two-piece dress that hung on the wardrobe door. It met her stringent requirement of no sequins, but even without any glittery trim, it was an outfit Meredith herself might purchased. The snowy watered silk shimmered with a luster all its own, and the exquisite beading on the three buttons and the low square-cut neckline of the short-sleeved jacket was handworked. The straight skirt stopped just above Paige's knees, but was slit high on one side to allow ease of movement.

In thirty minutes or so, she'd slip on that deceptively demure skirt and fasten those tiny beaded buttons. She'd walk out of this sumptuous bedroom for the last time to join David in the suite across the hall, then leave immediately for the honeymoon Adam had arranged aboard a luxurious yacht owned by a friend of his. Paige made a silent vow not to fall off the gangplank this time.

Now, though, she had thirty minutes to get ready. Thirty minutes to blend the best of Paige Lawrence and the worst of Meredith Ames.

Grinning wickedly, she tossed the towel aside and walked over to the bed. With unabashed eagerness, she plucked the lemon-colored lace teddy off the coverlet and held it up by its thin straps. She'd been waiting far too long for the opportunity to put this little baby to use. When they hit that yacht, both she and David would be ready—more than ready!—for immediate carnal copulation.

Shrugging out of her robe, Paige stepped into the flimsy scrap of lace and shimmied it up her thighs. She wiggled to adjust the divided strip of fabric that ran between her legs, a little shocked in spite of herself at the intimacy of the garment. She'd just slipped her arms through the narrow shoulder straps and was tucking the underwire lift beneath her breasts when the sound of the door opening made her spin around, both hands plastered against the front of her chest.

David stepped inside, still dressed in the tan slacks and blue knit shirt he'd changed into as soon as they returned to the hotel last night. This morning. Whenever. The bandage on his left shoulder bulged a bit under the shirt, but he showed no other signs of his recent wound.

"You can't come in here," Paige protested. "It's bad luck to see the bride before the ceremony. You're supposed to get changed in the suite across the hall."

"I'm going to," he said slowly, his eyes skimming her body. "I just came in to give you— Jesus, Paige, what *is* that thing?"

"It's called a teddy. I think. I've never seen one, um, constructed quite like this."

"Neither have I," he muttered. "It doesn't have any back."

"Not much of a front, either," she admitted. With a little spurt of daring, she dropped her hands. The stunned expression that crossed David's face sent a dart of pure delight through her.

"Good grief! Is that what you bought when you went shopping today?"

"No. This is—was—Meredith's. I've been saving it for a special occasion." Her shining, fresh-washed hair swept her bare shoulders as she tilted her head and smiled at him. "I think our wedding night qualifies as special, don't you?"

David stared at her for long moments. Then he returned her smile with a slow, crooked one of his own.

"Very special. But I don't think I can wait until tonight."

He turned, and the sound of the key snicking the tumblers in the lock thundered in her ears.

The old Paige, the shy, timorous one who had driven through the French Alps with an aching heart because she believed she wasn't woman enough for this man, might have protested. She might have reminded David that Maggie and Adam were waiting just across the hall. That Henri would be pacing the floor, all puffed up with importance over the fact that Paige had asked him to give her away. That the American consul might arrive at any minute, or the French magistrate.

This Paige simply shivered in delicious anticipation. They had thirty minutes, after all.

As David crossed the room, she wet her lips in an unconscious invitation. He stopped in front of her, his fingers reaching to brush the tip of one breast. She drew her shoulders back, and the underwire lifted her soft flesh even higher. The scalloped edge of the lace cup barely covered her nipples as it was. Paige's instinctive little movement exposed them completely.

David drew in a sharp breath. His eyes darkening with pleasure, he shaped her breasts, fondling them, worshiping them. Then he bent and brushed the soft mounds with his mouth. The sight of his dark head against her flesh sent a shaft of savagely primitive possessiveness slicing through Paige.

She wanted to wrap her arms around him, cradle him against her breasts as she had last night, keep him safe and secure from all harm. She now understood David's urge to protect her, to shield her. She felt the same, exactly the same.

His breath was ragged when he lifted his head. Paige saw the hot, urgent need flaring in his eyes, and her own rose in waves. His hands less than gentle, he searched her front for a hook or a fastening on the one-piece teddy.

"How the hell does this thing open?"

"It doesn't. It doesn't have to."

"What?"

"You're an engineer," Paige purred. "You figure it out."

With a half laugh, half growl, he drew her into his arms. Paige went willingly, eagerly. Her hands slid up the broad planes of his chest—then stopped abruptly when her fingers encountered the bulge of the bandage.

"Oh, David! We can't! Your wound!"

He drew her closer, nuzzling the side of her neck. "What wound?"

"You lost a lot of blood," she reminded him, hunching a shoulder against the tickle of his moist breath in her ear.

"I had a steak for lunch."

Despite her own fiery need, Paige stepped back. The memory of those desperate moments when she'd tried to stanch his bleeding was too fresh to ignore.

"David..."

"I'm here, sweetheart."

The look in his eyes almost melted her resistance, but she took another step backward, until her bottom bumped against the dressing table. She gestured helplessly toward his shirtfront.

"Doesn't it hurt?"

He nodded. "Like hell."

"Oh, David!"

Her heart aching in sympathy, Paige reached out to brush her fingertips gently over his poor, injured shoulder. He caught her hand.

"Not there." He redirected her hand to a spot considerably below his shoulder. "There."

"Oh!"

Paige had hoped this sinful little garment would have an instantaneous, erotic impact on David. It had. Her fingers pressed against the bulge in his slacks, and the hot, liquid desire in her own belly flowed into her loins.

Still, she was careful to avoid touching his shoulder when he swept her into his arms once more and brought his mouth crushing down on hers. He held her hard against him, his palms spearing down the small of her back to cup the bare, rounded flesh of her bottom.

When his fingers found the narrow strip that traced between her legs, he stiffened. The old David, the one who had always held himself rigidly in control for fear he'd hurt her with the violence of his passion, might have drawn back at this point. He might have undressed her gently and laid her on the bed, supporting himself on his arms as he surged into her.

This David took full advantage of the teddy's ingenious construction. Holding her mouth with his, he arched her against him and explored the moist dampness between her legs. Paige gasped as his fingers found the opening in the fabric and parted it. One, then two, blunt fingers slipped along her slick, wet channel.

She strained upward, her belly clenching as he stretched her, entered her, impaled her. She moaned far back in her throat. Or David did. She wasn't sure.

Sensation after sensation rippled through her body. She was sure she couldn't take much more when her brilliant engineer figured out just how to put that narrow strip of lace to even greater effect.

He twisted one thumb around the fabric and tugged on it, sawing it gently back and forth, creating a friction that had Paige squirming frantically. Wave after wave of heat shot out of her belly to her thighs, her breasts, her throat.

"David," she panted, dragging her mouth from his. "I can't... I won't..."

"You can. You will."

He reached behind her and swept the various bottles and brushes and combs on the dressing table to one side. Wrapping his good arm around her waist, he lifted her and set her on its smooth, satiny surface. The cool wood only heightened by contrast the fevered heat of her skin.

While Paige worked frantically at his belt buckle, he snagged his shirt and drew it, one-armed, over his head. In seconds, he stood before her, hard and rampant and hungry.

The old Paige might have waited for him to make the next move.

This one planted her hands on the smooth surface behind her, spread her legs wide and tipped her hips to receive him.

David surged into her with a power and a strength that took her breath away. The bottles rattled. A brush tumbled off the table. Paige arched her neck, throwing her head back as she wrapped her legs around his waist.

The savage thrusts slowed, then stilled.

Surprised, she opened her eyes.

He planted both hands beside hers, his chest heaving as he leaned over her.

"Who do you see, Paige?"

She struggled for breath. "What?"

Eyes as stormy as a winter sky bored into hers. "I warned you that we might not recognize each other by the time this mission was over. Who do you see now?"

"I see you," she panted, lifting a hand that shook with the force of her love to cup his cheek. "*My* David."

"Me, I do not like this!"

Red hair slicked down, scrubbed face scrunched up in a scowl, Henri folded his arms across his shiny new suit coat, with its jaunty red carnation in the lapel, and stared at the foyer.

"It is past the time they were to be here. Well past the time. The magistrate, he comes. The consul, he comes. But Mademoiselle Paige and David, they do not come." His scowl deepened. "The champagne goes flat."

Maggie twisted her half-empty flute in one hand and nodded sympathetically. "So it does."

She knew very well what had delayed the errant couple. She'd gone across the hall some time ago to check on them. It hadn't required any exercise of her linguistic skills to interpret the rough, urgent intonation in Doc's voice when he told her they'd be there shortly.

Shortly, of course, had stretched into *longly.*

Grinning, Maggie took another sip of the now sparkleless champagne. She'd known when she met Paige Lawrence in the boutique on the Croisette that there was more to the younger woman than met the eye. But the Paige who'd emerged these past few days had surprised everyone, herself included.

That once shy, demure young woman was now late for her own wedding because she was unabashedly enjoying her honeymoon.

A few moments later, the door to the suite flew open and a glowing Paige dashed in, followed more slowly by Doc. The bride wore the two-piece Saint-Laurent suit she'd purchased earlier today, but the side slit was twisted to the back and the jacket buttons were fastened crookedly. Instead of the white heels she'd chosen to go with the dress, she'd pulled on the same gold sandals she'd worn last night. She hadn't bothered or hadn't had time to put on any makeup, but this Paige certainly didn't need any. Her green eyes were huge, her lips red and ripe, and her cheeks were flushed with what Maggie guessed was whisker burn.

"I'm so sorry we're late," she said in a breathless rush. "David stopped by the suite to... to..."

"To give Paige her engagement ring," he finished smoothly for her.

Maggie turned to Doc in surprise. "Her engagement ring? Did someone fish her purse out of the bay, after all?"

"No. The emerald's gone, but I had another stone set for her this afternoon."

Shyly Paige held out her hand for general inspection.

Henri whistled, tilting her hand this way and that. "The stone is of a fine quality. If we are in need of money, I can get a good sum for this, I think."

David rested a hand on his shoulder. "Forget it. Paige and I will make sure you're not in need of money."

"I couldn't ever pawn this, anyway," she told the boy. "It's the diamond from the compact."

"No kidding," Maggie exclaimed.

"It was a wedding gift from Adam," she added, glancing at the tall, dark-haired man watching the proceedings with his usual cool air.

"From OMEGA," he said easily, strolling over to admire the square-cut diamond solitaire.

Maggie grinned at Paige. "So anytime you want to call Doc home, all you have to do is..."

"Press once to transmit, twice to receive," she finished, laughing. Her eyes sparkled as she grinned up at the man beside her. "Now who's got whom on a leash?"

"Before anyone does any more pressing," Adam suggested dryly, "I suggest we proceed with the ceremony."

Henri seconded his suggestion with a quelling look at Doc. "*Oui!* The champagne goes flat."

The civil service was simple and poignant.

Paige gripped the bouquet of white roses Adam had presented to her, somehow managing to look radiant and confident and shy, all at the same time.

Doc stood beside her, his eyes never leaving her face as he repeated his vows.

The maid of honor, positioned at Paige's left, translated the magistrate's stuttering half English, half Provençal phrasing for her whenever necessary. Maggie's throat closed at the look that passed between Paige and Doc when they joined hands.

Adam, at Doc's right, handed him the white-gold ring at the appropriate time, then stepped back. Paige passed roses to Maggie, who stepped back, as well.

Maggie tried not to stare at the tall, immaculately groomed man at Doc's side, concentrating on the service instead. But during each slight pause, she felt her gaze straying to Adam.

He hadn't purchased that charcoal gray suit in any boutique, she knew, or that red silk tie. They were hand-tailored in Boston, she suspected. Or New York. Or Paris. He looked so aristocratic. And so damned handsome, she thought with a small sigh.

No one would believe this wealthy, jet-setting politician had expertly worked the controls of a hovering helicopter just hours ago, his whipcord-lean body encased in black and his jaw darkened with stubble.

And no one would believe this calm, distinguished individual had icily torn a strip a half-mile wide off Maggie during the mission debrief. She buried her nose in the white roses to hide her grin, wondering if he'd *really* skin her alive if she ever swung out of a helicopter without prior jump certification again.

"And so, *madame* and *monsieur,* I pronounce you husband and wife."

Tucking the laminated card with the words of the service into his pocket, the portly magistrate beamed at the couple before him.

"You may kiss your bride."

Doc didn't need his permission. He swept Paige into his arms with a hungry, masculine fervor that made the magistrate blink, Adam smile and Maggie suppress a twinge of envy. Of their own volition, her eyes strayed to Adam.

When Doc raised his head, Paige laughed up at him, her face glowing.

The wedding supper was cheerful, noisy, and a tribute to Henri's taste. The head chef himself presented the last course himself, bowing regally when the small crowd applauded his spectacular flaming crepes suzette. Looking more like a royal duke than a head cook, the distinguished gentleman smiled benignly while his minions served the dessert.

"It was here, in Cannes, that the Prince of Wales first tasted flambéed crepes," he informed them importantly. "The dish was named for his companion of the night. A most ravishing woman, or so we're told."

He kissed his fingertips in a tribute to the glorious Suzette, a long-ago counterpart of Meredith Ames. Paige slanted David a private smile.

When the last crepe was consumed and the last toast offered, the newly wedded couple rose to leave. A shower of rose petals tossed by Maggie and a gleeful Henri followed them to the door.

At the foyer entrance, David shook Adam's hand. "Thanks for coming to Cannes. And for staying a few more days, to look after Henri for us. We'll take him off your hands when we get back.''

''No problem.''

''Just keep an eye on your wallet.''

''Roger.''

Henri's innocent brown eyes reproached him. ''*Monsieur!* I have retired from the business. *That* business,'' he added scrupulously.

David ruffled his red hair. ''We'll talk about your next business ventures when we return. See you in a couple days.''

''You will watch Mademoiselle Paige?'' the boy asked, trailing them to the door. ''Me, I do not like this idea of the boat.''

''I'll make sure she doesn't go overboard unless I'm with her.''

Paige didn't take offense at the assumption by these two males that she still needed looking after, since she knew very well they needed it, also. And she intended to provide it. For the rest of their natural lives. Smiling, she took David's arm.

Halfway out the door, she suddenly stopped and slipped her hand free. ''Wait! I almost forgot.''

She spun around and tossed the bouquet. The roses sailed across the room, heading right toward the tall, platinum-haired woman.

Laughing, Maggie caught them with both hands. She buried her nose once again in the soft, velvety roses, breathing in the heady scent of love.

When she glanced up, the laughter died in her throat. Adam was watching her, with an expression in his blue eyes that she'd never seen before. Maggie's heart slammed sideways against her ribs. Her fingers crushed the white roses.

''I have something for you, too,'' Paige told Adam with a shy smile. She came back to him, holding out her hand. His dark brows rose when she laid a small rectangular box on his palm.

"You're going to need this far more than David will."

A slashing grin creased his cheeks as he slipped the receiver into his pocket.

"I'm sure I will."

Paige wasn't sure just how or when Adam Ridgeway would manage to fit the laughing, fiercely independent Maggie Sinclair with a leash, electronic or otherwise. But from the look that flared in his blue eyes as they rested on the long-legged blonde, she suspected it wouldn't be long until he tried.

* * * * * *